Book Two: Becoming

LANA GOLD

© Copyright 2021 Lana Gold - All rights reserved.

It is not legal to reproduce, duplicate, or transmit any part of this document in either electronic means or in printed format. Recording of this publication is strictly prohibited and any storage of this document is not allowed unless with written permission from the publisher except for the use of brief quotations in a book review.

This is a work of fiction. Names, characters, places, and incidents either are the product of the author's imagination or are used fictitiously, and any resemblance to actual persons, living or dead, business establishments, events or locales is entirely coincidental.

ISBN: 978-1-7365152-2-8 E-book
ISBN: 978-1-7365152-3-5 Paperback

Chapter One

Cali Kistler was walking down Madison Avenue, nearly floating on air. She was still coming down off that rush of peeking into a place – an overall idea – that felt so deliciously illicit, and potentially powerful enough to engine her life forward. It was just after her transformative afternoon interview at Gillian Gladly's legendary bordello. There, she had finally faced head on, live and in-person, (no dithering, no denying) *exactly* how fascinated she was by the possibility of one day becoming a GG's girl.

I actually did it!

Relief mingled with a bizarre sense of accomplishment. But where did Jean-Chris, her wonderful friend/possible boyfriend, fit into all this? He would have to be put on a type of simmer setting, until she could sort out what was next (and best) for *her*. Now that she felt more strongly committed to quitting stripping (and finding her way back to school at her earliest convenience) she felt in a far too precarious lifestyle situation again.

Going 'all in' with Jean-Chris – she had the sense he

would love to go 'all the way' sexually with her, and emotionally, too – might not fit in with her ultimate plan to join GG's. She wasn't allowed to even consider returning there until she was better-educated, more cultured, and more sexually experienced…

She had been given two years to figure it all out. GG's words still trilled in her mind: *Return when you become the young woman I need you to be. The woman YOU need you to be. And not a moment before.*

As Cali walked along the shopper's paradise of posh boutiques, her head still spun with images of the almost theatrical 'stages' of the bedrooms where she might one day 'perform' and cater to people – well, men specifically – in an intimate way that might suit her quirky personality. She'd felt so accepted, nearly coddled there, by GG and her kindly assistant Kin. The beautiful, almost innocent-looking girls she'd seen standing outside in the garden laughing and talking were fascinating, yet approachable. They'd confirmed for her that hooking didn't necessarily turn you into a dragon lady.

She was relieved that she'd chosen to *at least* go and meet GG, and to explore the idea of one day becoming a professional sensual companion… But in having done so, the whole thing had just gotten real. *Really* real.

It doesn't mean I'm going to do it! And while I may be welcome back someday, GG said I'm not ready yet. So what next?

Swirling with nervousness, and not ready yet to sit down

with pen and paper, and plan out the next steps of her life without the financial safety net of stripping, Cali slowed her pace, trying to stay in the present. Standing in front of a highly reflective shop window, she looked at herself anew. An extreme makeover would eventually need to take place, apparently. And a mental one, too. Becoming a highly compensated escort meant a holistic approach, and involved a total mind-body-soul transformation.

GG had spoken of Cali not returning to work with her until she had displayed some accomplishments, some cultivation, interests and skills. So what exactly did she have to show for all her efforts *so far*? Because since she'd gotten off that Greyhound bus so many months ago, it had all been pretty basic: surviving, eating, not becoming homeless, showing up for stripping work – *tits up, chin up* – and making a friend or two (mainly Jean-Chris), attempting to eek some pleasure out of it all.

Now here she was, standing in the heart of Manhattan, after her visit to GG's… She was still alive and kicking, but who was she, really? How had she actually blossomed since she'd found her way to the Hotel Gram-Irving all those months ago? How would she introduce herself, if put into a situation where everyone was going around giving those little pseudo-resumes meant to impress and charm others?

"Oh, hello, I'm Cali Kistler: I once stole a bunch of gold from my dad so I could get here and go to a prestigious art school. But all I could do is manage to stay on living in a tiny room, without the school part. OK, that hurt, but I went with it… Then, when it looked like I might have to go back to Tightwad Hill again, I

worked as a nude dancer so I could keep living here (and that worked; maybe too well)... Then I lost my virginity, and I found out I love sex, and now I'm eager to sleep with different men... And yet I find I really adore spending time with Jean-Chris, who is so adorable, but he's maybe getting too close... but I digress!

You see, dancing's not for me: it's a shitty occupation filled with crap situations, and I need to have more luxury in my life. My main goal is to become a GG's girl, and make oodles of cash doing what I love best. But I can't do that till I get back to school, and make something of myself, maybe become bi-lingual...

"Ha!" Cali laughed out loud at all the ironies, the conundrum of it all, and retreated from the shop window, gasping a little. Utter ridiculousness! Everything GG had said about her was right: it was time to upgrade her life, class up her act, take some lovers, learn some languages, and finish her college education.

The slick, expensive stores beckoned with shiny, new things. But something about it all felt a little empty for her taste. Where was the hunt in it? Part of Cali yearned to visit the old scene at Rags to Religion – her mother Pearl's charity thrift shop for the church – where the volunteers were a revolving ragtag cast of rural and mature ladies, each a character in her own way. She thought lovingly of Vera, Eloise, Myrna, and, of course, her mother Pearl. Those old girls were always hashing out their problems with each other in the back room where they received and marked-up the goods.

Often enough they'd verbalized their joint fantasy about

the day a Degas or a priceless urn might come in, rendering them all free (from their shitty husbands, no-good kids and dull lives) to go on a round-the-world cruise. There they planned to kick up their heels "with some of those gigolos they always have aboard those ships!"

Growing up in the shop, Cali had developed a passionate taste for vintage clothes and all the interesting-looking used things that were hopefully previously loved. But mostly it was the thrill of the hunt and the hilarious crew of ladies who were supposed to be so churchy – and were anything but.

What would those churchy gals think of me now?

Her mind skittered to GG's again. There, it seemed there was a similar sisterhood in place. And men didn't mind if you'd already been well-loved, or well-worn, or widely loved. *Experience* wasn't necessarily a bad thing in that context. As a woman promising a taste of romance, you might have shagged with the best, but you just couldn't look 'hard' or act 'hardened.'

Stop thinking about this! Get on with things.

As Cali made her way slowly toward Midtown Manhattan, she observed the gestures, behaviors, and seeming habits of that subspecies of social, well-off women known as 'the ladies who lunch.' She yearned for delicious, gourmet food, and the time to savor it slowly with good company: smart girlfriends, perhaps… Or would a GG's girl sometimes leave the house and go out with the clients?

She knew she should be careful with money now that she'd committed to quitting topless and nude dancing. For now, she'd have to live off her cushion of savings, until her next steps became clear, and her hoped-for new living situation – her own apartment rental in Brooklyn – was a done deal. But she couldn't bear the thought, at least for today, of yet another meal of soup and crackers at the local diner, which seemed depressing and mundane. She decided to time her walk to coincide with the opening of the better restaurants for dinner. Maybe just to get a sniff…

Where would a successful GG's girl go out for a meal? Well, first there would probably be her weight to consider, and maintaining it, so it would need to be a place serving light fare. Next, drinking alcohol, especially anything hard, had an aging effect, and so she'd need to have no more than a glass of wine, if that. GG's girls were most likely very demure and discreet in their off time, and so the restaurant wouldn't be the hottest place in town: noisy and crawling with men on the make, out to get something for nothing, and girls hoping to hook up for the typical Manhattan one-night stand (with deep down hopes that he might be The One or that Love At First Sight may strike).

GG's girls, Cali reasoned to herself, were probably conservative with their hard-earned money, earmarking a certain portion for investment either back into themselves or in something with a yield. So the restaurant couldn't be too expensive, or, if it *was*, maybe a GG's lady would enjoy just a small bite at the bar. That way she could satisfy her tummy, and also absorb the ambiance of an elegant place, as well as statistically increasing her chances of meeting a high-caliber man for something *more* than a one-night stand. (The Cinderella fairytale wasn't a myth at all for a GG's girl, but something possible to attain; it was something that *could* become real if the right man was dealt with craftily and not indulged too soon).

Cali stood in front of Aquavit; it was the most subtle and elegant-looking restaurant entrance she'd seen on her walk, if ever. She looked down at her churchy outfit – the vintage floral prairie dress she'd hoped would endear her at GG's – and she felt immensely inappropriate and fussy. Even so, she wanted to have this experience, today, NOW, no matter what she was wearing. She'd intuited one particular thing from GG's (among many), and that was that some of the externals didn't matter all that much; it was how you carried yourself, how you projected from the inside-out, that *really* counted.

Met with a slightly snide welcome from the male greeter – after she confidently informed him that she was just there for a "snack and a drink" – she slid into a grey-blue velour stool at the bar. She was quite alone, as the low-lit restaurant had just opened for the dinner service. The solicitous bartender, wearing a bow tie, lit the candles on the bar, and handed her the menu. Reading it made her mouth water, but she kept her options to the appetizer section: each of which cost the equivalent of four soup-and-cracker meals at 'her' corner Greek diner.

From this menu of Nordic foodie delights, she chose a delicate portion of flower-shaped Gravlax salmon, served on a similarly-shaped Scandinavian bread, topped with a delicate dollop of cream and a small smattering of caviar.

Without being asked for ID, she was able to order a glass of dry white wine. She sipped at it, savoring it, observing how well it went with her meal; and all this while she monitored her posture and manners with a new interest.

She glanced round the restaurant: at the velvet banquettes and the starched linen-topped tables, each set with shimmering cutlery and minimal, but exquisite, Calla lilies. She observed as the space slowly received its patrons, clearly regulars, who spoke in hushed, reverent tones. She'd seen so many beautiful things today, tasted such fine flavors, and she yearned for her life to roll on in this manner, forever – with her as more of a central character, *not* an uncomfortable observer.

When the meal was done, she practiced paying the bill without thinking about it or 'feeling the damage,' such as a wealthy person might. "*I'll be back, Aquavit,*" she whispered as she left.

Chapter Two

It was a few days later, and Cali was relaxing in her Hotel Gram-Irving room after spending her time tucked away at the public library. She'd been dedicating herself to the pursuit of a grand re-organization of her life, setting her mind toward some higher goals –particularly college, having also visited various schools and speaking with their admissions reps, who'd been very welcoming, especially when she showed them the admissions letter she'd previously received from the Preston School of Design.

Her phone rang with a call from Tony. He'd been good about keeping in touch following her first time having sex with him; and she in no way felt used or abandoned or tossed aside after that night. She'd enjoyed the mental challenge of keeping him at bay: not clinging, not waiting impatiently for him to invite her on their next date. The sex with him had been so good (not that she was an expert judge of what was good or bad yet) that she was willing to forego other opportunities for sex with other guys, except for maybe Jean-Chris, who was in a class all his own. She was eager to see what erotic adventure Tony might come up with next.

He was an affectionate, but busy man who kept odd hours at his strip club Tony's Mr. Wedge. Knowing this, she always felt special when he called to check in on her, and special also because he wasn't looking to come over for a *quickie.* "Could we have lunch out tomorrow?" he asked. "I've got a free afternoon."

"Yes, but just one request. Could we… You know Brooklyn well, right?"

"Born and raised. My business might be in the Bronx, but my heart and soul is in Brooklyn. You wanna eat out there? I know a great place."

"Of course I want to eat. But would you drive me around and show me some cute neighborhoods, places to live?"

"Oh, do I look like a real estate agent to you? I'm not into role playin' but maybe for you I can get into it," he laughed. "What, you thinkin' of moving out of that rooming house?"

"Yes." There, she'd said it. It was out there in the open. It was scary to think of leaving the island of Manhattan and the chalky white womb (tomb?) of the Hotel Gram-Irving. But a bigger space, a bigger life (that cost about the same money or less, if she was to return to some form of school soon) was calling out to her. It would instigate a change. The kind of change that would be a base from which to launch into her plan of action to return to GG's a 'changed woman' someday.

"Good. I want you outta there, too. You should have a nice place I can come out and visit you at sometimes. I'll hook you up," he said confidently. "Tell me what you're lookin' for."

The next day, Tony did not disappoint on the food front. The quaint Italian restaurant tucked away in Brooklyn Heights was cozy, with low, wood-beamed ceilings, white tablecloths, fresh flowers and candles. For her date, and potential viewing of apartments, Cali's hair was styled in a smoothly curled, more 1940's look than usual; and she wore a fitted long-sleeved dress that hinted charmingly at her body beneath. It was a wonder her hair wasn't more damaged from all that 'teasing' during the stripping nights. Expensive extensions were off-budget, so she'd made do with making her thin hair look as full as possible.

The small space of Casa Como was curtained off from the midday winter sun by thick linen drapes. It felt as if it was open just for them as there were no other customers. Tony held Cali's hand under the table, and described it in a hushed tone as a place where "whether it's open or closed, it still makes money."

Without asking too many questions, Cali intuited this to mean that the owner was 'connected,' and the restaurant accounts were used to wash money from other sources; despite the delicious home cooking, the place didn't rely on customers for business. Given the outrageous complexity of the chef's Truffled Arancini, he *should* have more customers, Cali thought. Then, she dived into the Eggplant Rollatini that had just arrived: delicate, crisp eggplant layered between fresh mozzarella and San Marzano tomato sauce. "Mmmm. All I can say, Tony, is mmmm…"

I love to eat! Bring on the Michelin-rated restaurants, all of 'em! A little tremor of joy went through her: thinking that the lifestyle and earnings at GG's meant more encounters with fine food.

"Come have a drink with us!" Tony invited the chef, Renato, to sit down and share in a good bottle of Barbera – but he wouldn't. He seemed reverent to Tony, and proceeded to bring out dish after dish of goodies, until they were stuffed. Cali, in her new manner of cultivation, asked Renato a ton of questions about the origins of the dishes, the ingredients and the wine, which he happily chatted up.

While she was interested in knowing Tony better, and sharing bits of herself as well, there was a sense that their connection could only go so deep, conversationally speaking. With that in mind, she chose some filler to beef up their interaction, so that the lunch wouldn't be pulled under by lengthy silences. (In fact, she usually liked such moments – she and Jean-Chris often enjoyed them, and they never felt awkward, just contemplative – but Tony's style wasn't remotely contemplative).

Suddenly he said, "It'll be nice when we can get together more often, once you get settled in wherever you're gonna land." He gave her a good look-over, from head to toe. "And you look really pretty like that. I hate the too-sexy look. You look like you're going to a tea party, and it's good, I like it. Innocent."

"Thank you, that's nice."

"So what're you doing with yourself these days? You still dancin'? Ever see Ned around?"

"Unfortunately Ned and I parted ways. It was a conflict of interest type of thing. You'll be happy to know that I have *other* plans…"

"Oh, yeah? Tell Uncle Tony."

"Well, I hope it doesn't bore you."

"Try me."

Keeping an eye on his face for the eventual blank out – as she'd grown accustomed to experiencing with so many of the striptease customers, during their so-called conversations – she blathered on to Tony about the free Office Skills class she'd signed up for at the Public Library in Brooklyn. Once trained up, her plan was to apply for rather highly-paid work as an Executive Assistant through various temping agencies she'd learned were hiring. And the *piece de resistance*: she'd signed on for the next semester at The Design Arts Institute, a school she'd learned would happily accept her (and offer her a partial student loan) for credited night classes leading to an accelerated degree in interior design.

As she'd worked out this new plan, it had flashed through her mind to ask herself why she'd never figured these things out earlier, and decided to work as a temp or get back to school sooner. The truth was, she'd never felt as motivated before meeting GG. In any case, she felt a little grateful to the Universe for allowing her that gritty stint as a stripper: the *je ne sais quoi* it had layered into her personality, not to mention the street smarts and contacts it had given her (especially the one with GG).

She continued telling Tony about her life plan. "It's nowhere near as prestigious (or expensive) as the Preston

School of Design…" At this point, his eyes appeared to half close as he sipped at his wine. "But it's a step in the right direction, you know? It will all come down to my portfolio, and hopefully result in an internship with a good design firm toward the end of the two years. – You still with me?" she asked, as Tony seemed to snap awake.

Her thoughts suddenly veered to dear Jean-Chris. *He's* someone who would find all this incredibly exciting and newsworthy. Enraptured by design, art, and the intricate process of acquiring knowledge, he'd be standing up, clapping at the news of her personal turnaround. Meanwhile, Tony just mustered out a, "Nice, girl. You're doing good." And he squeezed her knee under the table, all the while stealing the last morsel of the strawberry-covered ricotta cheesecake off her plate.

Of course, when dealing with Tony (and probably Jean-Chris too), she conveniently left out, and would leave out indefinitely, any mention of her visit to GG's bordello and her aspirations to return there one day, as one of the girls. No need to complicate Tony's vision of her as that fallen angel now on the right path. She could always change her mind. In the interim, there was self-mastery and cultivation to attend to, if she even had a hope of returning to GG's.

After dessert, Cali half-hoped to walk around Brooklyn Heights with Tony, perhaps hand-in-hand, as she liked his style of holding hands: grabbing but not interlocking. But alas, he was quick to get them into the car. He nearly pushed her into his Lexus, before heading off for an introduction to his buddy Monty Miller at a realty office in Park Slope.

Monty sung the praises of the area: a bijoux, beautiful and convenient neighborhood of sloping, tree-lined streets edged with brownstones; each one charming in its own way, often with flower boxes and fanciful iron gates fronting them. There were two subway stations, a buzzing main street with restaurants, shops and services, and the crowning glory: Prospect Park, a bucolic, almost wild-seeming expanse composed of gentle hills, a small stream and lake, and just the green scene of relaxation and relief Cali yearned for in her life.

Monty and Tony were quite friendly, and so the 'apartment showing day' was more of a do-it-yourself venture, with Monty handing Tony several envelopes of keys with addresses or lock box codes on them. Tony and Cali showed themselves into several properties before she found the one she loved the best: a small 'alcove' one-bedroom in the back of a brownstone building, which overlooked a garden three flights below. The little formal entryway, high ceilings, wood floors, large windows and arched doorways were exactly what she wanted, and cost the same price as a month at the Hotel Gram-Irving. There was even a bathtub and, best of all, a fully functioning kitchen. (She suddenly flashed away to cooking Jean-Chris a proper meal sometime!).

She had enough saved up to cover the brokerage fees and several months' rent, and had an odd faith in the Universe that it would continue to provide, somehow. It would be OK; she'd never have to go home to Tightwad Hill again, which was beginning to feel like a figment of a distant bad dream.

"You like it?" Tony asked, sitting in the windowsill, relieved that the search might be over and they could continue with their play day. Cali strode around the empty apartment, admiring the place. She felt certain this was The One (even if Tony wasn't). She nodded and smiled over at him. "Let's go see Monty and do the paperwork."

"You like the apartment. But do you like *me*?" he asked, letting a naughty look cross his face. As she approached him, he slowly unzipped his jeans, and she noticed a hard-on bulging through his blue underwear. He pulled her to him, and she put her hand on him, grasping around his cock as their lips met. Leaning in close, she could feel more of his hardness against her lower stomach. This would only be her second time having sex, and she was ready to taste more.

"Is the front door locked?" he asked, as he kissed her, sliding his tongue into her mouth.

She imagined, then, what it might feel like to have it sliding again in the slit between her legs. "Yeah…"

"You don't mind if I'm a little… I'm going to tell you what I think you'll like; what you need."

"I don't mind." Ah, so this time would be totally different from the first time. No more "Mr. Nice Guy." She liked the concept of variety.

"Can I fuck you here?" he asked hungrily. At first, it sounded a bit raw and unromantic, but she decided she really liked it. Life didn't have to be a Harlequin novel at all times.

"Fuck me anywhere you like," she said, getting into the game.

"No. Fuck me *here*," he said, sliding down and crawling

over to where nobody could see inside the window. He pulled off his pants and underwear, and sat up against the wall, still in his shirt, spreading his jeans out beneath him, letting them act as knee pads so she wouldn't scrape herself on the wood floors. Displaying himself for her to jump on, he rolled a condom onto his erect cock, which was straining for her attention.

"Get on my cock," he growled, the words making her wet.

She hesitated for a moment. She'd been underneath when they did it before. She slid her panties down and off, leaving her dress on. Slightly unsure of herself, she approached. She could feel her legs rubbing together moistened with slickness; his cock looked so tantalizing, all ready for her to ride. Him showcasing it like that was making her crazy. "No foreplay today…?" she asked sweetly.

"Nah, get on it. I'll make you wet when I'm in," he said, as she felt her pussy pulsating with hunger to enfold him. "I want my cock inside you."

She kneeled down on him, gently lifting the skirt of her dress, and steered him between her legs to that place where he was already pushing, nearly bucking his hips to get further and deeper inside. It hurt again slightly at first, but then his hot cock rubbing across her lower lips felt so good. She guided him outside of her, and then back in again, spreading her wetness.

She became so wet, in fact, that his passage inside her was smoother and more pleasurable than she remembered it being the first time. Once her pussy lips were fitted tightly around his cock, and she felt him going the length of her, she let out a loud moan; and she slid back and forth atop him, clenching her legs around his hips.

An insane need to ride him without stopping took over her, and she mashed herself against him over and over. Each move brought increasing pleasure: him matching her movements with his bucking hips, and her bracing his shoulders for stability. She knew she should probably take more time, and extend this as much as possible, but it felt too good to slow down.

"Come all over my cock," he said, grabbing her hips, and driving his cock deeper inside her, letting her pump him relentlessly. "You know you want to."

"Oh, I do!"

As she continued riding him, she felt a huge, irresistible wave of pleasure overtake her, and he slowly let go, too. She covered her mouth by leaning into his shoulder, to suppress her moans and screams of pleasure as her climax approached from far away. When the delicious release finally overtook them both, she nearly bit into him, and she felt him shudder and moan.

As she held on to Tony, and their scorching interlude was cooled with some vestige of calmness, she caught herself thinking: *Fine practical research on the body mechanics of 'Cowgirl.' I think GG would approve.*

Tony snapped awake after some moments of seeming semi-conscious. "Let's go get this placed lined up," he said, and Cali sensed a slight annoyance in his voice that the rest of the afternoon would probably be spent doing paperwork, and not more fucking. She thought of something then.

"Tony, if you help me get a nice mattress here today, after I get the keys, maybe…"

"UH, huh. I see where this is going."

Chapter Three

Back with Monty, the real estate agent – while Tony waited outside the office – things were jovial. All of Cali's documents seemed to be in order, until he enquired about her lease Guarantor.

"But *why*?" she asked. "My credit is perfect; I have all the deposit, the certified rent checks, the first and last…"

"It's just a little precautionary measure we like to take in the case of 'self-employeds.' Could you ask a parent who has good credit?"

"No! God, no!" NOT that again: some stranger calling her father up, simply asking for his signature on something, and his "Go to hell!" zinging back. She felt a moment of hurt thinking of it. What the hell kind of wealthy father was he? What kind of rich man would make a daughter feel too horrified to ask for his help for something as simple as the guarantor-ing of a modest apartment lease? "Let me…" She motioned for Monty to wait, feeling a sting in her tummy. She hated asking anyone for *anything*. But this felt like *do or die*. The apartment was everything she ever wanted: it was all part of her grand plan to prepare for GG's some day, and she was *this* close… Tony probably had great credit, and he was a friend of Monty.

"Tony?…" she said sweetly, opening the office door to the street. It was already as if he knew it was coming. He nodded resignedly with a smile that was a little tighter than she liked.

"Guarantor you, right? You gotta understand that *nobody* can ever call me or call my house about this. They can't call me to collect rent if you don't pay it; this can't get on my credit report. Nothing, nothing can happen like that; nobody can ever find out. I like to keep things tight."

"NO, no. Of course not. I always pay my bills, no matter what. You saw my credit. I'm a 790."

"Let me go sign my life away," he rolled his eyes, making a move to go into the office, but smirked a little too. "You're trouble. You know that?"

She grabbed him into a hug. "Thank you!"

"I shouldn't be your guarantor, I should say no. But I can't say no to this pretty face," he said, pulling away.

"It's the last thing I want. I don't like entanglements."

"Me neither!"

"But I guess in life sometimes you just have to ask for help."

In fact she hated asking him. She really enjoyed his company, but she knew deep down he wasn't 'The One' and she'd be happy *not* to complicate his life. But what else could she do? Jean-Chris was a foreign national, and her rich, credit-worthy father would never agree. Tony was her only game in town. The trouble was, now she felt she owed him, and she hated 'owing.'

Damn my dad!

"Excuse me," she turned against the wall and collected herself, sniffing in, still feeling bitter about her own father's unwillingness to ever help her.

Breathe in the calm, breathe out the hate.

Tony pushed into Monty's office, and said, "I'll go sign. Then you go in and get the copies and the keys, and I'll be around the corner, waitin' in the car."

During the signing of the lease, as Monty fiddled with some Xeroxing, Cali held his adorable pet poodle, Tiberius, and fed him treats. She reasoned with herself that it was probably a good idea to offer some sort of reward to a man who just did you a major favor. Gloria Havistock, her childhood teacher, had once shocked Cali with the statement: "Men are like dogs! Exhaust them with play first, before you attempt to train them how to treat you."

Once everything was done, she joined Tony back in the car, and said, "So, after we get the bed from the furniture place, should we go relax on it for a while?"

In the course of setting up Cali's bed frame and mattress, Tony did a lot of grunting and groaning and futzing around with screwdrivers and tools, as well as slugging from a bottle of imported beer. Finally, he stood over the bed, proudly surveying his work, as if he'd just built a car engine from scratch.

"Mama mia. Finito! I am a genius."

"Yes. I'm amazed how fast you put that together. It's been hours."

"Hey, hey. Don't make fun of me. Get on the bed. See how you like it."

Cali laid down on the supremely comfortable mattress. He'd been generous and purchased something quite quilted with high-tech padding. Between the guarantoring and the mattress purchase, she was starting to feel rather beholden to him. Still, it was nice to be treated to things even if they had some implicit kind of price tag. She was willing to 'pay' because he had a lot of charisma and was so damn good-looking.

"It's nice! Thank you."

"Not like that. Try all fours…"

Hmmm… She turned over onto her arms and put her rear in the air, exposing her bottom beneath her skirt, which she'd hiked up over her hips. "Can I?" he asked, rubbing her bottom while sliding her panties down and off her legs, leaving her shoes still on.

"Mmm, mmm," she agreed, as he buried his face in her nether regions, getting her slick with his tongue and an excess of saliva. "You're still wet from before," he commented as she heard him unzipping his pants and rolling on a condom. Suddenly, before she could brace for the action, he was inside her from behind, jamming his cock as deliciously far as it would go. This was a first. They had never explored *that* before.

As he steadily pumped, going all the way out of her, and then plunging in again slowly, he reached around and played with her from the front. It all felt good, but whether she was sated from earlier (or this style of sex didn't quite agree with her) she felt a little disembodied from the moment (and from him) – as if she were watching them. Had she had more furnishings, and got herself a mirror, she might actually be watching them for real.

Reminder to self: buy a very large mirror for my bedroom.

She felt his pace quicken a bit, and she heard him grunting, like when he was building the bed. She didn't feel an urge to move toward her own climax, though – happy to enjoy the process of observing him heading toward his own.

"Doll baby, would you let me just fuck you till I come? I'm so close… I just wanna…" he asked, before releasing a guttural "Ohhhh God."

"Uhh, huuhh," she said, a bit too late. He collapsed on the bed with his pants halfway around his legs, and Cali smiled into the mattress. "Did you enjoy that, Tony?"

"Yeah. God! Imagine if I were a *real* handyman, you were my client, like, wanting your bed fixed, and *that* whole thing just happened."

On the way back into Manhattan with Tony, Cali struggled to think of things to talk about with him. She contrasted him to Jean-Chris. Maybe it wasn't right to do that, like comparing apples to oranges. But she half-feared that if their interludes continued, they would quickly start feeling mechanical, and potentially empty when he left. She'd start feeling like some quickie machine: someone he kept on booty call for his pleasure, all in exchange for having guaranteed her apartment and buying her a mere bed (although it *was* a nice mattress).

She puzzled over how her mind outlined situations in such transactional terms. After all, he didn't seem that into truly bonding with her. Was he the kind of guy she could call if she was ever very sick and/or needing a friend to take her to the hospital? What romance did they really have going? She struggled to find common ground and conversational paths that led to a deeper connection, or even mirth.

She observed herself sitting in the car, missing Jean-Chris. And yet, it felt so good when she and Tony... *screwed*. (She didn't know what to call it exactly – what they did together – but the amazing feeling of being possessed by him wasn't something she was ready to relinquish just yet).

"Tony, you know I really like you, right?"

"Yeah, hon. I know that. But don't fall too much in love with me. I'm not that kinda guy that can do that. I like the girls, all right? But I don't spread myself around. I'd like it if we could just have a regular thing. Something I could count on."

"Yeah, OK. But would you not call me Doll Baby? I can't get used to it. Just call me Cali."

"Yeah, sweetheart, whatever you want."

"Not like that either. *Sweetheart*. It's not personal. You know what I mean?"

"Yeah, I think I know what you mean, babe."

"Stop!"

"What else? With women there's always something else. What's the thing you *really* wanna ask me?"

"Well, ummmm... would you start teaching me Italian, like, on a regular basis?"

"Oh! Ya think I'm smart like that?"

"Yes, I do. I know you're completely fluent. So could you come over once a week and maybe give me a lesson? Force me to speak it, and correct my mistakes? I'll do my own work in books for the grammar, but just, I need the practice…"

"Aw, Babe. Yeah, I'd be happy to. Practice, ha!" he smirked, snorting. "Oops, I called you babe, babe. So that's what you wanna call our get-togethers: Italian lessons?"

"No, I'm serious. I *need* you. I want to be fluent in several languages in the next two years or so."

"Oh, you *need* me. I like bein' needed. OK, well can I bring over some eggplant parmesans or some pasta and wine, and we make an Italian night of it? Maybe Monday nights, when Tony's Mr. Wedge is usually a ghost town?"

"Sure. Bring your big sausage with you," she smiled, her eyes flashing down toward his lap.

She felt grateful that she'd already studied enough Italian that whatever he taught her would get her that much faster to fluency, therefore ticking off another of GG's boxes: that of "learn a few foreign languages so you can travel and impress the clients."

He looked over at her and laughed. "You're kinda nuts, kiddo. But I dig ya. I'm glad you quit stripping. It's good you're going back to school, and everything you told me about it. Even if the club's my bread and butter, I hated it that you were dancing. You're not that kinda girl."

"Oh, yeah? What kinda girl do you think I am?"

"You're a princess. You just don't know it yet."

Chapter Four

Once Tony dropped Cali back at the Hotel Gram-Irving, it was time for her to say goodbye to all that had been there. She could feel the keys to the Brooklyn place firmly in her hand; it had just gotten real.

Before heading to her room to start packing a few boxes and suitcases, she knocked on Jean-Chris' door, and heard a woman's laugh inside, as well as glasses clinking, and Jean-Chris pontificating on something, maybe telling a joke. "Don't answer that," she heard the woman say, as the voices went quiet.

"Who is it?" Jean-Chris asked.

"Cali."

Then, she heard him say, "I need to."

The woman replied, "Fine then, I'm leaving now!" Suddenly the door opened, and Darla – her hair wild, and her cheeks red – pushed past, smiling tightly as Cali made space for her to get by. "Excuse me," Darla said, unceremoniously as if Cali didn't matter.

"Hello to you, too," Cali sneered, catching Jean-Chris' eye inside the room. She leaned into the doorway for support, feeling very heavy. Despite her best attempts at liberal views, she felt a deep sorrow she couldn't explain. A quick glance revealed a messy bed and the stuffy smell of post-sex in an airless space. Facing the window, Jean-Chris raised it for more air, quickly tying up his rather Hugh Hefner-like robe.

"I'm sorry. I wasn't expecting you. I think we need to start warning each other that we're going to visit," he said, not turning around.

"No, I'm sorry. I should have called first. It doesn't matter anyway. I came to tell you something…" Cali suddenly felt like crying. She thought Jean-Chris was somehow hers, exclusively, even though logically she knew it wasn't true. Well, what did she expect? He was a young, hot guy – a charming foreigner – who seemed amusingly corruptible. Of course the too-old/hardened/trashy-for-him Darla would want to eat him for breakfast (like a sweet crêpe). Who *wouldn't* want him? The irony didn't escape her that she'd just spent the afternoon with Tony, who'd indulged her as well.

"Come and sit down," Jean-Chris pulled out a chair tucked under the desk, and Cali took a seat on it, unsettled.

His sleeping with Darla was *fine*; she was more pissed at how that big-tits, big-tattoos good-for-nothing had just treated her like a little girl, brushing by her like 'the big woman in the house.' After so many run-ins with her dad Dash, who'd condescended to her on a regular basis (and her mother who'd been patronizing as well, with all her *holier-than-thou* bullshit) Cali's ego was shot through and porous when people treated her like a little nothing.

"Should we go out?" Jean-Chris offered.

"Aren't you tired after *her*?" Cali chuckled, trying to cover up a second wave of wanting to break into tears. She made the motion of sticking her finger in a hole moving it back and forth, which she knew would be very vulgar and offensive to Jean-Chris' sensibilities.

"Do not insult me with this. My style is much nicer," he said, holding back a naughty smile, and speaking in a low voice so nobody could hear. "Please don't be upset with me. Darla is one-dimensional, OK? We take each other in like some people drink down a couple of glasses of whisky. It's very fast, very numbing, and we really cannot have more than two a week. We have a moment of satisfaction; there is nothing to talk about, really. She goes back to her room, or I go back to mine. And I am able to resume my studies in peace, while she returns to shaking her boobs and selling her Ecstasy."

Cali remembered that once in the dressing room of the Pussycat, before she was fired, Darla had mentioned she had a boyfriend, some guy named Benji, but: a) Cali wasn't sure if it was the truth, and b) despite her resentment about that nasty letter Darla had once sent to her mother, Cali dared not reveal this potential rival to J.C, lest she be breaking the 'girl code.'

"Listen. I don't have time to talk about Darla. Whatever. Fuck her. I've taken a really, really cute apartment out in Brooklyn. I'm moving out tomorrow!"

"Really? That is so strange. Darla is moving out, too. She'd come to say goodbye. I am losing both of you."

Suddenly, there was a commotion out in the hall, and Cali heard Darla's voice, "No, don't go in there! Benji, NO!!!"

But it was too late. As soon as Jean-Chris opened the door – to ask "What is happening?" – a punch came out of seemingly nowhere, landing squarely on his nose, and a chunky leather-clad guy took off down the hall with Darla. Cali shot up and looked out the door with Jean-Chris, who grabbed at his nose: rather astonished by this new development.

"You keep off of my Darla! She's comin' with me now. We're moving to Schenectady!" Benji yelled as he skulked away.

Jean-Chris, still reeling from the surprise knockout, managed to squeak out, "She was getting on me first!" It made no difference; they were long gone. "Fuck!" he shook his head, checking his hand for blood.

"Gosh. She stopped by to say goodbye by having one last screw? Weird. She's better off in Skank-nectady. And Benji, too," Cali giggled. She looked at Jean-Chris via the reflection in his mirror, smelling his colognes and playing with his tortoise-shelled brush & comb set, trying to seem light and casual.

"Ow! And just when I need ice, it is not here," Jean-Chris sat down on the bed, nursing his bruised face with watery ice from his malfunctioning mini-fridge, now encased in a paper towel that was quickly disintegrating with moisture. "Merde," he sighed, removing the soggy package, some of the paper towel left clinging to his face.

"So did you know she had a boyfriend?" Cali tried to enquire casually.

"Yes! But I felt very well compartmentalized. And I was comfortable keeping in my own compartment. You know?"

"Women can be very tricky," Cali confirmed, hiding a smile. "They do lie up the wazoo."

"But not you, I am sure," he rolled his eyes and sighed, pressing the towel to his nose.

"Never me," she giggled, and began playing with one of his unfinished architectural models made from popsicle sticks and toothpicks. She handled it in such a way that it made him nervous.

"Please don't touch that. It's my homage to Frank Lloyd Wright. His home was called 'Falling Water' but currently mine is an old pile called 'Falling Toothpicks.'"

"It's impressive, like you," she snickered, sitting down on the bed with him, before instantly shifting uncomfortably. Her undercarriage still felt a little sore from the two interludes with Tony, both within a few hours – especially the last one: getting nailed from behind so hard and so strong. As jealous as she may be of Darla, Cali would keep Tony a secret for now. "She's like a glass of whisky. Really? So you were *still* seeing her this whole time? You could do better."

"Let's not dump on Darla. I *would* do better, but she was hmmm… convenient. While the girl I *really* like has crazy ideas." Here he looked over intently at Cali. "This girl I really like, she's a crazy girl. She has visions of courtesans and being a bad girl dancing in her head. I'm not sure I could ever be someone serious for her."

"Oh, come on. Things are changing. I'm going back to

school soon, getting some new skills, and maybe, like, a straight kind of job." She dared not tell him that besides her design education, she had planned out a path of self-cultivation and development that might *also* prepare her to excel at the career of a high-priced independent call girl (with a solid start training at GG's).

"Wow! I want to hear every little detail about this. This is so wonderful!"

"But what's new with *you*?" Cali asked.

"I have a new part time job," he said, getting up to look in the mirror to assess the damage done. "It helps pay for school, but is also something I can put on my CV. It is so very boring for you to hear about."

"Nothing about you is boring."

He sat back down beside her. "I am assisting in a furniture repair shop, but a very high end place inside an auction house. I work on fine antiques, priceless *objets*. Maybe if I am lucky I will be laying my hands on, oh, Marie Antoinette's chamber pot or Winston Churchill's snuff box."

"Scintillating."

"Let's go to your room, and I will watch as you pack up. You have a better freezer than me; I need your ice! It's our last night together as neighbors," he said, grabbing his keys and gently pushing Cali out the door. "Naughty neighbors. It sounds so sexy, no?"

Back in Cali's room, Jean-Chris, being more analytical and systematic, proved to be a much better luggage-packer than her. Between applying ice and pressure to his nose, he did the best he could as she handed him various pieces of clothing. He neatly folded and arranged them into her suitcase, as well as filling some additional boxes with pieces she'd acquired since first coming to New York.

"Do you think we'll ever get back to the level of passion we experienced at the Turkish bathhouse sauna? When I, you know, just went in a little ways. Oh, it was so nice," he mused casually, as he held up one of her overly-decorated G-strings. "Do you dry clean these? How can they charge for this? It's so small."

"How could I forget that wonderful time…" Cali sighed. "No, I hand wash them with hair shampoo."

"Anyway, was *that* perhaps the apex of our relationship? Sort of our last hurrah before you become a bridge and tunnel person?"

"Oh, come on!" She came over and pulled the G-string from his hand. Wrapping it around his neck, she pretended to strangle him with it. He grabbed her to him, and pulled her into a long kiss, which then lead into her straddling him for more kissing. Unzipping his jeans, she descended to her knees, and reached through his underwear to bring him out to play. She took him all the way into her mouth for a few long, slow delicious strokes, as he leaned back in his own kind of ecstasy (and not one of Darla's pills). But then Cali stopped abruptly, giggling devilishly, and stood up. "Oops, I think you've had enough for one day."

"Don't stop!" he begged. "Why!!" he whined some more. "Why are you moving to Brooklyn and taking all your fancy lingerie with you!!! NO!"

"Yes. I must. This is to be continued: one night soon, at my new place. Okay? I want you to visit when my place is all pretty, and romantic and perfectly furnished, like… our little nest. It will be worth the wait."

"NO! Let this woodpecker into your nest. NOW, please? Chirp, chirp!"

"No. I've never made love with anyone in one of these Hotel Gram-Irving rooms. And I'm sure as hell not going to start *now*."

"You are such a perfectionist."

"Exactly."

Chapter Five

The following week, after moving out of the Hotel Gram-Irving, instead of waking to the sound of horns honking and garbage trucks rumbling, Cali enjoyed being roused by the sound of birdsong coming through her window. She took, too, lots of slow, contemplative walks in Prospect Park. Wasting no time in getting on with things, she spent a few days at the Brooklyn Public Library's adult education section, in the free Office Skills classes: getting her typing faster (Olympian faster, actually), as well as training on various software packages. Reluctantly pulling herself away from all the décor magazines at the library, Cali felt proficient enough to go into Manhattan and sign up to her new temp agency, Surefire Temps.

The Surefire Coordinator, who would pimp Cali out to corporations, was the snippy, thirty-something Misty Seemeister. Shifting uncomfortably in her squeaky office chair in a too-tight tweedy suit, Misty took her job – and talon-like fingernails – very seriously. They clicked along her keyboard as she inputted Cali's information.

Cali, who sensed she might have an allergy to working in offices, had been lured in by Surefire's promise of high hourly wages for her 'skilled' labor, not to mention the promise of flexible days and hours if she needed them. But she wasn't going to be just temporary. She was planning to go whole hog: working five days a week as a temp, and going to school four nights, once she got signed up at the Design Arts Institute, which was a state-affiliated school offering art and design classes in the evenings. With a student loan, she could now afford the tuition, and continue going forward towards a two-year degree in interior design. This would dovetail perfectly with her possible entrée to GG's, where she imagined she would find success, and quickly pay off her student debts.

As Misty typed away, Cali looked over the various documents and tax forms for her new employer. She leaned in to Misty, who pulled back uncomfortably. "The IRS will be tracking my income now?"

"Yessss," Misty seemed to hiss. "Welcome to America. Where have *you* been?"

"So," Cali continued, "Is my title 'temporary secretary,' or a 'temporary executive assistant'? I'm not sure what's the appropriate, politically correct and most current term for what I offer?"

"What?" Misty snipped. "What the hell are you trying to say?"

"What will I tell people *I do*?"

Misty stopped clicking for a moment. "California, you are a short-term, throwaway, replacement office helper who is instantly available to make scans and copies, type documents, create spreadsheets, get coffee, make and take calls, show your executive's guests in and out of the office… AND you are to ghost in and out of each assignment seamlessly, and without disrupting the job, OR DESK, or FILES of the person whom you are replacing for the short term. Breaks are at the discretion of your supervisor, and pantyhose are mandatory. Got it?"

"Oh, yes," Cali had nodded sweetly, "Great."

Misty's eyes were scanning over the next day's staffing needs. "Alrighty, you've lucked out. I'm sending you to one of the world's biggest pharma companies tomorrow. You'll be the third assistant this week, to the CEO."

"He's gone through three assistants already this week?!"

"NO. You'll be the third assistant. He has three assistants, and you're… the last – the least important."

"Ah, thank you for that distinction," Cali said, and Misty just rolled her eyes without looking away from her screen.

"Mr. Greenace is a great client of ours, so don't fuck it up."

Shut it, be thankful! She'd scored an assignment, at least for a few days; it would pay well and allow her forty minutes at the end of each day to get to night design school, which would take up most of her weeknights. And, of course, there would be homework all weekend. Her new life was going to be a grind, but a good kind of grind. Not the old 'bump and grind' kind of grind, like at Chesty's or Blastoff 69!

Dare she kick up her heels? Dare she jump for joy?

No… Cali hunkered down and gathered herself in. She

looked out at the lobby area and the other temps droning away, waiting for work, in their identical suits, stockings and low-heeled shoes. She dare not *be herself.*

A fleeting thought passed through her mind just then. *If I were at GG's, I could be more like myself. I'd wear blingy necklaces, strappy shoes and silky gowns. I'd flirt, laugh, finesse my charms and fuck. Yes, there'd have to be fucking strangers, but I suspect I kind of like fucking (maybe even strangers), and I'd make a shitload more money...* Onward, forward. This was just a piece of Cali's Master Plan. *I'm going to a cushy job in a skyscraper, not digging ditches in Bangladesh. Buck up.*

The next morning, Cali sat on a hard plastic subway seat as the train jostled its way underground from Brooklyn to Midtown Manhattan. She wasn't used to this kind of schedule, and felt comatose from getting up so early in the morning (nearly the hour when she used to return and wind down from her stripping gigs!).

Her navy blue polyester dress – another cheap thrift shop find she'd purchased in a bid to save money – made her yearn for better and nicer clothes. Ah, she dreamed of flowing dresses: lacy, flowery and possibly see-through. The pantyhose, which she'd been required to buy, were way too small, and were straining uncomfortably at her crotch. Her legs already felt itchy. Her low-heeled pumps, while practical, made her feel frumpy and all fenced-in. It was damn cold outside, too.

She snuggled for comfort into her 70's puff-sleeved, floor-length, down-filled coat. It was a wonderful gift from Rags to

Religion that her mother (and the volunteer ladies, who also sent cookies) had mailed her. She knew she looked a bit like she was sleepwalking in a sleeping bag, but who the hell cared, as long as she got that typing done and ghosted in and out of the scene quietly, filling in for people with *real* jobs.

Zorvis Pharmaceuticals was located in a towering building, which seemed to disappear up into a cloud. Cali looked up at the shard-like sliver with awe. Once cleared to enter, she shot up in the elevator, to the C-suites, her ears popping.

The woman at the main reception area took Cali's ID, and verified it against a list. Picking up the phone, she called someone. "The temp is here. Where should I put her?"

"You're making me sound like a sandwich," Cali complained, and the woman glared, pointing for Cali to go sit down and wait.

Soon she found herself stationed at the desk of the Third Assistant for Mr. Hank Greenace, who was situated in a plush corner-office suite, which had quiet, carpeted halls, light wood paneled walls and stunning views across Manhattan. The desk acted as a kind of barrier, blocking entry to the coveted space; it faced out onto a center group of cubicles containing the assistants of the executives who were housed in the surrounding airy offices with their floor-to-ceiling windows.

After a short introduction to the office systems by the Second Assistant, Katherine – a kindly-seeming woman of efficiency and class – the phone suddenly rang. Katherine stood watching as, slightly flustered, Cali pressed a flashing button and picked up.

"Zorvis Pharmaceuticals," Cali sung.

"It's HANK, the CEO!" the man practically screamed. "Who the hell are you?"

"I'm your third assistant. For a few days," she said.

"Well get your tookus the hell in here. I have my lunch order." Then his voice seemed to wilt into a childish whine. "I have to stay cooped up in here today. Fuck."

After he hung up, Katherine asked, "What did he want?"

"To give me his lunch order; he's dining in today. He sounds sad about it."

"You have 30 seconds to get in there, then."

"The countdown begins…" Cali said calmly, getting up slowly.

Katherine was panicky, however. "Did anyone warn you about Hank? His reputation?"

"No. 25, 24, 23…"

"He has a legendary temper. He's a screamer. Screams at everyone in this office and when he's home, too. But he's really good at what he does, obviously. That's why he's CEO. I couldn't work for anyone else now. He's so… direct. You don't need to guess with *him*."

"Ah. I know someone exactly like this." *My asshole of a father.*

Cali went slinking toward Hank's inner sanctum, pen and notebook in hand. She swayed easily down the plush hall toward the gate-like carved wooden door, trimmed with gold flecks. There, at the portal, she buzzed to announce herself as "Cali!" and was let in.

She entered Mr. Greenace's vast corner-office, which

even had room for a sitting area and tables holding a few model ships. As she came in, Mr. Greenace stood up, ever the gentleman. She was surprised to find that the man with the booming, cursing voice was actually a diminutive, totally bald man in his mid-seventies. This corporate titan, full of energy, brimmed with a dynamism and virile handsomeness that wasn't lost as a result of his advancing age. He was like a compact cross between Ben Kingsley and Bruce Willis, but with a wide middle girth and more lines on his face. She felt a slight twitch in her panties. She'd *always* had a thing for much (much) older men – and in this case, he was hot stuff.

"Take a seat. Let's discuss my lunch in detail," he said, sitting down. With a gesture of his hand, he invited Cali toward one of the soft caramel leather seats in front of his desk. "What did you say your name is?"

"Call me Cali," she smiled tightly, slightly unsure, as it often had been with her father, when he'd stick the knife in with an unexpected insult, insinuation or, at best, a belittling tease.

"Names are important," he mused. "And people love the sound of their own name. That's my first rule of business."

"Well, my full name is actually California."

"Ah, the sunshine state. You must be a positive person."

"I am, but I've heard that you, hmm, how shall we say: like to express yourself in a loud way. So please don't *yell* at me."

"*Yell* at you!?" he yelled.

"I don't respond to yelling any other way than yelling back, *and* I sometimes throw things. And I'm *sure* the people here wouldn't like that."

"Ha! You throw things too? Let me hide my ships."

"Good."

"OK, Cali. Lunch – back on track!"

"You sounded so sad when you said you had to order lunch in. Why is that?" she ventured.

He snickered a little, and laced his hands into a prayer position. Peering over them at her, he was almost squinting. She imagined that normally his regular third assistant or a lowly temp would just take the order, not show this much interest in him. Normally anyone this feisty and over-familiar might need to be put back in their place. But… seeming to be a decisive man, she already knew he would be nice in her soft yet strong company. She sensed that he liked bold women who he knew he shouldn't cross, even if she still appeared to be under twenty years old.

"Cali, it's like this. I, at my age, feel that my days are somewhat numbered, and each day that I must stay in this office at lunch, rather than go out and enjoy a walk, or a restaurant with a friend… I feel it's an impingement on my happiness. But in the interest of staying alive and continuing to steer this ship, I've been told I need to cut down on all my culinary weaknesses: the cheeseburgers at Peter Luger's, the steaks with Béarnaise sauce at Capital Grill, the chocolate profiteroles…"

"Ah, you like good food as much as me."

"I'm supposed to replace these meals with skimpy spa food, and have meetings three times a week with the personal trainer at the medical clinic across the street. So it's best if some days of the week I stay in, otherwise I find all the…"

Here he gave her a significant look, "*temptations* hard to resist."

"But you're not fat, you're *chunky*," Cali claimed with impudence. "Some might even venture to call you a hunk," she laughed.

"I'm a hunk of *something*," he nodded. "Some people think I'm a *piece of shit*!" He let out a booming laugh as she broke into giggles. He seemed to be liking her even more; puffing out his chest, he turned her way with more interest. Flattery could get a girl like her under his thick skin.

"So is it really serious, this condition?" she asked.

"They say I'm clogged with fat *inside*," he added ominously. "My visceral fat levels are through the roof; that's my gut. And my arteries are as congested as the highway out to the Hamptons on a Friday night."

"Ohhhh. Well then, as long as you're going to die soon, I think you should just get to eat whatever you want. As long as it's a steak salad dripping with blue cheese dressing and a chocolate chip cookie for dessert."

He smiled over at her mischievously. "Forgive me if I'm being too forward. Don't sue me for sexual harassment, OK? But you make a salad sound like erotica!"

"You should hear what I can do with a chocolate sundae," she laughed. She hoped that she was charming this man, and that he would suddenly be eager to know her *real* hopes and dreams: what she must be studying and so forth. She hoped he was thinking to himself: *what makes this pretty young woman tick and show up to work in a place like this? Dressed like that, she doesn't seem to quite belong in an office.*

He caught her discreetly scratching her itchy legs, clearly trying to resist but not being able to help it. "What's going on? Why are you scratching away like that!? A woman... God, I hope I don't get in trouble for saying this. Women should *not* touch and claw at themselves; it's not ladylike."

She made a mental note: *Don't claw or touch at self.*

"I know! I don't mean to, really, it's... I'm having an allergic reaction – a strong one! I believe they call it contact dermatitis. It's the synthetic fibers in these nylons that the temp agency made me wear. I've never worn them before; I always wore cotton tights if it's cold and..." she looked through them to her skin beneath. "I'm starting to look like a burn victim: my skin is all bumpy and bubbling up!" It was truly a dire situation.

He came over and took a look down at her legs. "You're a sight." Going to his open door, he made sure no one was looking or about to enter. "Get them off, NOW. I won't tell."

"Really?" she asked.

He pointed toward his private bathroom. "Jump in there and get them off before your whole body swells up. The *gall* of those temping people to require things like that!"

"Ok..." She did as she was told, and felt relieved immediately as soon as they were off – though it would probably take days for the rash to go down, and it would feel much colder that evening on her walk to her first night of school, sans nylons. Peeking tentatively out of his bathroom door, she asked "Safe to come out?" Holding her pantyhose balled up in her hands, she was glad that she'd worn such a long dress and panties beneath it.

"Yes, it's OK." He was right there waiting, and she sensed something new and eager in him. She didn't want to push it away, but she wouldn't chase it either. She'd noted the big portrait of his wife and family behind him. Mrs Greenace looked like the one who ran things at home, despite his rumored screaming.

Hank *was* intense, potentially volatile, and he was her boss (at least for a few days). *Who the hell cares*! Cali had already given this dynamic a lot of thought. She didn't put stock in adhering to all the "political correctness" of feminists seeking to reverse the sexual power politics.

She'd often pondered how the strictest of feminists were seemingly oblivious to the incredible power of their own femininity. Why did they so readily poo-poo the uniquely womanly skill of charming men with their beauty and sex appeal in order to enhance their lives for the better? They were missing out on so much fun and games! Why was it OK for uniformed officers to use any armament possible in conflicts – from hand grenades to Sherman tanks or even spytech – and yet in that good old 'war of the sexes' (still raging, it seemed, if one looked carefully under the glass ceiling) it was a social anathema for women to employ sexy powers in the battle against the patriarchy?

Fuck it. He wants me. And I want something from him: maybe his help.

Hank leaned down and examined her legs. "Oh! I've just noticed how pretty your pins are," he smiled, staying low, waiting to be kicked. Escaping any chastisement, he came back up for air to look Cali in the eye, and she gave him a promising but reserved smile.

Hank was harmless. He wasn't harassing her or making her feel threatened with loss of a job, so she didn't mind his interest. He was just another lonely man… who happened to be her boss for the day. He probably screamed at everyone, but he'd shown some caring interest and tenderness with her.

"That feel better now?" he asked.

"So much." Displaying the pantyhose balled in her hand, she said coyly, "Um, Hank… Could I leave these with you to dispose of discreetly? Katherine and your First Assistant would probably not understand if they saw me walk out with them. And your office maid may talk if I put them in your waste paper basket."

He chuckled, extending his hand. "Of course. But we have secrets between us now, Cali. Discretion is the highest form of honor you can give another human being. You know that, right?"

Discretion is the highest form of honor.

"I'm learning. But I think you could teach me a lot more about that. Lots of things, actually." She smiled, turning to walk out.

"Wait!" he said. "What are you studying? You're a student, right?"

"I'm at The Design Arts Institute. I was originally accepted at Preston, for the Foundation Year, for my large-scale floral mosaics. And I was planning to go there, but I got ummm… I lost my funding and couldn't go, and now I'm at the Institute."

"Don't say ummm all the time. It waters down the power of your speech. Just say what you mean without qualifying anything. I like it that you didn't burden me too much with your sad story, right now at least. Everyone has one, and it's best not to burden conversational partners with too much heaviness."

"Yes, sir."

Don't say ummmmm. Don't burden conversational partners.

"So I'd say you're a fighter. You rebounded quickly. And Interior Design. It's a cliquish cabal of witches, both male and female, is it not?"

"I'm not sure yet."

"The few interior designers I've been through with my homes, they seem to so often believe *their* taste is better than everyone else's, including their clients'. I *hate* arbiters of taste. I had to fire them."

"Does that make you an arbiter of hate?"

"Ha! Well what do *you* think of 'em? Designers who haul truckloads of shit in without your prior approval, and charge you for it! Then they pull a bad face when you complain that you don't like what they chose."

"I believe clients should be involved in their environments. If the client isn't into art and design much, then it should be treated as a consultative relationship. But if they have strong ideas for what they want, then more of an artistic collaboration is required. The great designers probably listen well and tastefully interpret their clients' passions and personalities – as well as their practical needs – without creating environments that would be embarrassing to *either* of them."

"Well put, young lady."

The phones were ringing, things were buzzing. "God, SHUTUP! I'm enjoying the hell out of this. Not some inane conversation about FDA trials, company secrets, or which of my useless kiddos can use the family jet this weekend."

"Thank you."

"I like you. You're strong, articulate. Make sure you stand your ground in those interior design classes, young lady. If there's a battle over the use of chintz vs. chinoiserie, I'm sure you're damn well gonna win it!"

"Ha! Will do," Cali laughed, trying to ease out of the office. His phone was ringing again. His First Assistant, Twyla, was hustling down the hall to make sure he got the call.

"Hank, it's them!" she waved her hands. "You aren't picking up!"

"I have to take this," he said. "Fuck."

The first night of school at the Design Arts Institute was quite daunting for Cali. Given her upbringing as an autodidact working from the public library, she had rarely attended a class with multiple students. Apart from a few drawing workshops, and rather slouchy seminars at the local community college as the token high-schooler, she'd not participated in much group learning.

Cali was shaking as the twenty-five or so students in her Interior Design Fundamentals class sat in a large circle, and took turns introducing who they were by telling 'one important thing about themselves.' Mr. Takaya – the rather stern, Japanese man who headed the entire department (and also taught the Fundamentals class) – listened in while arranging the various Introduction Projects the students had been instructed to bring.

"Hi, I'm California, but you can call me Cali…"

Her mind scrambled over what to say… *I want to be an interior designer, but I also dream about one day becoming a high-priced international call girl. Working in an office tower makes me feel dull, and like jumping out the window. I'd much rather be my boss's kept mistress…*

"I guess ummm…" – *Oops,* Hank had said, *No umm-ing, no qualifying.* "I'm really eager to make that transition from someone who could probably decorate an interior, to being a professional who can completely re-design a space and supervise renovations, moving walls around, all that. I think there's a big difference in the skill set, so I'm really happy to be here so I can gain that."

"Right on," Mr. Takaya said encouragingly from somewhere behind her, as he put the Introduction Projects on a board.

Cali looked around. Some people had that little sneering look cross their face when Mr. Takaya commented positively on her intro. Oh well, fuck them.

"She should re-design that dress," someone whispered loudly enough for her to hear. Ah, here was the cattiness and arbitration of taste that Hank had warned her about; it was already starting. She'd damn well better win that war over chintz or chinoiserie.

Everyone else seemed so stylish, and she felt self-conscious in her conservative, polyester blue office dress and bare legs. She vowed to find a nicer dress or a sharp-looking suit that might still pass the approval test for temp wear at the Surefire Temp Agency.

For the Introduction Project, the students had been instructed beforehand to embellish a small poster board with ten various items: it could be material swatches, photos and/or magazine clippings that were intended to collectively depict their personality through a visual medium, not using text or verbal cues. The other students were supposed to interpret the materials and the overall arrangement, and then guess at the personality of the student who'd anonymously done the board.

Cali's work included a carefully curated grouping of clippings of lush bouquets, a photo of one of her floral mosaics, a leopard print velvet swatch and a piece of rose pink chenille, two photos of heavily-curtained 'boudoir' décor (beds richly covered in silks), as well as richly-hued photos of very expensive Persian rugs. To resemble jewelry, she also had two 3D 'diamond drop earrings' – which were actually stick-on crystals arranged on the board.

As Mr. Takaya wrote down the students' impressions on a large pad of paper, Cali's introduction board came up. "Pleasure puss!" someone yelled out. "Femme fatale!" another said. "Do-me Queen," someone whispered loud enough. "Sex pot?"

"Guys!" Mr. Takaya said. "Do better. Be nicer."

"Luxury Lover – a sybarite!"

"Ultimate Romantic."

"Modern-Day Princess."

"I like it," Mr. Takaya said. "You see how the mood boards work? The person who did this board really did a great job of expressing her or himself. The personality behind it is nearly undeniable. Whose was it, by the way? I know I'm supposed to wait until the end, but I can't help myself." Cali feebly raised her hand. She could hear the air being sucked out of the room by the other students' jealousy. "*Are* those your qualities, Cali?" Mr. Takaya asked, and she nodded. "You see?" Mr. Takaya said, looking around. "Nailed it." He continued. "Now let's move on, and talk about why I REALLY had you do these mood boards! Let's start with… Cali - again! Hers is one of the best in terms of expression and concept, but it's a MESS, and therefore A FAIL."

He then proceeded to tear apart her work, and *most* of the other students' work, for the rest of the class. He touched his laser pointer at her project, and delighted in critiquing it for visible bits of glue, tape peeking out, seams showing, bad arrangements, unsymmetrical alignments, the slightest imprecision, the lack of neat cutting, etc. ("Scissors are prohibited here – X-acto knives ONLY!").

"Careless…" he shook his head, pacing back and forth. "Every year more and more careless. Why!? PRESENTATION is almost everything!" he whined. "If your presentation in my course isn't PERFECT, I WILL FAIL YOU!! And if you fail *me*, you will ultimately *fail as a designer*." It looked like it hurt him to teach this. He grasped at his heart, and practically growled, "You may disappoint me with your taste, or with your design choices or even how you present *yourself*, coming into my class looking like hell – I get it, you'll be up all night sometimes working on projects – but do not disappoint me with *how you present your work*! Now, go home and get to work on the next assignment! See you all next week. Start tonight so you don't get behind!"

Suddenly there was a mass stampede out of the classroom. Cali stayed behind in her seat, however: breathing deeply, collecting herself. Though she'd gotten more used to being around people, thanks to the strip clubs, any new social situations – especially if she were called out – made her head spin, and her whole body blush. And there was still a long train ride home this evening back to Brooklyn; then back up early for the train to get to Hank's office on time.

One distinctive woman in the class stood behind putting on her coat. She was a zaftig middle-aged blonde with a jolly, adorable face, and every curve pushing out of a very flamboyant vintage dress and cowboy boots. She stopped next to Cali. "I loved your introduction board," she said, in an evident English accent. "I feel like that inside too, like a femme fatale, but I didn't have the guts to show it."

"Oh, thank you!" Cali sighed, relieved. Compliments: the lubricant of civilization. "Well, you express it well with how you dress. And you're maybe the only one who didn't get in trouble about neatness. Your board was *perfect*."

"Oh, it's nothing. I'm a neat nick."

"Lucky you."

"Should we exchange numbers?" the woman offered. "In case one of us misses a class and needs the notes or… If you could just do my homework for me and I can say it's mine?" She snorted out an obnoxious laugh when Cali looked slightly alarmed. "Just kidding, of course."

"Yes, that sounds good. The notes part."

"Capital idea, I'd say," the woman said, writing down her name and number, and then handing it over, giving Cali a smile. "I'm Saffron, by the way. And if this class ever gets too bad, we could always go out for a drink after, too. Or slit our wrists with our X-acto knives. NOT SCISSORS," she laughed.

"Sounds good," Cali said, writing her info down for Saffron. "The drinks, I mean. I happen to see his point about the X-actos, though."

"Yeah, me too. It's a cleaner cut. More control."

Two more years of school to go, Cali thought, as Saffron left. She slowly gathered her things into her tote bag, wondering how she would ever go to work every day *and* attend classes in the evenings, with the level of production and perfection they would require.

There would be a lot of all-nighters and weekends 'in' coming up, and not the sexy kind. How was she going to fit a hopefully burgeoning romance with Jean-Chris into her life, *and* more of those hot trysts with Tony? Not to mention maybe getting more experience with some new guys (as GG had mentioned)?

Cali snuggled into her sleeping bag coat, feeling very tired and hungry all of a sudden. She wondered what in the world she would eat on her way back to her apartment: a good old slice of affordable pizza, no doubt, from Mr. Smiley's on the main street of Park Slope. Then she'd take a bath, before passing out in her bed.

The next morning at Zorvis Pharmaceuticals, Cali had barely gotten to her desk when she heard Hank's muffled, prolonged yelling as he berated someone inside his office. After some time, one of the male executives emerged, red-faced and rubbing his temples.

Suddenly Cali's line three rang, and she picked it up promptly. "Hello Hank, how may I help?"

"Let's discuss lunch! Come in."

She grabbed her notebook and a pen, and was into Hank's office in under the requisite thirty seconds. She looked slightly less frumpy than the day before, having been inspired by Saffron's bold outfit – and Hank's unabashed flirting. She'd decided to wear a loose wooly cardigan and the long vintage dress she'd worn on her lunch date with Tony. And leather boots, which would hide the fact that she was wearing cotton tights and not allergy-activating nylons.

"You feel better today?" Hank asked. "Less itching?"

"Yes, much," she nodded.

He looked her over, but in a nice way. "You look like you're on your way to church."

"I could use a visit to church. After my first class last night, I need the prayer. Brutal! But I remembered some of the things you told me yesterday, especially about how to speak, not saying ummmm, and it made a real difference."

"Good." Hank invited her to sit on one of the plush chairs in the sitting area, rather than across from his desk.

"God, these people kill me! You know what corporate intelligence is, Cali? It's my internal CIA. We have to make sure our precious formulas don't get into the wrong hands. You've seen *Tinker, Tailor, Soldier, Spy*, the movie?" He plopped down into the chair opposite her.

"No…"

"Well, see it. Excellent movie. We've been fiercely protecting the formula for our new hard-on patch, but I suspect – no, I have direct evidence – that there's a leak in the information pipeline. And I think the mole is my Chief Chemist. Fuck." Hank peered down the hall to make sure his other Assistants weren't coming in. "Some other top secret business." He pulled out a luxurious-looking small gift sack from under a table. "You'll need to open this here," he whispered. "And tuck it into your notebook…"

"What?" she said. "I can't."

"Yes you can."

Before she could truly protest, she'd already reached inside and pulled out a flat package made from velveteen-textured paper covered with curvy lettering in French. Realizing it was a pair of 100% silk thigh-high stockings, edged in a wide band of exquisite lace, she faced a sudden dilemma. She quickly took in the blatant symbolism in the gift, and what it might mean for her life, her studies, perhaps her ability to be much, much more comfortable – if she played it right.

Shall I reject this outright, and go temp somewhere else, and hope that in my absence he still wants me and comes chasing? Or do I hold tight and see what else is on offer (it's got to be more than stockings!)…

"Silk. Not nylon. They're from a store here that is based in Paris. *La Petite Coquette,*" Hank said, carefully monitoring Cali's face for any sign she might scream out in horror. She softened her eyes to let him know he was so far doing well. She clutched her hand around the gossamer fabric sack containing the gift.

Oh my God, I've passed that La Petite Coquette shop window; all the pretty things made me salivate.

She enjoyed the feeling of keeping him in suspense as she suppressed a smile, admired the lace, and wondered if she'd need a matching garter belt to keep them up or not. She probably would, as they were old-fashioned silk, with no synthetic stretchy fibers or elastic on top.

Why hadn't Jean-Chris or Tony or any of the guys at the strip clubs ever given her such an exquisitely thoughtful little gift before? Were they insensitive louts? Hank, even if he was a bit older… well, he looked great in his tailored suit and cuff links, and his chunky body hinted at a dynamism she could only imagine. What kind of sexy imagination did he possess that could come up with such a thoughtful gift and the boldness to give it to her, here? She liked him. A lot.

Discreetly tucking the flat package into the depths of her yellow notepad, she looked him in the eyes, and said, "I love them, *love* them. Thank you."

That's all it would take for Hank to know that he'd been right about Cali: her willingness to become special for him. She imagined him reflecting that he should have bought the matching garter belt. And for her: what *this* was, it was so much more different than the short-term 'relationships' and overt transactions she'd known in the harsh surroundings of the strip clubs. But yet, some small part of it felt the same and familiar. She'd pleased him, and now he was signaling he wanted something more. She wasn't sure what, but she wasn't opposed to it (yet). Wasn't this what being a pampered, discreet courtesan was all about?

This – a secret relationship with Hank – could possibly be an excellent training ground for discovering what it means, and what it requires to be 'special' for one man, who in return would possibly make her life richer, and easier, and still leave her time to pursue her goals. A relationship with Hank might be like *GG's lite*.

"I'd like to invite you for lunch next Monday," he said. "Somewhere private."

Don't be too easy to have. Don't say yes right away.

"You know, I can't be away long," she said. "Surefire Temps is probably moving me to a different company, and they're keeping track of me."

"I'm being kept track of, too! It won't be long, just a lunch, a chance to… Depending on how it goes, it might become something we might think about on a regular basis. What do you think?"

Hmmmm, it all sounded safe enough to her. He wasn't a predatory wolf disguised in sheep's clothing. He'd shown his wolfish side and filed-down fangs to others (like the possible mole who just left his office) but he was a softy inside. His gift of a fine pair of silk stockings could only indicate there would be uber-private dealings and discussions that might lead to some action with this handsome older gent with money to burn.

"Well. Go on. I'm listening…"

As she pretended to take dictation, Hank laid out the exact instructions as to how and when she would discreetly enter the nearby five-star Wendell-Astor Hotel, and happen to find her way to his suite, whose number he would call her with (there were never to be texts or emails between them).

"I'm going to give you some gift cards later today. And over the weekend, I want you to go buy a new coat. That one you left in yesterday made you look like a refugee who got lost from a camp. Ladies shouldn't dress like refugees. No offence against refugees, they dress for their circumstances, but I think you know what I mean. And your dress yesterday? I've seen dusting rags with more style. And, while we're at it, I'm sending you over to Frederick Fekkai for your hair, and am setting up an account. Wait! Holy hell, no. That's where my wife Esther gets *her* hair done. No. Go get a style and blow whenever you want, but not there. I'll take care of *that* with a different gift card. When I see you next week at the hotel, I want you looking like a million dollars. Like a girl without a care in the world. One should always dress at the level they want to be paid."

The idea of an initial makeover thrilled her (though it was more superficial and less intense than GG's suggested surgeries). The Design Arts Institute may have just started, but 'Preparation for GG's' was officially under way as well. Hank would be her first practice 'client.' She eagerly wrote down some notes to transfer into the little notebook containing her most intimate thoughts, which she kept tucked deep in her purse.

Ditch anything that resembles rags or refugees.

For my "on" times, rethink my wardrobe from places like Rags to Religion.

Look like a girl without a care in the world.

Always act like I'm worth it.

Dress like how you want to be paid.

Be someone special for Hank Greenace, and learn it to perfection.

Kindly request he provide the garter belt and the panties that match the stockings.

Chapter Six

The following Monday when Cali walked through the Wendell-Astor Hotel on her way to visit Hank, it was a whole different story than when she'd first walked into Zorvis Pharmaceuticals.

Her long hair was cut well, smoothly coiffed and blown under. Now all one color, she'd become a cool blonde with a few discreet highlights built in for depth. Under a long, black cashmere swing coat with a wide belt, she looked adorable in a well-fitting navy blue suit, with a white ruffled blouse beneath, frills peeking out of the sleeves. Her low navy heels had small gold buckles with the double C's (as in Chanel). And completing the picture of an elegant young lady: a rich blue leather handbag with a gold chain.

As Hank greeted her in the room, and walked around her admiring the transformation, she was grateful for the experience of a few hours of unbridled consumerism he'd given her over the weekend, with the gift cards. It was truly addictive. She was at the point where she couldn't decide what she loved better now that she'd tried both: flirting and having sex with attractive men… or shopping for clothes and beautifying herself. Could life ever become some outrageous, heady concoction of *all of that*? She hoped the answer might be a resounding *Yes*.

Stepping inside Hank's suite was the *real* beginning of the story she'd felt long stirring inside her: the one about becoming sparkling and educated, but also possibly *a courtesan*. Although they hadn't touched each other yet, and though the 'terms' of their agreement would never be obviously stated, she decided to trust in him, to latch onto the powerful attraction she felt toward him, despite their vast difference in age and stations in life. Whatever support he could give and whatever he wished to offer would be enough.

These thoughts were still in her mind when he gently took her coat off and laid it on a chair. Leading her into the living area, he dropped to his knees, and clung to her around the back of her legs. "You are my God-ess," he professed. "Would you ever design to show me a special favor?"

"Maybe."

She sensed nothing S&M or Slave and Master about being asked this request. It was just an impassioned, adoring plea for…? She wasn't sure what, but being called a goddess was great, and she liked how he'd stated everything in the language of old romance novels. A 'special favor' usually meant s-e-x.

"Hug me!" he pleaded. Rising, he gathered her into his arms, and she returned the hug, a little reluctantly, not sure what to make of his vast pendulum of self-expression. "HUG ME!" he commanded. Grabbing him, she gave him the squeeze of a lifetime. He whined into her shoulder, as they were nearly the same height. "I never get hugged..."

"Aww. Ohhhh." She was slowly becoming enlightened. Getting adoration for just being a feminine creature was quickly becoming Cali's secret top-shelf elixir of choice, like a plant-based violet-flavored liqueur, or a rum that was redolent with a coco-nutty Caribbean flair. She kind of liked the hugging, too. It had a great effect on her. Her mother had hugged her only now and again, and her father never. Being held in a long embrace by a loving, expressive man seemed to soften some of the hardened jadedness that had snuck into her soul while dancing on bar tops and raunch-filled runways while guys threw wadded-up money at her. She cuddled in.

"Why couldn't I have met you earlier in my life?" Hank whined.

Because...*any earlier I wouldn't have known how to appreciate you.* She'd needed to go through the grinders of the Pussycat and Silkies (not to mention a shootout at a greasy garage) in order to cherish a man like him. But she'd save her stripping tales for a much later time, or maybe never. He might not want to know those kinds of things about her. *Less is more, where your sordid past is concerned* she'd read somewhere in a book on how to capture men's hearts and have them groveling at your feet.

When they finally pulled apart, Hank wiped some moisture away from his eyes.

"I smell..." and Hank came in closer, then sniffed at his own clothes. "You shouldn't have done that," he said, shaking his head. "Perfume! Fuck!"

That morning Cali had nearly doused herself with a gorgeous new fragrance she'd purchased with one of his gift cards, hoping it would last until noontime when they met, but Hank was not a fan.

"If my wife caught wind of that…what is that? It's wonderful! I love it! But…"

"I understand. I'm sorry, I had no idea. It's Hermès."

"She knows, by the way."

"Knows what?"

"That I need this. I do it with her approval. We don't exactly sit around dinner discussing it, but she's given me permission to go out and get what I need. She's a tremendous woman: the best wife and mother a man could ask for. Physical warmth was never her forte, however. Once the children were gone, well, she *really* checked out on that part of life, but she's never left me in the lurch. I've got her blessing, and I've got *you* now."

"Wow. I don't quite understand, although I guess I do." Her mind shot quickly to her father Dash's relationship with Lacy, and her mother's begrudging, bitter knowledge of it.

"I don't expect you to understand everything; you're still a kid. It's a thing about being a mistress. Remember when I said the greatest gift you can give a man is your discretion?"

"Yes."

"This falls into that category. Don't wear perfume again. I wouldn't want to throw our meetings up in Esther's face. Now, let's see what else you've got on… *under*."

Hmmm, this was all a bit more direct and contrived than

Cali preferred. With Jean-Chris, and even Tony, passion, love (whatever you wanted to label it) it flowed. Clothes were removed without instructions. There was always some flirtation; conversations were unpredictable, excitingly volatile sometimes, with J.C – and mind-numbingly inane with Tony, although he made up for it with the satisfying force of his fucks. In this case, Hank was acting as a Director, almost as if next he'd yell out: "And action!"

Cali did a slow striptease for him. It felt familiar, although there was no music playing, and no crowd watching her. She slid off her jacket, and unbuttoned her blouse. Walking toward the couch, she indicated for Hank to sit down and enjoy the show. Taking care of a gracious man here, in this private room, was *so* much better than catering to louts in the seedy environs of Blastoff 69 or Chesty's. She tempered down her true abilities to dance, not wanting to give him any hints about her recent past. She fumbled a little on purpose, and swayed a bit awkwardly, as if this were all new to her.

"Go on," Hank urged. "Own it. I love it."

As the clothes came off, she revealed an exquisite one-piece teddy with garter straps, from La Perla. It was in pure white Italian lace, which coordinated with the white silk stockings Hank had gifted her when they first met. This made him smile.

"So essential. You've done well. The perfect lingerie – it just brings everything together. You are a gift!"

"Thank you."

"Lunch? I'll talk. You eat."

He led her over to a table spread with silver covered trays, and lifted them up simultaneously with a flourish. She'd so dreamed of having a buttery lobster roll and truffled fries or a cheeseburger with gouda and sugared bacon, also with fries on the side. Maybe both. Instead, what could best be described as elevated rabbit food nested on their plates with some white vegetables shaped to look like small eggs.

"They've given us some radishes," he sighed. "Radishes give me gas. Fuck."

"I get the logic of yours. But what is *mine*? I was so looking forward to really *eating*."

"NO, Cali. If I'm going to cheat death with a healthy diet, you are too. We're doing this together. You do fattening foods on your own time. I'm lying to my secretary about where I'm at when I'm with you: A PRIVATE GYM followed by a spa food lunch. So I'd better get the body to prove that's where I was."

"Oh," Cali tried to hide her frown with a smirk, but failed. She picked up her fork.

"I saw that. Do not frown in the presence of any man you wish to enchant, young lady. The uptick of a woman's smile is directly proportional to the hoisting of a man's mast, if you know what I mean."

"I think I do," she giggled.

No frowning when Hank – or any lover – is around.

"Come sit," he said after 'lunch,' patting the couch beside him. "I couldn't stop thinking about you, and this, all weekend. It really got me through," he sighed. "And knowing I will see you on Friday too, it makes my week so much better." He pulled a bottle of water from an ice bucket and poured out two glasses.

Could I not order champagne or a lemonade? she thought to herself.

"I have to offer you water. We're a 'dry' company. If the boss is caught drinking during work hours, it sends the wrong message to all the chemists who have to stay sober for the sake of science. So, did you enjoy shopping this weekend?"

"Very much so," she smiled. "I was a little sad. It reminded me of a very nice woman I knew growing up, who taught me a lot about feminine things. She was my father's girlfriend, her name was Lacy – but she died pretty young from skin cancer, as a result of too much tanning. I was so broken up over it. He was too; I wasn't sure if he was going to make it."

"Cali, I don't mean to be rude, OK?"

"What?"

"When you meet me, we're here to just be in the present, to talk about the present, or, frankly, whatever *I'd* like to talk about. And sometimes all I want to talk about is *me*. This is not a therapist's couch for you. It may sound harsh, but I don't really give a damn about your past or what feelings were brought up for you. You see, the average man – and I'm not average, but I mean most men like me – will give out little hooks about what *they'd* like to talk about. Usually for men, they want to talk about themselves. It's *just how we are*. It's up to you to 'hook on' to those hooks and use those to help steer the conversation."

"Oh!" Her mind scrambled. Jean-Chris had never acted that

way, and he was a guy. He'd seemed to care very much about her past experiences, and to listen carefully to what had shaped her, and what she was feeling as they spent time together.

"Don't get me wrong. That's just a rule for this context, for what we have together. *Here*."

So this is one kind of world, and out there, was another. Whew. It was starting to sink in, finally, that within these types of relationships, there was a type of stage, and the actors did not break the 'fourth wall' by breaking character. To Cali's mind, it was comforting, and insular, to know that – if she didn't want them to – the men she potentially might entertain, could be barred from entering the inner recesses of her life, her mind. That was a relief.

"Oh. I'm such a ditz."

"Hold on, young lady. Ditz!? Please, never let me hear you say a bad word about yourself again. It's, well, hell, all I can say is I don't like it! Don't do it! Whether it's just a form of modesty or you really believe bullshit about yourself, I never want to hear you slander yourself again." He slugged from his water. "Sorry to be bossy, but I'm the boss here, and I won't have such a lovely flower like you talking that way about yourself. It's lies. And I hate liars."

"Yes, Hank. Could we… hold hands?"

"I'll hold hands with you," he smirked, grabbing hold of her hand tightly, kissing it. "I might even play footsies with you. How do you like that!"

Later that afternoon, after their hugs had resulted in giving Hank an intense hand job to cap off their day together, Cali rode out to Brooklyn on the train. She wrote the following in her little purse-sized notebook:

Discretion is the greatest gift you can give another person.

Never too much perfume or, better, none at all.

Own it. Be it.

The connection between lovers is one interior world, outside is a separate world.

Lovers who support you are never to be your therapist. But be a therapist to them.

Don't say a bad word against yourself.

Though it may only be a hand job, infuse it with some love.

Chapter Seven

On a Friday evening after Cali's intense first weeks of work and school, and the Universe's wonderful insertion of Hank into her life, she was ready for a little R&R. There had been a fabulous new development: Hank had ended their first appointment on a promising note.

"This is the only time we'll *ever* speak of this matter; I don't like to talk about money. Before I see you on Friday, please go and set up a Paypal or some such. Write down your information for me, and put it in an envelope. I need you to set yourself up as an independent contractor, my uhhh… consultant."

She'd pretended to be puzzled. "Why, Mr. Greenace?"

"I *may* want to wire you something every once in a while," he had growled, softly, and she'd smirked.

After classes, she met Jean-Chris in front of the Hotel Gram-Irving. Cali enjoyed knowing that it was no longer her home but, instead, the entertaining, interesting place that had once sheltered her when she'd first become a New Yorker.

"I've missed you," he said, grabbing her into a hug.

They seemed to pick up right where they'd left off: in a delicious limbo land between teasing, petting and foreplay, and the imminent 'going all the way' as a fulfillment of their longing to connect on an even deeper level. They held hands, and took a good walk into Greenwich Village toward a target Japanese restaurant. As they did so, they debated the pros and cons of Cali's recent move out to Brooklyn, and hashed out his dilemma between focusing on antiques vs. architecture. They also reviewed her decision of going to a 'lesser school' than Preston, which cost much less and allowed her to work during the day. Finally, they rambled into the question of: if having sex for sex's sake was actually ever a good idea, particularly in contrast to making love with someone via a so-called loving relationship.

It was all a bit of a ploy on Cali's part to prevent herself from mentioning her evolving relationship with Hank. She wanted to keep away from confiding in Jean-Chris about this new mutually beneficial relationship with someone who could mentor her in preparation for being a courtesan in future (hopefully without Hank knowing he was contributing to her 'delinquency').

She looked over at Jean-Chris. "Love complicates everything. Can't sex just be for fun, or, God, you're going to hate me for this, but a transaction, even? Must it be such a heavy, meaningful thing?"

"I am not a good judge of this. I am so easily seduced. I usually don't make any distinctions between love and sex when women just want to have their way with me."

"Of course. It sounds like you've had a lot of lovers so far, besides Dump 'Em Darla?"

"Hmmm, love is not a word I would associate to describe what I have known with some of the ladies. I was sort of in the right place at the right time…"

"Oh, like last call at a bar? When some women will go home with *anybody*?"

"That is very flattering, thank you, but no. Can *you* tell me about having sex, with a more deeply, um, personally informed opinion?" he teased.

"Screw you," she sighed.

"Let's hope!"

Once they were shoeless and seated in the Japanese restaurant in one of those booths sunk into the floor, Jean-Chris confessed this was his first time having Japanese food.

"I've saved myself for you, in a culinary sense," he smirked, perusing a menu that had him a bit confused. "Have you saved yourself for me?"

"I'm not telling you. Every time is like the first time. Alright?"

A waiter with a sizzling platter walked by. "That's hot and dangerous. A lot like you," Jean-Chris laughed. "And what have you been getting up to out in Brooklyn? Have you, you know…?"

"Just never you mind."

"I can't stop thinking about it, actually. Whoever you had your first time with, he is a lucky fellow. Maybe it was that guy, the one who was in your room that time when I heard you crying?"

"Sneaky. I'm not telling you. Now tell me about your new job!" she said, as they clinked glasses, and quickly downed the hot saké that had arrived.

"So, I'm here tonight having Japanese *with you* because my new boss asked me to go out to get him lunch from the Japanese buffet today: this buffet. It all looked so good, the sushi; it's so beautiful and fresh, and I was thinking 'I should try this myself some day. Why not tonight, with Cali?'"

Here, he launched into a story of how he'd brought his new boss a whole bowl of the light green super-spicy wasabi condiment, thinking it was a sweet dessert, like pistachio or lime pudding. On being offered it in this way, his new boss, completely unreasonable and angry, had accused Jean-Chris of trying to kill him (or steal his job if he was out sick).

Jean-Chris sighed, "I *do* want his job, *someday*, but I think I would choose a more effective way to kill him than a savory sauce made from a root vegetable. But now I will try this offending thing myself..." he said when their first plates of sushi arrived, carefully transferring a small amount of the wasabi to his plate.

"Hoo boy, that's hot," Cali said, her nostrils flaring as she tasted it, quickly taking a swig of her cold water.

"It is like a fire-cracker going off in my mouth,' he concurred, using his chopsticks to mix condiments. "I think it must be mixed with this soy sauce to be bearable."

Then they dove into the incredible sushi. Cali savored every bite; it was easily now her favorite food. "This is a little bit of heaven in my mouth," she smiled.

"I like that you like to try new things. Have you tried

anything *else* new, lately?" he ventured, chuckling. "Have you made *amour* with anyone interesting?"

"I'm not going to tell you what you want to know!"

Later, some fortune cookies arrived, and Cali insisted that they add the words '*in bed'* to the end of each fortune. "What does yours say?" she asked, as Jean-Chris carefully opened his cookie and read it, chuckling.

"Yours first."

"Mine says: You will find a new position soon (in bed)."

They broke into giggles. "I have tried many already. I am not sure if something will feel new," he confessed. "But it probably feels new with new people."

"Oh, fuck you. Why'd you have to bring that up?" Cali frowned.

"I am sorry," he hung his head. "You are right. Rude. What does yours say?"

"Rude is right. Mine says: always seek new adventures and you will never be bored (in bed). Ha! There!"

"Ohhhhh! You dog. It is so easy for women to have adventures. I have really had to work hard for the few I have had. Begging, almost. Like a dog."

"Huh. I don't think so. I think Darla just tossed herself to you like a scrap."

This began an interesting discussion of Jean-Chris' secret jealousies of the things women get to enjoy, like "anytime" access to new and strange lovers, if so desired. He also claimed that silky things against the skin were one of his main sore points. "Women can feel head-to-toe silk, but a man? Hmmmm... This might need to be something done in secret. But under no circumstances do I wish to wear women's underthings."

"I know what I'm getting you to celebrate your new job!" Cali exclaimed. "Let's go, now."

After Jean-Chris paid the check, and Cali gave him a nice hug thanking him, they nearly ran out of the restaurant as she led him to a nearby store where she knew they had a selection of silky pajamas.

"Pick a pair!" she encouraged, running her hands over the array of colors and patterns in the shop. "Something that really says, 'I am Jean-Chris and I feel silky,'" she laughed.

He came along and ran his fingers down her hair sweetly, tugging a little. Leaning into her ear, he said "*This* feels silky to me. Oh! You want me to choose my pajamas, not your beautiful hair. Well OK!" He went about picking out a pair of red wine-colored, shimmering PJs that would fit him beautifully, while leaving enough room to stretch out during sleep, or...

Soon they were in his room at the Hotel Gram-Irving, making out madly and nearly tearing each other's clothes off. Backing her against the wall, his hands strayed all over her breasts.

"Your room is a mess," she sighed. "But I understand you're busy," she teased; she was the queen of slobbery herself. Throwing her dress off and sliding out of her boots, she revealed a red lace bra and panty set.

"It's always like this. But, I am not a slob. Not like you.

You are a slob pure and simple," he teased back. "*My* mess is a reflection of my many, many varying interests. And you look *delectable*."

"Uh, huh."

"So I think it's OK if we make love now that we won't be living together?" he asked, taking both her breasts into his hands and launching his lips onto her neck.

"I'm not so sure," she said, as he grazed her neck with his tongue, and once again ran his fingers through her hair, making her feel like giving into any demand he may have of her. "Remember at the steam room when I put it in, just a little ways? Can we…?" he asked, assuming she'd know exactly what he wanted. "God, I think of it every day."

Though yearning to experience him, she thought to herself: *I've just played with Hank today (though we didn't go all the way; close enough). And Tony has 'reserved' his Monday night with me next week, two nights from now. Before that I'll see Hank again earlier that afternoon. What KIND of woman am I, really – being comfortable with this much action with multiple men, none of whom I love (apart from maybe Jean-Chris)? Isn't it a blatant hint that I need to start getting paid for what I love doing best, i.e. monetize my appetites? Maybe, though, I could keep Jean-Chris as my freebie, my 'favorite'?*

She hated how calculating she felt, how coldly rational. Weren't matters of the heart the *last* place to be so reasonable and minimalist? At the moment, giving in completely to a passionate, all-in relationship with Jean-Chris felt so potentially messy. It probably meant giving up Hank's financial support, and her plan of going on to GG's (someday). Going 'all in' with Jean-Chris would require more struggle, more time in offices, more juggling of her conflicting wants. It felt mentally exhausting already, and all he was doing was kissing her neck! It felt very, very nice, as he went lower, and tongued her nipples.

"PLEASE put on your new pajamas," she urged. "We need some kind of barrier between us. Tonight is not the night."

"Damn! Why not?" he asked, sliding his hands over her bottom as their lips found each other; while their tongues intertwined, he guided her hand to his raging hard-on.

"It's a secret skill to master…" she whispered breathlessly, now that he'd found a way into her panties with his fingers, tantalizing her into a state of utter wetness. "We need to pace ourselves."

"But I could never have enough of *you*," he moaned. Feeling his hard girth in her hand, she squeezed a little, and he groaned in desire. "Can't I put it in, just a little, like before?"

"Pajamas on, then we'll talk," she insisted, and so he stripped sexily for her: putting them on as she watched. She enjoyed taking in his lean physique, his muscled buns, imagining how good it would feel to press them while he fucked her sometime, soon.

"There," he said, sitting down on the bed. "Come and sit on Santa's Lap. Tell me all your wishes. Tell me some of the naughty things you've done while we've been apart."

No way. Whatever she might reveal, Jean-Chris would tease her mercilessly, initially hiding that he felt hurt or jealous. Then he'd probably pout a bit, then devolve into sulking. He could be so heavy at times. His seriousness about her was one of the reasons she preferred to keep this light.

What to do? *Drop to my knees soon, before I can't say no, and get him into my mouth…*

His cock was so appealing, and so was he. She climbed into his lap in her underwear. Pressing her pussy to his cock, she nearly came from the pressure it put on her clit; she could barely contain rubbing up and down on it, imagining how great it would feel if he would actually, or accidentally slip inside.

"I have something for you, too. A gift," he said, between long, sensuous and slow kisses and caresses that were turning her pussy into an absolute waterfall. She hoped she wouldn't stain his new pajamas with her juice.

"I think I know what it is," she said, grabbing around his cock.

"No, really! I have something. Reach in my PJ pocket," he encouraged.

In doing so, she drew out a pretty vintage bracelet with sparkling, pastel faux stones arranged into vines and flowers. Just her sort of thing. He'd taken notes on her taste in the past, as they'd wandered around the vintage stores in the East Village. "It's soooo beautiful!! How did you sneak that into there? I was watching you get dressed."

"Magic fingers."

"Oh my God. It's totally, totally gorgeous. I'll keep it forever!" she smiled, securing it on to her wrist. Jumping into his lap again, she straddled him.

"Keep *me* forever?" he asked, burying his face in her neck before finding his way to her lips again. She felt his cock straining against her panties, ready to slide under *and in*… but she knew that shouldn't happen, not tonight.

"Now *I* have something for you." She dropped to her knees, ready to take him into her mouth. She eagerly tore into his pajama pants to gain full access to his cock, and her mouth closed over the head of his rod. She felt the interesting sheath of skin slide back and forth (he being uncircumcised), but he stopped her, grabbing her shoulders.

"Let's not do this. I don't like how this just happened, the order of things. I'm sorry, you will think I'm a fool."

"What? Did I do something wrong?"

"NO, it's just… first I give you a bracelet, a gift, and then right after, you get on your knees to service me. I guess it doesn't feel right."

"It's not servicing – I'm totally into you! I *want* to. It's not because you gave me something. If I were more sensitive, I would say this is becoming insulting."

"I don't mean to insult you! It's my fault. I should have waited to give you the gift at another time. Then there would be no question."

"No question of what!?"

"That this is a kind of symbiosis: a transaction. Oh God, I am digging myself in."

"You are. A transaction was the farthest thing from my mind. But now I see what you're seeing, and… God, that's just not how it is."

"Come, let's lay down and talk." He laid down with her

on the bed face to face, but she sat up, fidgety, wanting to get home.

"You've treated me like a whore because you can't get it out of your head, all the things I've told you about me. Even if I *were* one, and I someday *may* be, you have to know that I treasure this bracelet and *you*, and all the fun times we've had, and I think of you as my most special friend."

She got up and gathered her clothes as he said, "I am a pig. I am so sorry. There is no point in you staying. I've ruined everything."

"I forgive you. It's no big deal."

"I have treated you badly today. I will make this better."

"You haven't treated me badly, but I need to go."

He pulled her to him, and kissed her on the top of her breasts lovingly. "Please forgive me. If you want to see me again, you know where I am. I don't know where *you* are in Brooklyn. I'll understand if you never wish to see me."

"I *do* want to see you again," she said, quickly dressing. "I want you to visit me when my place is all set up better. A romantic nest for us." It seemed as if she were making her intentions for a proper relationship official.

"Just call me?" he said. "I miss you. It's not the same here without you."

"It wouldn't be the same over there without *you*."

She opened the door, and quietly shut it behind her.

Chapter Eight

That night, after arriving at her bare apartment – which was devoid of all but the basics like the bed and her clothes in the closet – Cali looked online, and noticed that Hank's mysterious shell company had generously sent her a gift infusion of cash into her account. He'd named the entity Power2U Charity. It looked like she was indeed the beneficiary of enough funding to make a difference in her life. Whether it would come in weekly or monthly wasn't clear yet. Even so, she felt inspired to trust in the Universe that the sum was a weekly gift, and to go out shopping accordingly.

Being so well-rewarded for her care and hugging of Hank was gratifying; it was, as the British sometimes say: *moreish*… Like certain snacks one can't stop eating, she wanted MORE. The jolt of cash felt a lot like that first (and last) inspiring sniff-up of cocaine on her first night dancing. Getting 'paid' so well (though she preferred to think of it as getting 'gifted') felt soooo good. It made her feel confident and bold. Unlike the coke, however, this was a 'high' that could be repeated, and wouldn't necessary ruin her life with addiction – as long as she could maintain Hank's interest, and keep their rapport crackling, enticing him sexually and always satisfying his need for hugs. Hopefully the gifts would keep rolling in on a regular basis.

The next morning, at the local flea market in Park Slope, Cali arrived very early in the morning to beat all the professional treasure hunters. Flea markets, thrift shops and any kind of junk-filled place hiding décor-booty was just her kind of territory. Invigorating! Plus, she felt giddy and flush with cash as she perused the stalls of 1920's antiques, some good quality pastel-colored vintage rugs, and a few exquisitely-shaped seating pieces that would go well in her new rental. Of course, they weren't perfect and needed some costly re-upholstery work, which required the purchase of some pricey yards of luxurious fabrics.

Cali returned to the ATM, and also drew out some cash off her new credit card. She went (what her mother might call) 'hog wild' on furnishing her new place. Running through her starting cash from Hank so quickly, she justified that this was only the beginning; there would definitely be more coming in. A niggling little voice in her mind reminded her of something she once heard Sugar say in the dressing room at one of the clubs. *Easy come, easy go. Black market money don't wanna stay at home.*

Well, she was putting her money into her home: creating a pretty, inviting environment for herself (and the many lovers she imaged she might practice with there). It would be a comfortable, charming cocoon from which to some day emerge as an accomplished, educated, and cultivated butterfly – possibly ready for GG's, and with an interior design degree in hand. Wasn't furnishing her first apartment to perfection a major part of practicing to be an interior designer, too?

Once her furniture at the antiques market was paid for, she called 'Clark Gents: The College Hunk and Handy Man Service' who advertised hauling-help online. The male customer service person was completely reassuring, and said they could send someone immediately to help move the furniture from the flea market into her new apartment.

"Great, call you back!" Cali hung up suddenly because something occurred to her, but she still felt a little unsure about it and wanted to think it through. Perhaps *now* was as good a time as any to try out bit of 'seduction practice' on one of those total strangers or 'unattractive men' – as GG had described them – who would no doubt cross her path one day as a courtesan. She'd surely be required to treat them kindly and perform for them, despite their looks, little hang-ups, or whatever. She assumed that GG had solely been referring to men who were physically unattractive (or not her type). Dealing with men behaving badly, as in those who were mean or had rude manners, etc… that was surely a lesson for another time. Hopefully it wasn't tolerated at GG's at all; those kind of men *wouldn't be tolerated personally by me*, she thought. Some trepidation whipped through her, then, thinking about the potential for violence against women that lurked around every corner: straight life or not.

She suddenly thought of an analogy. How could she – as someone seeking to cultivate herself as a courtesan with sexy super powers – at a very basic, purely physical level, ever learn to blindly take a chocolate from the variety candy box, and not put it back if she didn't like the way it looked/tasted, etc.? How could she learn to eat the distasteful candy in such a way to have the candy think that she was savoring every bite of it/him? Wasn't this the essential art of the thing, of being a consummate (and professional) seductress? She probably wasn't ever going to be ready for GG's until she mastered *at least* this basic.

She called the Clark Gents back to complete her service request, and this time a woman answered. When they were done with the details, Cali said nervously, "This may sound weird, but please don't send someone too handsome. You know, my boyfriend gets very jealous when the movers are too good looking." She felt herself blushing as she lied. "Please just send over one of the guys who is good at lifting, but doesn't look like any permutation of Superman, or Clark Kent. Know what I mean? Not too…"

"Got it," the woman interrupted her. Cali could almost hear the eyeballs rolling up into the woman's head, as in *What the fuck*? People in New York could be so curt, sometimes making her feel like such a fluffy airhead.

"Thank you!" Cali said, but the woman had already hung up on her. She hoped she would not be too disappointed. Perhaps she wouldn't be able to sleep with someone too unattractive and inappropriate as she wouldn't be able to bear it.

Seeking out a not-attractive fellow was a complete reversal to her usual secret anticipations about the hopefully handsome, shaggable and noncommittal men who might some day show up to help with various handyman tasks. Today, her challenge to herself was to welcome, spoil, craftily seduce and 'make this guy's day' no matter what he looked like (and if it was clear he didn't have a girlfriend, of course). *Open the chocolate box and take a bite (of whatever).* She bristled with nerves, but felt firmly on her path to self-education in the seduction realms.

Jean-Chris called while she was waiting for Clark Gent to arrive. After apologizing for his behavior the night before, and finding out she'd already engaged in some retail (or secondhand) therapy, he asked. "Why didn't you ask me to help you choose the antiques?" before adding, "Wait. Cali? How are you affording all this? Cali...?" He sounded suspicious, fearful even, of her answer.

She sighed loudly. It really wasn't any of his business, and of course he was linking it to the possibility that she was maybe back to stripping or now up to turning tricks. "I had some savings left over from dancing."

"But don't you need...?"

"What I *need* is to get on with my day. Can I invite you out when I'm ready for a visitor?"

"But of course, Cali."

"Bye, handsome – have a nice weekend!"

She fiddled around the apartment, waiting nervously for Clark Gent, who might soon become her second lover (or technically third, if 'a little ways in' with Jean-Chris was to count for something). She'd taken care to wear a tight t-shirt that showed right through to a lacy bra, cute jeans, and durable sneakers (if she'd have to be involved with helping out). Soon enough the intercom buzzed, and she heard footsteps coming up the stairs.

"You must be Clark," she said, opening her door, eyes closed, determined to smile big at whoever had shown up.

"Live and in person. Are you still asleep, uh, Miss Kistler?" the man laughed.

When she finally opened her eyes she wasn't disappointed, but actually charmed by the guy. He wasn't movie star handsome, but stocky, cute and cuddly: a guy in his twenties whose puppy fat wasn't yet a thing of the past. She'd lucked out this time!

"Hiiii!!" *Whew, I've pulled a tasty caramel from life's box of chocolates.*

Behind Clark Gent, stood his heavy-lifting assistant. A naughty thought of entertaining both of them at the same time flashed across her mind – but the other guy wore a marriage band on his finger. Besides, *that* idea of two dudes in tandem was way out of her league! For the moment.

They were there to look at the space, door width and such, then take her over to the flea market to pick up her new armoire, a chest or two for the living room, a cocktail table, a love seat, an overstuffed chair, a dining table and two cushion-y dining chairs.

Once they were at the flea market, as Clark's helper worked on wedging a dolly under the ornate carved wood wardrobe Cali had purchased, Clark whistled, "This is humongous! You must have a lot of clothes. Do girls really need all those clothes?"

"City girls do, yes."

"You a city girl? You strike me as a country girl gone city. With a vengeance."

On the return drive (the assistant sat in one of the chairs in the back, probably holding on for dear life as Clark bounced the truck over the local potholes) Cali learned that Clark Gent was the CEO of Clark Gents, and an enterprising college student who actually had a lot of Clark Gents contracted under his brand, using their own vans and giving him a cut of every job. His only requirement was that they have good driving records, and be respectful, brawny lifters and happy haulers.

"What does your girlfriend think of all this?" she tried to ask coyly but he returned it with a sly, sidelong glance.

"Ha! ME? I try to meet girls all the time on those apps, and the minute they see me in person at the coffee shop, if I even get that far, they just order an espresso. When a girl likes you, she'll order something big and fluffy at the coffee shop, with a lot of whipped cream on top; she'll take her time, get to know you. You can watch her licking all that cream off the top of her lip. Nope, with me they take one look and just order a small drink. Have you heard of a drink called a Ristretto? It's *half* an espresso! 'Bye! Nice meeting you! Got my little Ristretto here! Oops, it's already gone. Gotta go!'"

"Aw…" Cali laughed at his funny but sad take on things

out in the harsh urban world where physical looks and first impressions seemed to count for everything. It hinted at his hurts, but also at that unremitting human need to connect, to find love and acceptance. "I don't see how this could happen," she insisted. "These girls are probably just so intimidated by your intensity, your sincerity, how busy you must be running the Clark Gents."

"No. They take one look at my huge tummy, and they think it'll be like climbing up on a huge gummy bear – which it is, but hey…"

"You're as sweet as a gummy bear, too, though, I can just tell. And that pretty much overrides everything."

"Well, at the moment nobody's riding, I can tell you that much."

Once in her building, Cali took note of Clark's brawn as well as tight buns as he single-handedly carried her loveseat up the stairs of the building. He was indeed husky and had a man's muffin top around the middle (call it more of a Bundt cake top), escaping out from under his t-shirt. But he was cute as could be, with long eyelashes, deep dimples and a mischievous smirk.

While moving in the wardrobe, a lacy pair of panties dropped from a hanger on the wall. They had been put there on purpose to subliminally work on whomever Cali might seduce. Clark picked the piece up, and pulled it over his head, wearing it like a scarf around his neck; it put Cali into a state of giggles.

"It's the next best thing to having a woman's legs

wrapped around my neck, oops, did I just say that?" he laughed. "I'm working on my political correctness. Don't sue me for sexual harassment during a move-in just cause I said the way I feel when I get around panties. And tiny panties, too!! I'll bet *you* don't even own a pair of granny panties."

"Were you *hoping* for granny panties? I could probably find someone's grandma somewhere."

"Let's just get our minds back on getting you set up in here."

Once everything was in place, as his partner waited out in the truck, they took a lemonade break, and Cali teased Clark Gent a lot – the two of them sat on top of the kitchen counter. "It must be nice to lift stuff without needing a weight belt. Like, cause you already have a *natural* weight belt," she said, gently poking at his tummy.

"Hey! Some women call me beefy. I have something to hold on to," he laughed. "They're luuuuuv handles. Haven't you ever heard of them?" He hopped off the cabinet, offering his hand to help Cali jump down safely. She took hold eagerly, and he made a little dance move, twirling her around. "I should probably go now. It was fun moving you in."

Her eyes flashed; it was time. "Can I give you a tip?" she asked, coming in closer. Her heart was beating madly, and she realized this was the first time she was putting the full-on moves on a near-total-stranger, an 'unsuspecting' guy.

"What's on your mind?" Clark Kent responded. "What did I do wrong? What's the tip?"

"No, not *that* kind of tip: *this* kind…" She forced herself to simply reach out and touch him; it seemed such a feisty thing to do: initiating a hookup without a prelude or a pretense. She rubbed her hand along his arm – which felt mottled through with sheer brawn – and found her way to his hand. Grabbing it gently, she led him to her bedroom, pulling off her t-shirt and bra with the other hand as he watched from behind.

His eyes popped when she turned around topless. Practicing a more seductive, come hither voice than she'd articulated before, she said, "So could you stay just a little longer?"

"You havta ask? Hell yes! Whoo! So you really don't mind my gut, do you?" he said, throwing off his t-shirt, and almost kicking off his tennis shoes.

"No, I love it! I love a good gut," she laughed. Waiting until he was undressed and his eyes were on her, she slid off her tennis shoes, and removed her jeans slowly, revealing a skimpy pair of lacy panties. She slid these down her legs and spread slightly, giving him a glimpse of things to come.

"Oh my fucking GOD!"

"Come over here," she said, laying back on the bed, taking his cock in her hand. Mmmm: he was meaty and hard. Her pussy twitched with anticipation, and the pleasure that must be in his cock somehow transmuted across her body, entering her; she felt her lower love lips heaving with heat and wetness. As she stroked him, with each pass of her hand, he got harder and more swollen, and she leaned back, waiting for him to jump her. He managed to reach over to his jeans, and extract a condom from his wallet, and then slide it on. "I thought this rubber would never see the light of day! Now it's goin' into the dark again!"

She marveled at how empowering it felt to ignore petty fears, and to leapfrog over her own sense of shyness and reserve: initiating sex on her terms.

"Are you sure this is real?" he asked, laughing nervously, now poised above her. He wasn't the smoothest of lovers. In her limited experience, he seemed a bit clumsy, but his sense of excitement about getting seduced distracted her from any further analysis. "I can't believe this is happening. Can I go in?" he asked, his cock now poised to enter her.

It was a rather intoxicating feeling, having the ability to put this young man into such a state of fantasy fulfillment. But a little bit of education was needed. "Would you play with me first, till I can't take it any more?"

"Oh yeah!" he said, nearly tapping his head. "I almost forgot. This is such a crazy surprise. Sorry! I'm so freakin' overwhelmed, like a kid in a candy store!"

"And I got the gummy bear." This seemed to make him puff up with pride. Sliding in beside her, he attempted to kiss her awkwardly on the lips. This wasn't really what she had in mind. Kissing was so intimate; it was something she might only accept with Jean-Chris – or Tony if he insisted. Kissing was certainly too intimate for Clark, or *this*. "We don't need to kiss. I'll be OK," she tapped him on the back.

"Let me rub it on you, all up and down. Promise I won't go in until you're begging for it," he said, guiding his cock to her pussy. She enjoyed the feeling of him pushing in, landing on top of her clit, where he gently rubbed her up and down, holding firmly around his cock, making it feel even harder. His gut helped things along by pressing in on her clit too, and she decided she would always like men with a belly for this very reason.

Slowly, slowly, he rubbed the head of his cock against the length of her flower, pushing in ever-so-slightly. She moaned. It felt really nice.

"Like it?" he checked in. Good boy.

"Yes, very much," she sighed. Her pussy lips clutched around him, sucking in for more, as he kept up a slow, steady pace of rubbing up and down along her now well-moistened slit, dipping in slightly at her entrance. As he teased her relentlessly, she pushed his hand away, and caught him around his back, between her legs. All in the name of some practice, this kind of sex with a near stranger felt so delicious. It was just a one-off, just to enjoy his cock, and to give him the time of his life, and understand better and better what makes men tick (in bed, and other places).

Practice makes perfect.

After a nice long session of this rubbing outside of her, she invited him in for more. "Give it to me now, please!" she begged, ramping up the drama, injecting into her voice that it was life or death here: his cock inside her something she couldn't live without, something she'd die from if she couldn't have. She was also testing the sound threshold of her bedroom, "LET ME HAVE IT, CLARK!" she cried out. (Hank had told her once, "People love the sound of their own names." Now was a good as time as any to put that into practice).

Good. The walls seemed thick in this early 1900's building. She could have more lovers, yell more, and come loudly a lot more if that was what the hell she wanted. *Fuck yeah!*

"Yes, ma'am! Ooooh man, don't you worry Miss Kiss…tler, getting' in RIGHT NOW." He finally indulged her by plunging his cock deep into her, sinking into the tight lips that hugged around him, enveloping him in an ether of warm pleasure. He closed his eyes, plunging in again and again. Overshadowing her with his body, she enjoyed the feeling of his hard, fat cock ramming in and out of her, and his belly pressing on her pleasure zone.

"God, you feel soooo good," she cooed, half wondering if it was too much melodrama for the circumstance. "So fucking good! Clark! Fuck me!"

"Yeah," he growled, eating it up. "I'm glad I got to move your stuff in. And move into *this* tight little place. Like a studio apartment for my schlong."

"Ha! You're hilarious!" She felt like giggling uncontrollably, which made her pussy vibrate around him even better. She was getting slightly habituated to his movements, realizing it was time to shift position slightly to vary the pressure, and move toward the inevitable orgasmic pleasure she was about to enjoy. She wanted him to keep fucking her, but with a bit more grinding action focused on her clit, getting more of his girth to stuff her pussy with its greatness. "Move up," she dared to say, half-wondering if she'd be tossed out of bed for being bossy, but that wasn't the case.

"Yes, m'aam," he said, as he got on his knees more and

hoisted his cock deep into her again. In it went, deeper now, and with more of his girth forced inside her, filling her up deliciously. He grinded away at her in a circular pattern, relentlessly drawing her into a state of a rising tide that would soon engulf her in a wave of pleasure. "Oh, Cali. I'm gonna blow," he warned, as she felt him slow his movements. She braced herself, and moved her hips up and down on him. His cock pumped her in and out, and she felt her pussy flower into a magnificent orgasm as her hips met his, and they came together. He groaned in release as she screamed into his chest. "Dream come true," he sighed, trying to come back to the real world.

Later, he dressed hurriedly, citing the fact that his partner was still waiting outside in the truck (probably sleeping in the back by now). "Am I ever gonna see you again?" he asked. "Like on a date?"

While it had certainly been delicious, and fun, to seduce him, it might be necessary to keep young Clark on the back burner; definitely not at the front, in a hot, boiling pot, where her thoughts of Jean-Chris so often bubbled away. "Probably not," she sighed, not offering any excuses but making herself sound regretful.

"Hey," he offered, "If you ever move overseas, could we shack up in a shipping container together? It'd be like an end-to-end total moving service, with um, a lotta good stuff in between."

"Ah, well you know what they say: it's not the size of the craft that counts, it's the motion in the ocean."

"HA, Oh my God, you're nuts!" he laughed.

"I'll definitely call you next time I move," she promised, handing him a generous tip from a little box. Despite everything, she wasn't the sort to offer sex instead of a cash tip for a job well done. Everyone worked for money, in the end. Anything less was less than classy, to her mind. And being classy was all part of preparation for GG's. "Please share that with your partner," she said.

"Will do. It's been grand." Pulling his baseball hat on, he tipped his cap her way.

"You seem like such a neat guy. Just keep being yourself, and I'm really sure the girls you meet at the cafe will start getting those tall drinks with lots of whipped cream."

"Thanks," he said, and slipped happily out her door, cash in hand.

Chapter Nine

It was some weeks after Cali's momentous first private date with Hank, and she was already settling well into her role as his secret 'kept' mistress. The fringe benefits weren't exactly life-altering, but they were life-enhancing. As it turned out, Hank's wire-ins of funds were more sporadic and less impressive than she would have liked. They were unpredictable, too, which seemed done on purpose, intended to keep her on her toes. They certainly weren't the weekly allowance she'd counted on and at first assumed (as was reflected in her initial spend on furnishings).

She was actually quite into 'the red,' as the budgeting calculations done in her little notebook revealed. This was confirmed by her new credit card statements, which now arrived regularly in the mail. Still, she was managing fine; her credit wasn't crashing at all, and eventually everything would be paid off if she kept up her visits with Hank. It was just going to take a while.

Hank's gifts were still helping her to have two days a week off temping. She used the time to spend on homework for design school, and she was certainly keeping up now. She reasoned with herself: there were other, more intangible benefits to spending time with Hugging Hank. He was teaching her all kind of things about being a lady, a person, and about being an exciting, bubbling companion (one who reads the paper every day, and keeps up on the stock market, Hollywood scandals, and anything else that might be conversational fodder). That was what preparing to be a GG's girl was all about, right?

She and Hank's clandestine meetings were heavily weighted toward hugging, and Cali enjoyed the big dose of affection, as well as compliments – often followed or preceded by constructive criticism. She was discovering that he couldn't maintain an erection for long. Knowing the bad science behind rushed FDA approvals, he refused to try his company's still-experimental patch for erectile dysfunction, known internally as Project Liftus. Hand jobs were just about the only thing that got him off. Most important to the man, other than hugging, was interesting conversation. She provided both in abundance, keeping him sated yet keen.

Hank had once said they were never to speak of money, and she held firmly to this dictate of his. Still, she was dying to ask for more (and some good room service food during their visits, not just that skimpy spa food). *Just a little?* It felt impossibly risky. She might lose him. Do mistresses go on strikes? Do they demand raises? Do they decorously hint for more gift cards? She didn't feel quite 'professionally' ready for the level of manipulation needed in order to get more cash (and that lobster roll with shoestring fries she'd seen on the menu at the hotel).

Perhaps there was another way of increasing her funds, that didn't involve a big ask from Hank… Something that didn't involve him at all. Just one of those quick infusions, or a small, sudden windfall that would bring her bank account back into balance, and she could quickly eradicate the accruing debts that now felt like little weights, keeping her down.

Sometimes in the streets of the City, she'd marvel at the rather overweight people here and there, wondering how they had ever reached that state of grotesque obesity. But she had only had to remind herself that while *they* may be physically fat, *she* had bloat too, and it was only getting bigger. She had the financial kind of fat growing on her, but you just couldn't see it (fortunately). Didn't mean it wasn't there.

She longed to reduce or throw off this bloat, to start anew. That involved being better-behaved financially and a much better steward of her money. It was probably easier to be a good steward when you had more money to be a steward of, she thought. She'd been on a kind of high, and gone on a shopping and self-care binge when she'd first received her gifts from Hank. But she had grossly miscalculated exactly how far it would go (or how often it would keep coming). GG wasn't ready for her yet (or she wasn't ready for GG's) but the more she thought about it perhaps there really was another way – besides returning to yucky, exhausting stripping or sporadic nude modeling gigs at Barry's Art Loft – to infuse her life with some more cash (and never go astray again!).

She needed something more interim. A bit like temping. A stopgap that involved less commitment than entering GG's, but was also less tricky to find than another corporate titan desiring a secret mistress; that was an opportunity that had relied on luck, and had just fallen into her lap (or had she fallen into his?). Sugar daddies like Hank didn't seem to grow on trees (*Or maybe I don't know how to shake the trees yet*).

Maybe just a little dabbling from time to time in the hotel bar seduction arts wouldn't hurt. Or NO, just this once? Just until school's out and I can secure a well-paid internship at a design firm, or... She steered her thoughts away from definitely returning to GG's someday, because the more she did her classes the more she reckoned she might feel differently about all of that by her college graduation. In any case, bar seduction would certainly provide the kind of education GG had once talked about.

That night, when Cali returned to Midtown Manhattan dressed like she meant to be paid, it had started raining heavily. She found shelter under her huge umbrella as she made her way to the rooftop bar of the Penultimate Hotel near Central Park, avoiding puddles in her best shoes (and lingerie beneath).

Hank had taught her well: she was dressed simply and conservatively but with hints of sex, like a touch of lace peeking out from her décolleté and bouncy, bed-roomy hair. She looked like the kind of young woman a man would be proud to ask upstairs to a room, possibly 'in exchange for a consideration,' as Cali's old novels had discreetly described the act of prostituting oneself.

Walking through the maze-like lobby of the Penultimate, staying calm while pretending not to look for what felt like a hidden elevator, Cali felt a great appreciation for her interludes with Hank. Rather than this nerve-wracking feeling of so obviously hunting for a paying stranger, she yearned for the same comfortable feeling she often got when discreetly making her way to Hank, knowing he was waiting for her up in the room.

It's education. If you don't take the risks, you don't get the rewards.

When visiting Hank in the afternoons, in the interest of discretion, she'd always bypassed the velvety, cavern-like ease of the Wendell-Astor's hotel bar/lounge, where she intuited there were probably professional girls looking for dates. But tonight, once on the right elevator, she exited and headed right in to the Penultimate's rooftop bar, which was housed in an atrium-like space, with the rain pelting down and sliding down the glass. She eased into a seat at the circular, zinc-topped bar trimmed in precious woods. She felt herself shaking and self-conscious, and a huge part of her disliked not necessarily being in control of whom might seek her out for 'company.'

Nursing a non-alcoholic mojito, Cali wondered if it seemed obvious to anyone what exactly she was doing there. Before she could become too self-conscious, a man sitting across the bar motioned to ask if he could come over next to Cali and take a seat. She nodded discreetly, *Yes.*

Once he was close, Cali saw he had bags under his darting eyes, love handles, jangling jowls, and expensive golf clothing hiding a paunchy tummy. "Are you…working?" he asked, leaning in.

Cali quickly summed him up: nerdy, desperately horny, probably harmless, a wedding ring, easily affording the Penultimate's jaw-dropping nightly rates. She turned back around and sighed. Hank had a lot more appeal to her than this guy. Wasn't there supposed to be more of a *Pretty Woman's* dashing Edward Lewis in this adventure? Her heart fluttered with the thought of her handsome Jean-Chris, and how much more fun they would be having right now if *he* were there beside her, instead of this specimen with little man boobs poking through his golf shirt.

"Possibly." She smiled sweetly at the man, having learned by osmosis from her short time visiting GG's that one must be nice to all kinds of men, regardless of their physical presentation. It's why she'd given Clark Kent a ride, after all. Being good at escorting meant making men feel accepted and desired, no matter how they looked. How they *treated* a lady was more important, and would be evaluated to determine their suitability.

"What are you asking? The gift?" he whispered.

She quoted her price in his ear. It was much more than she usually made in a whole week temping, and approximated what Hank had placed in her account to make their visits rewarding. It was a fairly outrageous ask considering she: a) didn't really know what she was doing, and b) didn't know what fees she might fetch at GG's, i.e.

going rates for companionship. But she'd give it a try. "Is that gift OK with you? For an hour?"

"That's fine," he said curtly. "I'll be waiting for you in Suite 704. The door'll be unlocked."

Cali didn't love his lack of warmth or easy conversation, but that didn't make him a potential serial killer – and serial killers didn't usually lodge at the Penultimate, she was sure of it. Should she evaluate his treatment of her based on his blunt style alone? Not necessarily. Plenty of strip club guys were shy and not into buttering a lady up. So this one would be just something, *someone*, to get through. It would take no more time from her life other than the next hour. There was no pretense of romance here. But: it was money she didn't have in her pocket an hour ago. And now she would. She already had big plans for those funds.

She felt the palpable sensation of going from 'nearly broke' to 'less broke' to… 'well on her way to her rent and expenses being pre-paid for the month!' She would go, too, from 'never turned a trick' to 'turned a trick in a hotel once.' Jean-Chris' words from their first date suddenly haunted her. *Why are you so eager to get rid of your innocence?*

A short time later, Cali was in Mr. Darty-eyes' room. A stack of large bills sat on the desk untouched (Cali had read in a fictional diary of a call girl that it might be best for a high-end professional to act like the cash doesn't exist, and only collect it discreetly at the end of the date).

"Get undressed," he said.

Soon enough, Cali stood in her lingerie before Darty, who

kneeled before her in his underwear. She motioned toward the minibar. "Would you, ummm... like to offer me a drink, or something? Shall we sit and talk for a little while first?"

"No."

"OK. So what brings you to town, Mr. I-don't-know-your-name-but-we-met-at-a-bar?" She was trying to be light and friendly, but Darty was very serious, all biz. She was almost scared by his abrupt manner. The diary of a call girl had also said that in the US, where prostitution is illegal, the undercover cops were never very chatty, either, and often a little hostile and unaffectionate; they had a disdain for the women they were about to arrest. You could always tell a cop, the diary said, because they hated hugging the girls.

"Might be nice to get to know one another?" she said gently. "Let's hug a little!"

"Don't try to impress me with your intelligence or charm, or whatever. I'm not a cop. I'm saying it out loud so it's on the record. I'M NOT A COP."

"OH." Cali felt deadened, although she was relieved that he wasn't a cop. He didn't seem to have any need to treat her like a human being, like a lady, like someone special. Why bother to have a civilized, sweet conversation with a woman you pay? She hated Darty instantly.

He slid down the top of her teddy as she bristled, and she took it the rest of the way off, with no desire to please him further, apart from the basics to get her money and get out. He was now admiring Cali's body as if she were a statue. It was off-putting.

"Jesus, you're not perfect but you'll do! Not that it's any

of your business, but to answer your question: I'm here because my wife is having a bunch of cosmetic surgery. For her fiftieth birthday. Head-to-toe tune-up. My treat."

"Oh. That's a nice thing to do for your wife."

"Yeah. I'll say. She's in the special unit recovering now. She'll have about three weeks in compression garments, bandages, drains, all that stuff. She looks like shit now, all black and blue, even the whites of her eyes are blood red."

"Oh, gosh."

"But one day she'll look great again. She's a beautiful woman, you know. It's why I loved her. Turn around. Let me see your ass."

Why you loved her? Cali turned around so Darty could see her ass but NOT the furious expression on her face. He loved his wife – for her looks? That was it?

"Lay down. I want to eat you. I love eating pussy." Wasting no time, Darty got to his knees, spread Cali's legs and dove in.

As much as I like oral, the sooner this is over, the better. Cali closed her eyes and stiffened as his tongue slid in and out of her: she couldn't even *fake* any pleasure. She bristled at the gall of this very unattractive man prompting his wife to have all this surgical work, while he himself continued to resemble a bulldog eating a bee! She felt herself palpably losing her temper. She wanted to throw something – a vase, perhaps, but mostly him – out the window.

"Like it?" Darty asked, still licking away, and now masturbating himself.

She thought to herself about all the various men she'd

met at the strip clubs. Wasn't it amazing how some could be unattractive in a traditional sense, but yet so charming, so kind? Just like her chubby hauling guy, Clark Gent. Wasn't it crazy how fun conversations and charm outshone outer shells – to the degree that, during the lap dances she performed, she'd sometimes yearn to sleep with some of the men, to be closer to their spirit, their kindliness, their sense of fun humor. Character was destiny, she'd concluded to herself, and she imagined the same must apply to the women at GG's, and soon perhaps her, too. Her looks were not perfect (although they could be more perfect if she herself went the suggested surgery route) but personality was *everything*... She would need to remember that.

"You coming?" Darty asked, just as he started to become breathless, excited.

"Uhhh...." Cali managed, faking it in a way that would never win an Oscar. "YEAH! Coming!"

Faking it with a butt-faced, rude man like Darty is only rewarding bad behavior. No positive reinforcement here.

"That's it, come for me babe. I'm gonna come too!" He stood up and wanked himself while struggling to speak as he aimed to come on Cali's stomach. "See? My wife. She can have all the cosmetic surgery in the world she wants to. But I gotta tell you..."

Cali waited for the next asshole-ish thing out of his mouth as he rubbed himself out. Here it was: "There's just nothing like... getting something strange. A new young body... Strange stuff... Aaaarrghhh Uggggg..." Darty came quickly with a gross grunt.

SPLURT.

Cum on your belly: physical evidence of a job well done. But otherwise, she felt like a complete failure as that engaging, sought-after, quickly-beloved companion she dreamed of ultimately becoming. This little toad had blocked all her efforts at charm, real caring or conversation. *Fuck him.* Cali grabbed a Kleenex from the bedside table and wiped away the evidence. She would soon be free of the man. Unconnected! Unattached!

Am I really free though? Isn't this a moment with a man I'm not fond of, that I'll need to erase from my memory?

Cali would rethink her 'rogue' adventures from now on. Maybe it was much better to screen men at the hotel bar over a long drink first, converse a while – even part ways and come back together later at another date and time – and make sure it was as pleasant as can be. Be extra discerning. Let her asshole meter do its thing before taking a chance on another fucked-up encounter like this one. Thank God he hadn't wanted to be *inside* her, transferring his negative energy in *that* way.

This was probably why one trained with madams like GG first, to avoid these types of situations as much as possible, to allow those more in the know to screen the clients first, and to reduce the risk of unpleasant encounters that must weigh on the soul after a while.

"Your cunt tastes great, whoever you are," he said, turning on the TV.

Cali sat up quickly. Wanting the hell out. "Gee, thanks. Can I…?" She grabbed her purse and clothes, strode into the bathroom, and shut the door behind her. She leaned back against the door, composing herself, then went to the sink to wash up. She imagined the intimate post-mortem evaluation of this evening that she'd have with the philosophical Jean-Chris, if only she could ever tell him about this… and if only he'd truly understand. But he wouldn't.

"Here are women, all over the world, spending billions on their collective beauty, on pleasing their men, subjecting themselves to every kind of risk and pain – and then an asshole like this one comes along and sums it up thusly: no matter what she does, or how she looks, I just want to fuck something strange.

Strange stuff.

And here I am, selling that putz my 'something strange.' Not only does it make me ashamed of myself, it makes me terrified of ever becoming someone's 'old familiar.' Someone's 'Not so strange.' Shit. How utterly unromantic!"

Cali shut the water off. It had to get better than this. This was beginner's bad luck. She'd *never* do this again. Soon she was dressed again and coming out into the living room, where Darty was waiting in his bathrobe. He was eager to get Cali out the door. He opened it.

"You were great, thanks."

Before he could close the door behind her, and while safely in the hallway, Cali kept the door open with her hand. That old poisoned juice, her temper, was coursing through her veins now, and there was no stopping it. He *had* to be put in his place.

"What?" he seemed supremely annoyed.

"Could I mention something?"

"Yeah, what?"

"Um. You should really do something about those big bags under your eyes, and those hanging jowls. Maybe a little surgery to tighten things up there?" Darty attempted to close the door but Cali quickly pushed it open with all her strength, and continued, "And you know what? A PENIS IMPLANT! You could really use one. Cause your WIFE – you know, the one in the HOSPITAL right now? – she's probably thinking how nice it would be to be with a new and different cock. Something younger, maybe a lot bigger. You know: SOMETHING STRANGE!!!"

"You fucking cunt! You little WHORE!" He slammed the door.

"Yeah, I am, motherfucker!" Cali felt herself revving up into an unstoppable rage. She slammed the closed umbrella into the door, assaulting it as if she had a bat. "GO TO HELL! GO TO HELL! GO TO HELL YOU ARROGANT, ENTITLED MOTHERFUCKER!"

Only silence from inside the room. And then he was by the door again, "You forgot your money. Now that you've called me a motherfucker, why don't you come in and get it?"

Oh fuck. I forgot to take my money!

"Slide it under the door, now, fuckhead."

"No."

"Take a good look at yourself in there! You're no prize, MOTHERFUCKER!"

"YOU seemed to enjoy yourself! Getting some cunny!

You should be paying *me*. Oh, you left money for me in here! I see it right here!"

"YOU FUCKER!!"

She was still assaulting the door, screaming, "Motherfucker, give me my money!" while the security guys caught all this on camera. Watching in their office, they were mesmerized, slow to take action.

"Bring the animal tranquilizer," one joked. "We got a wild one on the seventh floor."

"Rubber bullets?" the other one snickered, looking over the night's footage to track her quick trajectory from hotel bar to Darty's room. "Sheesh, this one struck a deal at the bar at 8:20, and by 8:31 she was in his room. Smooth operator."

Cali stopped for breath during her rampage, and suddenly realized that – as an esteemed guest of the hotel – this nameless darty-eyed guy behind the door held all the cards. By wandering in the Penultimate's hallowed hotel halls, *she* could be considered a trespasser.

God forbid she got arrested and got a record because of that asshole! If you're going to get a record, better to get it for doing something more meaningful or beneficial.

Eeeeeeeks!

She made a quick diversion toward the fire escape staircase, and rapidly made her way down to another floor. God forbid he'd call hotel security. They could easily be waiting for her at one of the hotel exits. "Jesus, FUCK!" Cali's heart beat fast as she ran down all the fire escape stairs, exiting by a side fire entrance.

She suddenly craved a stop-off at a nearby Mexican restaurant she knew, for a few Margaritas on the rocks. There, she could hide out and mentally make sense of all this. She would be able to calm down and examine all her inner feelings about this incident through the pale, lime light of a good drink with quality salt on the rim. The tart fresh liquid would trickle down her throat; maybe she would have a chicken chimichanga to accompany it.

However, instead of slipping off into a burrito, she found herself greeted by a couple of hotel security guys who'd also called in New York's finest cops. "Drop the umbrella, and move away from your weapon. Put your hands up where I can see them," the Stallone-look-alike cop rolled his eyes and sighed.

"What weapon!? It's *an umbrella*!"

"According to the man you just attacked, it's a weapon," he said, as Cali dropped it to the ground.

"I didn't attack *him*. OK? I was attacking his *ideology*."

"Oh, his ideology."

"Yeah, I was just going for his door. He's a turd. He's like a little turd all dressed up in golf clothes. Like a garden gnome with a pot belly wearing a striped Greg Norman shirt."

"Quit while you're ahead," the cop instructed, sliding the umbrella away with his foot. "Turn around for me."

"Come on!" she resisted slightly, but knew better than to give them too much trouble.

"Sorry, but we need to take you in." He got behind her

as she slowly put her hands behind her back.

"God! You need to understand. He had all the personality of a gnome's turd, too, that's how bad he is: a little piece of shit on shit toast."

"Right now, you're under arrest for trespassing and a possible attempted assault here." He handcuffed Cali gently. "It's all on video."

"Free ride, though," the other cop shrugged, as he held open the car door while she ducked inside and took her seat.

Chapter Ten

On the ride over to the station, Cali felt deeply ashamed of herself. She was: a) regretting she'd undertaken hotel hooking, and b) sorely disappointed in her lack of ability to collect her pay, as well as, c) ashamed of her ineptitude to emotionally handle a relatively harmless man like Darty. He hadn't laid a hand on her, and in fact, had only sought to give her pleasure. His only offence was being a horny dude, if a total douchebag, with antiquated, sexist views of women. His only real mistake was in feeling that he could express his shitty opinions to Cali without recourse. (Her seeming like someone he could share with, *was* worth a point or two to the positive).

Had she only showed some self-control, and been smoother, been more accepting of that turd's outlook on life – faked up all the way, of course – and had she only kept her mouth shut, and her own opinions to herself, she wouldn't have forgotten to take her money; she wouldn't have totally lost her temper, and wouldn't be sitting in a cop car now, arrested, headed toward God knows what else was to follow.

There was a reason GG had emphasized the mastery of emotional self-control before she ever stepped in to the house to work with more men like Darty.

Now I know why.

At the police station, in the holding cell for the night criminals, Cali clung to the bars that faced into a larger visitor and officers' area. She thought of whom she might call if given the opportunity: who was the most important person she could ask for help or consolation? Jean-Chris was on the top of the list, but the more she thought of it, the worse of an idea it seemed.

Over the last few weeks, as she'd fixed up her place, spent oodles of money, obsessively decorated, and then madly applied herself to her school projects – focusing as well on her twice-weekly meetings with Hank, plus a weekly Monday night romp with Tony – Jean-Chris had seemingly been quite engaged with his own life, too. He often complained there weren't enough hours in the day for the auction house job, or griped about his struggles with architectural software, and how difficult it was staying creative and original when it came to writing up trip reports for the many museums he was required to visit.

He'd called her frequently to catch up, but an actual in-person meeting, now that they lived so far apart, had eluded them for many weeks. It didn't mean she didn't like him any less; it was more of a question of when (and how) he could fit in. Now – inside the holding cell, and feeling extremely tired in this grungy, noisy jailhouse – she allowed her mind to float away into her now-cozy bedroom, which was fitted out with nice white linens and a canopied bed, covered in fine white cotton. It was there that she planned to soon 'fit Jean-Chris in' to her life in a more intimate way – after a good sleep... or would she be held in this cell forevermore?

She imagined for a moment what it would be like if she and J.C could finally take it all the way. Spending time with him, and enjoying their intriguing, funny conversations, their passionate and teasing interludes, all of that had been a true pleasure. He was exactly the kind of guy a girl could really fall in love with and cling to. If that's what she wanted. But could she *cling*?

She was hungry for more of him, that was for sure, but she wasn't entirely sure he was the kind of guy who'd ever be willing to share her with others for very long. And she wasn't entirely sure, either, that she was done experimenting with all the new and different men who might be coming her way. The process of gleaning experience was an enjoyable one, and being exclusive with one guy (as great as Jean-Chris may be) might officially mess that up.

"Hey, what you day-dreamin' about over there, Miss Priss?" A female cellmate was now enquiring.

Tearing herself away from her dreamy thoughts about how delicious Jean-Chris might be in bed, Cali perceived that some of the other, tough-looking ladies in the temporary lockdown were now circling her – and she was still in her comparatively fancy evening outfit. The scrappy bunch, possibly in the same girl gang, tried to figure out who they were looking at. "You one of those high-priced hookers?

You get busted?" one asked, getting a little too close to Cali's convincing cubic zirconia stud earrings.

"No."

Not yet a hooker? Or briefly, yes, I was one tonight.

"No, man!" another lady joined in. "This girl here, she's more like someone who stole from her company. Like, the accountant. That what it is? I just know it. Like a bedazzler, that's the word, right, girls?"

"An embezzler," Cali corrected her. "A Bedazzler's a machine for blinging up your clothes."

"A smart one here. Smartass."

"Thank you. It's really easy to remember. An *embezzler* takes *away* your bling. And the Bedazzler puts it all back. Snip, snap!" Cali laughed nervously. "Those things work great on denim. You ever try to trim your jeans with one…?"

"Funny. We got a funny." The 'leader' was standing a bit too close again, so Cali sashayed away. The leader stalked her anyway, and Cali clung to the bars while the girl looked at her earrings. "Well, I like the bling in your ears. You feel like giving me a gift tonight? Take 'em out. You know, just so I could have a look?"

"Oh. These?! No, please. These earrings are two carats of the highest graded diamonds, and were handed down through my family," she lied. "I'd be lost without them!"

"Well then, that's what I'd like the most, if you wanna buy my protection," the woman showed Cali her sharpened molars, holding her hand out for the earrings.

To buy a little time, Cali acted as if it was difficult to get them out and hand them over. She tried to make casual conversation. "What's your name, if I'm going to give you my favorite earrings?"

"I don't share my name with someone who may become my sex slave up at Rikers."

"*Ewwww*. I mean, not *ewwww* about you. Anyone would be flattered to be *your* sex slave. But I really don't want to go there. Do you?"

"I been there before; it's not as bad as all that. The time went fast. I didn't have to cook or clean." The leader admired the earrings in her hand, blowing on them, and giving them the old diamond fog test. The rocks were steaming up as fast as the nervous sweat on Cali's forehead. "What the…? These ain't priceless diamonds! You missy, prissy little liar. You lied to me!"

"No! My jeweler lied to me. I'm as shocked as you are!"

"Missy Prissy gonna get herself in a whole peck of trouble," the leader sang out.

"No. Now I'm not as prissy as I look…" Cali insisted, as the woman came at Cali's stomach with a resounding punch while the other ladies rallied her on. "Ooooof…" Cali hunched over in pain, just as someone else stepped up for her turn to sock her in the gut. "Guard!" Cali tried feebly to scream, as the pain bounded through her intestines. Worse – fear about her very survival had paralyzed any fight left in her. She cowered and slid to her knees, hunkering down on the floor. "Please don't hurt me," she cried. "Please, I'll do anything" she sobbed, as the pain from the punch and fear about more reverbed through her entire being.

Suddenly, a forceful female voice bellowed, "BACK

OFF! That's ENOUGH! Remember who you are: children of God! You want more time in the hold, everyone? Or to be free and every dream become a reality? Back off her, bitches!"

From Cali's point of view, bent over in pain, she saw various pairs of feet in assorted shoes back away obediently. She looked up through the bars at her savior. There, standing in a black leather jumpsuit, vintage two-toned Puma high top sneakers, and sporting an impenetrable knife-and bullet-proof jet black vest, was none other than her former bachelor party dancing partner and fellow stripper: Sugar. Brown Sugar, as she was sometimes known, or – as she liked to call herself – Sugar Brown. The memory of saving Sugar from a gang rape on a rainy night in a greasy garage flooded back to both of them as they reunited, locking hands through the bars.

"Sugar!?"

"Sweetcakes?!"

"Shortcakes. Yes, it's me."

"Saved-my-bacon-Shortcakes! What the fuck are you doing here!? Forgive my language, girls. The Universe forgives but it doesn't forget."

Cali grasped on tighter to Sugar's soft kid-leather gloved hand. "What are *you* doing here?" she asked.

"I'm a jailhouse chaplain. There's a lot of us from different faiths coming in, but I'm here most of the nights. I minister to the girls. Tell 'em about a better way. Whew, they were 'bout to blow the guts out of you." She looked in and addressed the women loitering around in the cage. "Nobody touch my girl here. She's a divine being of light, and I have her to thank for bringing me here today. If y'all wanna know, this one here ain't afraid to pull out her Glock, and take down some cock. She's special forces to the power of pussy, got it?"

"Yeah, yeah." The women backed off and talked amongst themselves.

"See? That's Divine Timing. And that's what I'm teaching now," Sugar said with pride.

"You're teaching now? That's amazing. I'm so impressed. That was fast!"

"The Universe don't know no bounds of time. After I detoxed, it didn't take long before I started my own church. But I don't call it that. It's the Divine Mind Study and Worship Center. Wait a minute. I stole something from you that time I stayed with you at your lodging. I gotta show you something; hope you'll let me keep it…"

She pulled out the postcard she'd pilfered from Cali's Hotel Gram-Irving room the last time they'd seen each other. Cali, still holding her stomach, and trying to catch her breath, read the words again:

"My Dear Daughter, never forget that Jesus Loves You, and I Love You, and I am Praying for Your SALVATION and a PLACE IN HEAVEN. Don't lower your STANDARDS. Use your GOD GIVEN TALENT for the GLORY OF GOD."

"That's amazing. Gosh, my mother! You keep that one. She sends me one nearly every week."

"And your soul still ain't saved in just the way she likes it, neither? Gots to be just the way *she* likes it. *Her* religion.

Or you ain't ever good enough. No room for true spirituality to flow through a person when they've got all that guilt, all those rules."

"Yup."

"Hmmm, I know you, Shortcakes… You lost your temper out somewhere tonight, didn't you?" Sugar guessed. "You gave in to your lower self. You lost control. Somewhere in there you accepted less than the best, and it manifested – probably in the form of some asshole man."

"An asshole man, yes, and I lost a lot of money, too. He owed me for a service rendered, and he just sort of ripped me off. If you know what I mean."

"Uh, huh, I think I do. But you see, that's just a symptom – somethin' within reflecting back to you, of where *you* been short-changing *others*. But forget about that part. *You* did it, whatever you're in for. You're in here. Your best thinking got you here."

"Yup."

"And your best thinking's gonna get you out. You start visioning for release and respect, and I'm gonna pray right along with you. Here, take my card. Come to my church down in Greenwich Village as soon as you can. We got a real musical Sunday worship service, and Wednesday night is a study service. It's a nice group of people. There's great abundance everywhere for you. Just gotta open yourself up to it."

"Oh, thank you Sugar. I'm so glad you're here."

"You comin' to the service then?"

"Ohhhhh, church never really was my thing," Cali

sighed, remembering attending her mother's Pentecostal worship where the 'Holy Rollers' spoke in tongues, and fell down drunk on the spirit in the church aisles, while Reverend Mitchell talked trash about: 'Jezebels and fallen women.'

"My place is nothin' like you've ever seen," Sugar assured her. "The Divine isn't something out there, it's in here." She pointed to her heart. "But if you come to my place, you can meet up with it, you can be with it, know what I mean?"

"I do," Cali nodded. "I think I really do. I promise to come. Someday."

"Fair 'nough. Ha! Me and Shortcakes, dancing together again, in a way. But we can't do this alone. You got representation in here? A legal Beagle with a keg of somethin' to help pull you out from under the rubble that is now your life?"

"Uh! Ha! Geez. I don't feel like it's rubble yet. But no, I have no idea who the hell to call. I'm just kind of dazed and confused."

"I'll hook you up right now," Sugar said, calling out on her phone. "I got a guy on speed dial; loves helping the girls out. He's sparkin' up a career as a celebrity legal defender. Just got a rock star babe out of jail for some kinda misdeeds. He's gettin' a name now, but I'm sure he'll help you out. Not cheap, but worth a penny." Before Cali could say thank you, it was all arranged.

In no time at all, Cali saw an officer approaching the cage with Mr. Clive Vogelnest. It was an old-sounding name for a young-ish, totally bald and super good-looking short guy in an expensive tracksuit and a diamond earring in each ear. He looked a little too much like a thug from the 'hood, and way too sure of himself, but she'd accept that if he could get her out of jail.

Despite all the bravado, she liked his hustler moves: there was something of the boxer to him. He shook her hand, and gave her an aggressive look-over, like he was about to devour her. "It always amazes me what you pretty girls get away with…" He winked, and the noise of the jail gate clanging shut behind her drowned out the rest of what he said.

After hiding away in a small meeting room, introductions were made. She liked how he seemed almost apologetic about his smarts and his law degree from a prestigious university. After a few details of what had occurred, Clive offered a short, impressively cunning strategy on how to present her side of things to the judge, which Cali approved.

"We'll work out my exact fee later, depending on what kinda shit the judge and the defense throws at us. But basic: it's a few thou if I get you out tonight," he stated. "You gotta few thou on you?"

"No. It's stashed away at home." *But it's all I have.*

"Mattress money. I like it. Good. After you're unshackled, and I mean that in the purely metaphorical sense, I'll give you a ride home, and you'll get me the cash, and you'll promise never to be naughty again. Till the next time," he smiled, challenging her.

"Till the next time…?"

"It's just in you girls' natures to be bad. The sooner you

acknowledge and embrace that you're a bad girl, the better you'll feel. Now let's go see the Judge."

She stopped him for a moment, as his words reverbed in her being. "What did you just say?"

He repeated it. "*The sooner you acknowledge and embrace that you're a bad girl, the better you'll feel.*"

"What you just said was so profound," she said, still reeling.

"Call me a philosopher. Let's get in there."

Their legal strategy actually worked, and was helped greatly by the video, and the fact that the hotel's attorneys couldn't get very far if Darty, the 'offended,' was ultimately reluctant to have any part of something public that might expose his cheating to his wife. After some paperwork, Cali was let go.

She and Mr. Vogelnest headed off to Brooklyn together in his long, sleek BMW Series 7. Smelling of leather, it was paid for by guilty and innocent criminals alike. "Like it?" Clive asked. "So much better than that peeling *pleather* in the back of a cop car," he smiled and laughed.

It did feel nice to be out of the fray, and she enjoyed Clive regaling her with stories from the legal trenches – but his voice was loud, and she was suffering from a jailhouse and gavel headache. "Do you have any Tylenol?" she managed to wedge in, as he reeled off personal episodes from the courtroom drama of his life.

"Tylenol is a well-known aphrodisiac. I hope you know what you're doing," he said, giving her a sidelong glance, while keeping his eye on his lane on the Brooklyn Bridge. "In the glove compartment, sweetheart."

Cali quickly fished around, found the bottle, and swallowed three as if they were candy. Either the placebo effect took over, or the Tylenols really were aphrodisiacs, but she realized she was horny as hell. If there was the possibility of dragging this Clive up into bed this evening, to top off one hell of a day, she'd surely go for it.

Nothing like a good bang to take the edge off a cluster headache.

"I know what you're thinking about me, Cali. You're thinking, how can this guy defend some of these lying, cheating, murderous scumbags that come through his office like the rats and roaches that infest this city every time we put the garbage out?"

"No, I wasn't thinking that…" *I was thinking about how I'd like to feel you inside me tonight.*

"Well, it pays damn well. We all prostitute ourselves in one way or another. But I'm not just in it for the money. I simply believe that every person good or bad is entitled to a fair trial. It's the cornerstone of our democracy. I don't represent a client. I represent *democracy*."

"Good, that's great." *I wonder if you have a nice dick and know how to use it. I'm so stressed out, and dying for you to come upstairs and fuck me to help me forget this day.*

"And I'm sure as hell glad when some of 'em do get what's coming to 'em, motherfuckers all! More are bad than good. I *know* when they've done it. But I've never thrown a fight. I get in the ring, and I slug it out on their behalf till the end. As I did for you today. You happy to be free? Have I served you well?"

Yeah, and now you can serve me more of you upstairs. "Yes, Clive. Thank you. You're certainly relentless." *Do you fuck relentlessly, too?*

"I AM a relentless motherfucker! Glad someone finally noticed!" he nearly screamed as they pulled into her neighborhood. "Now girl, you just go upstairs, take your time, count it all out, and I'll be down here waiting to receive my tribute."

"I'd prefer it if you would join me upstairs to receive your tribute. I'm scared, you know. What if I break the law again on the way in there?" she smiled, looking ahead.

"Oh, you're scared?" He asked, getting it, putting his arm around the back of the car seat, and pulling her to him. "You scared of *this*?" he asked, plunking a big kiss on her lips, guiding her hand to his cock, which was now ballooning out of the stretchy fabric of his track suit. "You sure you can handle *all* this?" he asked, her fingers barely fitting around his raging hardness.

"Oh, yeah," she whispered. Boom. He wasn't afraid to jump over any shyness and reserve, and to just hop into bed. Learning to be more and more like that was what it was going to take if she ever wanted to become a high-priced call girl. Call-girling wasn't always about crock pot romance, she'd once read; often it was just about getting down and dirty within an allotted period of time, more like a microwave... Tonight with Darty had been a great example.

"I just have a few terms and conditions in my fine print, as a guy: I don't stay all night, and you still have to pay me in cash," he said. "And I don't like a lot of talking; I need silence to perform. From you, at least. The less you say, the better."

"Fine. I want you out of my place as soon as we're done. And stop bragging."

"Ouch! Fine."

Clive Vogelnest, despite his hard edges, was a complete gentleman. After parking the car, he opened her door, took her arm in his, and walked with her to the outer front door as she nervously fumbled with her keys.

"Sorry, can I just say one thing?"

"Yeah. You're breakin' the rules, but go ahead."

"I'm so tired after everything that happened today," she sighed. "Long day."

"Should I go?"

"No way."

"Good. I'm going to make you more tired," he smiled. "And then you can sleep me off."

Whew! Now THAT was confidence.

Once upstairs, Cali left Clive with a glass of water, and excused herself to jump quickly into the shower. But soon there was a knock at the bathroom door. And soon after that the nude Clive pushed Cali gently up against the shower wall with her hands locked behind her, arrest style. His hard, condom-covered cock pressed into her ass as he reached around and rubbed her pussy, diving his fingers deeper at intervals, while she moaned.

"You're wet! Is it OK?" he asked in a low growl. "You've been so naughty that I have no choice but to punish you with my… love baton. Can I?"

She couldn't help but giggle at that one. "Hell, yes," she agreed, as the shower water bounced over them both. He spread her legs apart with his, and bent her slightly, before plunging his cock inside her puss with one long thrust that filled her up perfectly.

"God, damn!" she called out, feeling his relentless thrusting pushing her toward the shower wall. He allowed her to release her arms, and she braced herself. Pushing back on each of his aggressive thrusts, she enjoyed the slightly painful feel of him ramming away inside her, and she adjusted to his motions. *Nothing to be afraid of here, just surrender to the fantasy.*

"Admit it. You were bad."

"I was…"

"No talking!" He pulled her head back with a light yank on her hair, and kissed her neck as he kept thrusting, letting her pussy know who was boss here. This went on for a good while as he brought her nearly to climax, but then pulled out, or pulled back, before plunging inside her from behind again. Suddenly, the shower water stopped. "Get out. Go to the bed, and get on your back," he commanded. "Whatever you do, don't dry yourself. I need you wet because I'm going to fuck you more, naughty girl," he pretend-sneered, with a sweet smile.

Feeling delicious anticipation, she entered her dark bedroom, and she laid down on the bed, still dripping wet in every way. Before she could even get comfortable, she felt him pounce on her, spread her legs with his, and shove his cock inside her; this time even deeper and even more relentlessly with his thrusts.

"This OK?" he asked. "I'm not being mean. I'm just, I like everything intense."

"Do it," she agreed.

He rammed at her with a steady rhythm, and she quickly rode up to an unavoidable, delicious orgasm that made her feel like a twig captured in a river, about to go over a huge, plunging waterfall. When the climax hit her, she cried out briefly, and he covered her mouth with his hand, but didn't stop fucking her for a second.

"I'm not stopping. You know why? You have more in you. You know why?" he asked, groaning as he changed position slightly to come at her pussy a slightly different way. "You're a bad girl who loves sex, you love fucking, you'll fuck anything that moves, and you can't get enough, and you love my big cock, just pounding away at your tight, wet little pussy," he growled. "I wanna fill up this pussy with my cum. Not really, I still got the condom on. But you gonna let me?" he asked, picking up a pace that was bringing her closer to another overpowering orgasm.

"YES, I LOVE IT!" she agreed, before feeling his hand over her mouth as he said, "What did I tell you? Shut up and take my cock."

She loved dirty talk like this. So far, he was the first to fully engage her in it, and he could do it all he wanted. The more he talked, the more she was about to blow, and so was he.

"I'm warning you. I'm fucking that little wet, hot, tight pussy, and I'm not gonna stop, I'm not stopping," he groaned as she felt his whole body stiffen; hers matched it as she strained toward a second imminent release into another flowering fireworks of pleasure. "Here it is… Aaaarrrgh!" he yelled out as she felt his cock explode, and her pussy muscles spasmed deliciously around him, electrifying her whole body with a sex-induced high.

Jesus. No wonder female troublemakers and naughty rock stars keep this guy on speed dial.

Later, after Clive had enjoyed another shower, this time alone, he emerged. As he dressed, Cali handed him his envelope stuffed full of nearly all the cash she had in the world. She'd ground down to nearly zero. He handed Cali several business cards.

"When you get in trouble again, call me. And have your friends call me, too."

"I'm sure I won't be…"

"Nah, nah. A girl like you can't help but get in every kind of trouble. Remember: good girls may get to go to heaven, but bad girls get to go everywhere. And sometimes going everywhere requires a criminal defense attorney. A *celebrity* criminal defense attorney like me, I might add," he laughed.

"Thank you. I'll remember that," she snickered.

After her door clicked shut, she sat down on her couch as his elegant car purred away quietly into the night. After all the excitement of the evening, she felt a bit let down to return to the quiet of her apartment, and face the empty piggy bank.

Now I'm nearly broke, for real.

For a moment she thought of calling Jean-Chris, to

confess all that had gone wrong today. Though he was a friend (almost a lover!) she knew better, and no need to burden him, especially this late at night. Something like this would never happen again. He could never know about her overspending, or her failed foray into high-priced hooking, getting ripped off by her first 'client,' royally losing her temper, then the expensive night in jail (followed by amazing sex with her talented defender Clive).

"Self-sabotaging!" he'd no doubt say.

Fuck him, he doesn't know what I go through. *I'm complicated.* She'd never ask him to borrow money, give shelter, etc. – no matter how bad it might get. Nobody must know. *I shall maintain my prestige (in his eyes, at least). Whatever it takes.*

Chapter Eleven

The following week, Saffron and Cali were at school, seated at the same table, working on an assignment that used gouache paint colorations inside a series of boxes to illustrate how colors can look very different depending on what is placed next to them. "Like how we act different with different guys!" Cali whispered Saffron's way, mixing up a fire engine red. Oops, what if Saffron was a lesbian. "Or girls?"

"Yeah – I'm completely like that, with guys! Do you have a bloke?" Saffron asked, keeping quiet enough not to disturb the rest of the class, as everyone worked diligently on their assignment.

"I have…" Cali hesitated to answer, in case Saffron was one of those really conservative women who'd drop her in a second, citing severe disapproval of her burgeoning 'alternative' lifestyle. But just looking at Saffron, in tonight's flouncy dress with her boobs nearly popping out of what must be one of those demi-cup push-up bras, it seemed unlikely. "…A sugar daddy. And I have some other special guys. I feel like I'm starting to collect them."

"*I'm* a collector too," Saffron whisper-giggled. "I'm like the freaking Frick Collection of fucks! *Such* a shagaholic." Her eyes were round as saucers, and she had a saucy smile to go with them.

"Quiet, please," the teacher called out.

Cali had already texted Jean-Chris earlier to see if he felt like going out that night, and he'd accepted. Well, the more the merrier, Cali thought, so she wrote "DRINKS? After class?" on a piece of paper, and slid it Saffron's way.

Saffron gave a two-thumbs up to that.

Once they were bundled up and walking across town toward the East Village, Cali and Saffron didn't stop dishing on men, and talking about sex and girly stuff like what skin creams were best for the chillier days. Being about twenty years older than Cali, Saffron had the benefit of life experience, so she did most of the talking.

She'd been married three times already, had no children, and had just moved to New York from London. "And I completely decorated about ten different apartments and *huge* houses in the process," she boasted. "Those were my babies. So I do know my way around décor. As for the technical stuff, the real nitty-gritty of I.D? God, well, I can see my studies are going tits up. I just hope I can scrape a pass! I just want to monetize my decorating and social connections, and the degree will certify me. But, fuck if I care about bloody field measuring, mock-ups, scope-of-work orders and all that bollocks."

"It might serve you well to care," Cali said softly, but Saffron blathered on.

"For the first time in my life I feel free of overbearing men, and wifely duties –I'm free!" Saffron gushed. "Who's your favorite shagfest right now? By the way, where are we going?"

"You seem like someone who likes a bit of fun," Cali hinted. "Just going to stop by and pick up a friend of mine who would like to go out with us."

"Lover? The guy we're picking up."

"No, not him. Right now he's just a friend. But I have this other guy, I've slept with – Tony – he's in his forties, a super cute Italian guy. He owns a strip club."

"You met him in *a strip club*, this Tony?"

"OH yes; I danced topless for a little bit. That's how I met him."

"God, I love New York. I'm meeting the most interesting people. But you're so young! How does that happen? Do your parents know? Are you in love with Tony? And, most important, will they have a strong Lemon Drop martini where we're going?! I'm dying for a good drink – or ten!"

Gosh. Saffron has a ping-pong ball loose in her brain, Cali thought to herself. She was a bit glad when they veered into the side street, Hotel Gram-Irving in sight. Answering all those questions required a level of discussion that was deeper than she wanted to go. Getting through the first few months of design school and the temping work was cause for celebration, not more self-examination!

"You'll love the drinks where we're going," Cali promised, approaching the front desk window at the Hotel Gram-Irving. The usual guy, Ferrell, was on duty; he seemed halfway glad to see Cali.

"What have *you* been doing?" he asked, giving Saffron a long glance before looking over at Cali. "Trade in all those guys for *this* dream puff?" This made Saffron laugh out loud.

"Is that your way of saying I'm fat?" Saffron countered.

"And was that your way of saying I'm a slut?" Cali asked.

"You're not skinny, honey," he nodded over to Saffron, and then looked Cali up and down. "And slutty does not even begin to describe *you*, Cali."

"OH MY GOD, SHUTUP Ferrell!"

"HA! Just kiddin' around," he started laughing, seeing how riled up he could make Cali.

Just at that moment, Jean-Chris came out of the elevator, greeting them. He looked handsome in black jeans, a grey turtleneck sweater and a charcoal wool coat.

"Jean-Chris, I'd like you to meet Saffron." Cali said.

"Hello. I have heard so many nice things about you…" He winked at Cali, the truth being he'd never heard anything about Saffron.

"Cali didn't tell me you'd look like a compact Cary Grant!" Saffron said, hooking arms with J.C, and leading him (alone) down the front steps. Cali watched helplessly from behind them, now half-wishing she'd left one of them out of the evening plans.

"Where to?" Jean-Chris asked.

"Drinks!" Saffron nearly sung out, seemingly inspired by having a hot young guy within pouncing distance of her.

Delphine's had a secret door like an old-style speakeasy, and once they found it, they pushed in, soon finding themselves ensconced at a candlelit table. Several rounds of Lemon Drop Martinis in, Jean-Chris and Saffron started chatting about their favorite public-access gardens hidden away in Paris. Cali sighed. Her life hadn't been rich enough yet in travels to share in such knowledge. *It's coming*, she thought to herself as a DJ took his place at a nearby platform, beginning to play the evening's sexy lounge music.

"You were going to tell me all about your sugar daddy!" Saffron said to Cali over the music, leaning in. Jean-Chris' ears perked up and he heard every word. Though he was firmly tipsy, his senses were sharp enough that his eyes laser-beamed into Cali's.

Looking away quickly, she laughed, "Oh. It's silly. I don't think it's anything serious," she lied.

Jean-Chris looked away, too. Cali could see by his twitching face that there were little raging fires sparking up inside him. She watched as he tried to douse them with a long swig of his cold drink.

"No, tell us about him: Mr. Sugar!" Saffron said.

"Yes, tell us," Jean-Chris said, smiling tightly, leaning in.

Cali's heart was sinking. She never wanted him to know that she had sunk to this new "low:" that she'd agreed to meet Hank on Mondays and Friday afternoons for one-hour visits that he could discreetly build into his busy, often-questioned schedule. (Hank had promised they could have more time together by going away on business trips, but they could never really be seen together in public).

It wasn't a lot to ask of her considering that she found Hank attractive, both in body and mind. She also admired his sense of personal discipline and his sort of code of success she hoped she could pick up by osmosis. While their relationship could technically be called transactional, or even prostitution, it bought *time*, her most valuable resource. It wasn't prostitution – it was a gift! The thought of Hank's patronage was incredibly relieving to Cali. Her "twice a week" with him was a deeply personal, practical choice; one she'd hoped would stay entirely private. But now Saffron was damn well forcing her into a corner!

"So, is your sugar daddy old, rich and wrinkly?" Saffron goaded her. "Or more like a young Christian Grey type, like in *Fifty Shades*? Is he a little mean and ties you up, literally? Do you have a lucrative contract?"

Cali looked over to Jean-Chris. She bit her lip and looked down in regret. *Lie to him, or tell the truth and suffer the consequences.* "It's top secret," she clipped.

Gracious-as-ever, Jean-Chris quickly changed the subject, and drew Saffron into a conversation about her feelings on the décor and embellishments at Versailles. Once that had been exhausted, and many other topics covered, he asked, "What next, girls!? Midnight pierogis at Veselka, anyone? A nightclub?"

"It's been fun. But I think I've had enough," Saffron conceded, pushing away her last (and ninth) drink. "Would you mind seeing me home?" she asked him. "I'm Upper West Side. Or… your room is so much closer. I could just crash there tonight and, uh, like that we could keep on partying into the wee hours, no worries? I could buy some rum, or… where do you get coke around here?"

"Cocaine?" J.C seemed a little shocked.

"*We* could see you home," Cali said, and Jean-Chris suddenly looked very impressed with her assertiveness. "We'll drop you in our cab before *we* head out to my place in Brooklyn?"

"*We're* going out to Brooklyn?" he asked curiously.

Saffron protested, "Oh, no. That doesn't make any sense, two opposite directions. I'm sure there's a way…"

Cali sat there amused as Saffron seemed to have a brief alcohol-infused mind fart as to: a) exactly how to get herself alone with Jean-Chris pronto, and, b) how did he and Cali suddenly go from 'just friends' to 'overnighters in Brooklyn' in the space of a few hours?

"Just get me into a cab,' Saffron snarled. 'I'll take care of the rest." She looked over at Jean-Chris. "Can we exchange numb–?"

"No!" Cali insisted, and he looked away, pretending not to hear. "He doesn't have a number. Very low tech guy. Still uses wax seals and carrier pigeons."

Jean-Chris smirked. No doubt he felt a catfight coming on.

Saffron shook her finger at Cali. "You're very pro…" (Here Saffron struggled drunkenly with her vocabulary) "…Pro-*prietary* for someone with a sugar daddy. Professional, too."

"That's enough."

"*And* an Italian lover. Some skeezy strip club owner, Tony? O Solo Mio!" she sung out, off key.

Shit.

Cali looked over at Jean-Chris, who started whistling and looking around, once again like he didn't hear a thing. But she knew he couldn't stay this way for long. He leaned in and spoke in no uncertain terms in her ear. "This reminds me of that time when we were starving and you ordered some lasagna for us to share. It was all hot and bubbling, but no, you decided to keep it all to yourself. 'Fuck Jean-Chris!' Let him order his own meal or eat his hand."

"Where is this going?"

"Were you ever going to tell me about this Tony guy?"

"God! No, nothing to tell. It's nothing, really. Just getting experience. Learning uh, the language. Italian, you know."

"Experience!?" Jean-Chris tried not to raise his voice. "You've traded bliss with *me* to practice on the pole of some strip club owner! I thought you were done with all that. The stripping *merde*."

"He's not like that, exactly. He's just someone I hook up with…"

"This Tony is probably married, too. All the Italians *are*," Saffron reminded them in a drunken slur. "Never met an Italian who could keep his dick in his Zegnas."

"Impossible," Cali shook her head. "I don't think so."

Jean-Chris interjected, "You don't seem convinced. Do you *know*? For sure?"

Cali glared at Saffron, who seemed amused by the beginning of a lovers' quarrel.

"It's time for you to go now, dear. You're shit-faced. It's getting embarrassing."

"Not as embarrassing as your immoral lifestyle," Saffron lobbed back.

Cali suddenly scooted out of her chair, as if about to throttle her, but restrained herself by putting her hands on her hips instead. "You should talk – rich divorcee brat, collecting your check every month!"

"It's blood money; I earned every penny with that prick!"

"Girls!" Jean-Chris yelled, holding Cali back. "Manners!" Saffron stood up and slammed down some cash on the table. But he stopped her, pushing the money back towards her, which she tucked away in her purse. "MY treat tonight," he sighed. "Women don't pay when I'm around. I think you two need a 'time out.' Into your corners, everyone," He was trying hard not to laugh at them.

"Nice," Saffron said. "Thank you, Jean-Chris." She turned to Cali. "See? You've got yourself a gentleman. Too bad you treat him like shit." She pushed her way out the front door of Delphine's. Swaying on the curb, she wildly waved down passing unavailable cabs even though a lighted cab was headed right toward her.

Cali came outside to make sure she didn't fall down. Soon after, Jean-Chris came up behind Cali, and slid his arms around her waist. "I am over this, OK? It was just a shock, to hear her talking about your 'lovers' in that way. Is this Italian *molto romantico*?" he asked gently.

"Yes," she nodded. "He's nice. But there *are* other cultures to experience."

"OK," he sighed. "So I am very late coming to the party."

"No party. Just there's a right time for everything. And for you and me."

They watched in amusement as Saffron carefully made her way toward the incoming cab, slamming herself and only part of her dress in. She rolled the window down. "See you at school next week, slag heap!" Saffron yelled, laughing to herself, as the cab sped off.

Cali had to admit to herself, she'd drunk quite a bit, too, and the street was spinning. The subway this late was out of the question. She wouldn't feel safe alone in a cab being that drunk. The night ahead was taking on a lonely, sinister demeanor. "I wasn't lying when I said it back there. Stay with me in Brooklyn tonight?" she asked. "I'll make us brunch tomorrow."

"*You* are cooking?" he asked. She suddenly realized that thanks to her association with Hank Greenace (and her gross miscalculation of his generosity), a lot of the crockery and proper china – the flatware etc. – was now in place; other pretty things, too. She could practice her hostess skills on Jean-Chris. Food being the way to a man's heart, and all that, these were all useful and charming skills for a courtesan to have.

Chapter Twelve

As Cali and Jean-Chris rode out to Brooklyn in the taxi, they held hands – but she knew he must be able to feel her energy, her appetite, for him flagging. She'd admitted to being very tired after the first busiest months of her life. But she knew she was coming across as pre-occupied with other things as well, as she stared out the windows at the passing sights. It was probably pissing him off quite a bit.

She imagined that to Jean-Chris, it had probably sounded like she was juggling of a lot of men these days. The Sugar Daddy, The Italian… Meanwhile, her mind was on what they'd all discussed about Tony. Could it be that her "noncommittal" lover was actually *married*?

All the pieces were starting to fit together clearly: Tony's "unavailability" in more ways than one. His perpetual reserve and distance was notable (apart from when they made love). But even when they'd slept together, he'd objectified her a little too much; she'd allowed it, chalking it up to preparing for the objectification she might experience one day at GG's: a part of the gig, as she understood it. His being married explained his discretion when she'd danced at Tony's Wedge, and how he'd never invited her for a visit to his personal home. He'd rented that boat when she'd had her first time with him, and they had a few stolen afternoons, but only in discreet 'family' restaurants (like the totally empty Casa Como). It all made sense, especially his never taking her out for a cocktail in the evenings after their interludes.

Tony was so unlike Jean-Chris, who seemed so transparent and eager to be her boyfriend: sharing the tiny corners of his mind with her, offering sincere love, a future perhaps. Tony was…

Married.

She must have *known* on some level, but refused to truly *see* it. And now she couldn't *unsee* it. Damn J.C and Saffron! They'd gone and spoiled some of the fun of her flying blind. She struggled momentarily with the seeming immorality of the thing, this sneaking around with a married man, nibbling from the plate of another woman. But she was by no means in love with Tony. She wasn't chasing him. Theirs wasn't a meeting of the minds – any 'friendship' was a sort of pretense to their body parts colliding, and her greedily ramping up on her Italian language fluency, in preparation for some dreamed-of trip to Positano or Lake Como, in her vision of herself as a world-traveling call girl.

How ridiculous, she thought to herself. *I can just go to the Italian Institute for classes or jump on an online Italian conversation course! But no – no juicy cock there (unless there was a hot guy in the class. Hmmm… when do I sign up?). No,*

*I had to go and get mixed up with a married strip club owner with both police AND mafia connecti*ons! *Will I get a horse head in my bed if I stop hooking up with him?*

God, I'm ridiculous. Una stupida puttana!

Wasn't this behavior the kind of thing she'd grown up with, and integrated into her being as somehow acceptable? The dearly departed Lacy was her father's girlfriend, and her mother went along with it all, for reasons of her own. Wasn't she herself the gal who'd interviewed for a position in New York City's most expensive and exclusive bordello? So why was she suddenly feeling so guilty and moral all of a sudden? Wouldn't most of GG's clients be married? Were the interludes with the married Tony just practicing for that?

I'll deal with that shyster Tony later, she thought. Meanwhile, she slid her hand over Jean-Chris' way and gave him a guilty smile.

"I'm feeling strange," he suddenly admitted, just blurting it out. "Think how horrible and lonely I'll feel if you toss me out at 2am tomorrow or whenever you tire of me?"

"Oh, darling J.C, I don't think so. It's not like that. I'm just exhausted. I've never experienced times like this. So busy; so stressful in some ways…"

"Then why did you invite me out if you cannot give me your best?"

"It was the best I could do?"

"And you know how both of our lives are right now. Every second is counting. My homework is immense. Immense! If we spend tomorrow together playing in the morning and brunching and I return home late… It's very difficult for me. Even *amour* with a beautiful woman I adore is not worth it if I am to fail all my courses."

"I know. It's the same for me, too. I'm living in a big 'time and money crunch.' Wait. Did you just call me beautiful and adored?"

"I don't know what I'm saying. It was very wrong to enjoy so many of the lemon martinis without having a few glasses of red wine in between."

"No, I distinctly think I heard something about adoration and attraction."

"Why do you tease me like this? You were so jealous of Saffron. It's the *only* reason you suddenly wanted to sleep with me, to have me stay over. Because *she* wanted to stay over at my place."

"No, it's not like that. I… Whoo! Don't get me wrong. I think about shagging you all the time. I just wanted it to be perfect when we finally…"

"What's not perfect? *We're* perfect. We've lost so much time, playing games. There was always my room or your room. Or some private corner at the Turkish Bathhouse after that man thrashed you with those leaves, but nooo."

"At the hotel, that would have felt like we were living together! Imagine how awkward we would have felt every day after, seeing each other like that. Like, *uggg married* people…" She scrunched up her face.

"Uggg? Being married is probably very nice, Cali. You'll see some day."

"You try it first and let me know."

"Ha, ha. And now we're living far apart and you still

don't seem very eager to see me or make love with me."

"It hasn't been *that* long since I left the hotel! My lifestyle. My apartment. It wasn't *ready*."

"Stop making excuses. You were busy with your sugar daddy."

"No. I was getting used to not relying on stripping. And I was going hmmm straight."

"You, Mademoiselle Kistler? 'Going straight'? What is this *load of caca*? You do not have anything straight about you. Everything is like…" And with this, he made some crooked motions with his hands. "I do not even want to begin talking about this 'sugar daddy' in your life. I am furious about him. I hate him. This is no sugar daddy. This is a shit daddy."

"You know something? Fuck that Saffron and her big mouth! Bitch can't keep a secret. She's completely broken the code of girls. Good girlfriends keep secrets, and she's therefore not a good girlfriend."

"She's just jealous of you. You're probably far more talented than her, apart from the other obvious things, like, how pretty you are, and having *me* in your life. When you were in the bathroom she actually had the audacity to open up your portfolio and take a quick peek through. Right in front of me! You need a lock on that thing. She rifled through it like it had state secrets inside."

"Really?"

"Really. It was a little shocking."

"Why didn't you tell me when it happened?"

"At first I wasn't sure. Maybe it's something you interior design students do: share your work with one another. And

I didn't want another Heimlich incident getting us thrown out of Delphine's, like what you did to Darla at the diner."

Cali remembered the rather delicious feeling of getting revenge on Darla by crunching her ribs, and squeezing her nearly to death under the pretense of saving her life with a faked-up Heimlich maneuver. *Shit*. She suddenly felt gutted. Everyone around her seemed to be lying to her in one way or another, all except for dear Jean-Chris.

Once they were upstairs in the apartment, he looked around and complimented her on the charming new space; he was impressed she'd managed to secure it for herself at the same price as her room at the Hotel Gram-Irving. He changed into her oversized plush bathrobe, which he barely fitted into but which provided a bit of comfortable covering. She changed into a modest vintage Laura Ashley nightgown garnished with satin rosebuds and white lace; it was long-sleeved and high-necked – completely Victorian – and left a great deal to the imagination.

"Sorry, I'm still searching for the right lighting. I'm trying to keep to a budget now" (*Now that I'm almost broke*) she said, looking around at how her bedroom was pitifully mood-lit with the light from the kitchen. Jean-Chris leaned against the wall with his arms crossed while she climbed into bed and collapsed against the many pillows.

"So. Tell me. Does this old man you have managed to seduce with your sweetness, your humor, your curvy body – does he want you to be exclusive with him? He must be *very* in love with you."

"No. It's just a Monday and Friday afternoon thing. Lots of boundaries and perimeters, rules and regulations. He's very regimented. He runs one of the world's largest –"

"Who cares what he runs or what he owns. So because he is so anal and so powerful, I now have an option for the other days of the week? And what about the Italian?"

"What about him? If you come sleep – just sleep! – and be quiet for the rest of the night, in this big, nice bed with me, I may give you an option for other days."

"Oh, that is very kind of you. My choice of a day." Jean-Chris came and sat on the edge of the bed. "Give me your feet. Feet out. I will rub them while I ruminate on all this. I cannot sleep until this is settled. Lotion?"

"Over there, on the dresser."

He got some lotion on his hands as Cali tucked her feet out. Grabbing hold of them, he began giving them a wonderful massage. "So. Let me analyze this logistically. First, you left stripping behind. 'Oh, Jean Chris, I've left it all behind, I will never strip again…'" (Here, he mimicked Cali's high, breathy voice). "Then, a short while later, you go to work in the corporations. I am thinking you will be a very fast typist, you'll answer phones and do some good work. And on the first day, the President of the company or whatever he is, talks you into becoming his kept mistress. *Mon Dieu*, I do not want to think of this."

"Think of what?"

"What you could be capable if you could ever hold a straight job for more than a day!"

"Yeah, better if you don't think about it all."

"You do know what you are slowly becoming, no?"

"It doesn't seem to bother you that Darla was selling illegal drugs. But *me* lighting up some old guy's life who helps me with school on a very part time basis; *that's* giving you hives?"

Talk about hives! God forbid he ever found out about her failed hooking venture at the Penultimate Hotel, losing her temper with Darty and landing up in jail, with a large legal tab to pay. She'd keep that one well-hidden lest he dredge it up from the depths of her being, for a closer look at every moldy carbuncle. *No more hotel hooking.* She'd promised herself never to attempt something stupid like that again, (without the benefit of more experience at GG's).

"You're very hypocritical, you know that? You knowingly continued fucking Darla, even though you knew she was seeing that guy Benji."

"Do not wiggle out of this by talking about Darla. She existed in another dimension. When her bag of Ecstasy was sold each night, she simply had her wicked way with me, and then she would go see her, uh, other boyfriend. She had more needs than he could fulfill."

"Benji. Ha!"

"Yes. I had no idea that Benji would be so jealous about something so casual. Our hearts were not involved, me and Darla."

"Yeah, you never met Benji until your face was introduced to his *fist*."

"Never mind this. I want to go back to… What's his name?"

"I'm so tired of talking about Hank," Cali said, sitting up in her bed. "Would you please go turn off the light in the kitchen and shut up about my life?"

"Ah, Hank. The Wank."

Soon the light in the kitchen was off, and Cali heard Jean-Chris' bathrobe fall to the floor. He slid in next to her; her back turned away from him. Gently raising her gown over her body, he pressed in close to her, his arm finding its way around her waist and his hand finding hers.

"Never mind about this rod of hard steel pressing between your legs. It will still be there in the morning if you want it. And we can still stay friends even if you are committed to becoming a courtesan to this guy Wank."

"Hank. Please, I'm sleepy. It's too heavy to talk about this right now; you've drained me. Nothing is ever easy-breezy with you."

"You know why I am hating this? I am hating this because as long as you are like this, it means we can never fall deeply in love. As long as you insist on having these other men, and I can't offer you what you need, the financial part, *we* can never be. And it makes me feel so weak, so far from my dreams… But let's just sleep."

"You're talking too much. Don't think so much. Let's, Shhhh. Don't worry about what I need. Just be my friend," she said, enjoying his delicious warmth, the wood, and drifting off into a night-long cuddle with Jean-Chris.

"Be your lover?"

Zzzzzzz…

Chapter Thirteen

The next morning Cali was alarmed to find that Jean-Chris wasn't there beside her. She sat up in a mild panic. *Did I say something wrong? Did I make him feel bad? Was this too much too soon? Did he not feel wanted enough?* But after looking around for a note, she noticed that the apartment keys that had been laying beside her purse were missing. She breathed a sigh of relief. He would be back.

After a head-to-toe freshening, just as she put the finishing touches on a gorgeous 'morning look,' the door finally squeaked open, and she heard pots and pans banging, and grocery sacks crunching as he made his way past the bathroom to the kitchen. "I've been to the flea market and the grocery store. How do *you* feel?" he asked. "We, meaning the royal we/me had too much to drink?" He put down a sack, and placed two heavy pots onto the stove.

"No, I feel pretty good. It was nice. I've never spent the night with anyone before."

"Ah. I have been part of a first for you. May I say you look very beautiful this morning? But first I must make the breakfast without distraction. OH! I used your toothbrush, but first I pickled it in a jar of alcohol and then after purified it more with some bleach I found under the sink. I am terribly afraid about this MRSA."

"I noticed you are a little germ phobic. Is that why you put my remote control into a plastic Ziploc bag? Don't you think that's a little presumptuous? You don't live here, you know."

"I don't know who did that. Here is my problem…" and here he leaned against the counter, as there was nowhere to sit in the kitchen. He motioned for her to enter his arms and she did. "I am embarrassed to say: I could only afford to do something practical for you this morning. I cannot *also* take us out to breakfast, as I will run out of cash until the auction house gives me my stipend next week. I thought if I bought the right omelet pan at the flea market and some supplies, you will keep the pan for a long time, and it was all the same price as going out. I hate that this is all I can do at the moment."

She felt his pain. He probably felt quite strapped, especially after paying for the girls' multiple drinks the night before, without blinking an eye. "That's OK," she said, touched by the gesture. What he'd done for her – going to the flea market and the grocery, and now cooking – had required so much thought and effort, more so than some older, more successful man would probably have put into their morning. A guy like Hank would have just snapped his fingers and a breakfast, consisting of a single slice of avocado with a dash of salt on it, would have appeared.

"Eating in restaurants can be very, how do you say, like a passing experience one forgets?"

"Fleeting?" she suggested.

"Yes. Like this I have a new apartment gift for you to use always, *and* we can eat something. Here."

"Oh, thank you! This pot and pan are very nice. Enamel! You have a good eye."

"I practically grew up in the flea market, my favorite uncle was a *brocanteur*."

As he told her stories from his childhood in Paris helping his uncle with his antiques business, he prepared the ingredients for ham and cheese omelets to be served with a freshly-baked French baguette, still warm in its paper sack. Cali was suddenly struck by a depth of feeling – dare she call it love? – for the guy whipping eggs up in front of her. It was a deep admiration and yearning for him, some desire for a connection and intimacy with him alone that she couldn't shake off easily with her usual practical, material reasoning. She morbidly toyed with what it would feel like if he walked out into the street and was struck by a car. She would be *devastated*.

Up until now she'd touched bodies with a few men, but never touched souls. Whatever else was going on in her life – all her petty desires to get ahead, all the addictions forming and attaching her to material things – for a moment they fell away and she saw only *him*. She stopped his hand from turning on the burner on the stove. "About these passing experiences that one forgets…" she said as she took his hand, leading him to the bedroom. Undressing each other, they laid down together on the bed, and he took her face into his hands, kissing her neck. "I hope you won't forget *this*…" she said.

He spent a lot of time kissing her, his tongue exploring her and hinting at what his cock might do, once it was deep inside her. Biting her lips lightly, his hands roved over her breasts as he caught her nipples between his fingers and ever-so-lightly squeezed, sending a rush of pleasure down below. After a long delicious interlude, kissing and rolling on the bed, he held her still, and she felt his head descend as he took her clit between his lips. Squeezing down, he sucked her in, before plunging his tongue deep inside her, alternating with caressing her lower lips with his, before delving again into her pussy with his tongue, which she felt from time to time flicking around her asshole, bringing her to a new heights of pleasure, but not to the point of coming.

He poised her on all fours, and she relaxed into a fluffy pillow, braced for his entry from behind. As he slid on his condom, he was visually enamored by the image of her like that. He took a moment to admire her, and was completely allured by the curvature of her hips, the small of her back arching in anticipation of receiving him, her pink pussy lips glistening: knowing that when he pressed in the perfect place, she would eagerly take him in.

He slowly pushed his cock inside her, and sank into her, as she arched her back and felt his hot, hard rod filling her up. He stroked her hair and pulled it back lightly with one hand, as the other fondled her lightly in front. Kissing into her neck, he delighted in hearing her moan. She enjoyed every hard inch of him as he gently nudged further inside her, and then pulled out again, only to return a few seconds later with another delicious entry.

His lovemaking, as he slowly pumped inside her, was very deliberate and sensual and embracing. He was taking into consideration, based on what had been revealed to him the night before, that she may still have had limited sexual experience; he wasn't sure. Almost in answer, she felt herself putting on some light 'inexperienced' theatrics to disguise some of the newfound skills she'd learned with Tony, Clark Kent and Clive. But in so doing she felt taken out of the moment. Jean-Chris was not someone she should fake anything with. She could be herself, she reasoned, and stopped faking a lack of experience.

As his thrusts became more intense, she forgot about other men, faking and anything else that might take away from this perfect pursuit of pleasure with the most adorable guy she'd ever met. She pumped back on him, enjoying the feeling of him in her, on her, and with her. She just went with it, and would deal with any of his inquiries later.

She became saturated with his immensely romantic energy, as he turned her over and covered her in kisses. She thought fleetingly of Tony and the contrast between his and Jean-Chris' style. Tony had been a technical marvel: using his hands, tongue and cock as tools of pleasure. But he'd been a bit detached from the whole experience. With Jean-Chris, she felt that he was losing himself in her, and was using pleasure as an expression of some deeper well of feelings.

As he gently circled her nipples with his tongue, she gently stroked his cock up and down, eager to have him inside her again. She felt herself losing her own grip on reality, diving into the experience with him. He led her into further pleasures as he descended to her love flower again and circled there, too, gently with his tongue for what seemed forever. Then, as she writhed in pleasure, he plunged his tongue deeper in and out of her over and over, and brought her to the edge of coming before sliding his body along hers and gliding on top of her.

He slowly entered her as she wrapped her legs around him, and they rocked together slowly but steadily. She felt immensely adored, almost *too* adored – was this going to complicate things? – as he brought his lips to hers and kissed her again, deeply. She reveled in the weight of his hips bearing down on her, and how the hard bulk of his cock filled her up with each thrust. Over what seemed a long period of holding her in a tight embrace, he steadily increased his rhythm; her hips rocked and met his with a delicious force, which they could both no longer hold back.

"Jean-Chris!" she whispered into the morning as she gave in to coming. She felt him also losing it, and the bed fell away in her imagination so they were suspended a few moments more in a free fall toward a mutual climax that made them both shudder and moan. They clung to one another hard, until their grips on one another grew lighter.

They stayed entwined for a long time after that, their bodies relaxed, but their minds beginning to race. She couldn't help it but to say, "I adore you. I really do" – even though it might bring about consequences. (*What was he thinking covering MY remote control in plastic!?*)

"So will you still like to see me again?" he asked playfully.

"I think I would like to, yes."

"May I see you *tonight* then?" he ventured, hiding a joking smile.

"Ummmm, no. Don't you have homework to do *back at your place*?"

"Yes, but I could do it here. In fact you have a lot of room here for me to stretch out with my drawing table. We could do our work *together*. I could even move my things over, just a few books. Your fridge is much nicer and bigger." It was taking everything for him not to break out into a laugh.

"Mmmm, that all sounds nice but, if you haven't noticed, I'm a bit of a lone wolf."

"I knew you would be this way," he said, rising and getting dressed. "So resistant to becoming *a couple*."

"Oh my God, you're kidding me!"

"I am!" he laughed. "Were you afraid I was getting, how do you say…?"

"Clingy?"

"Clingy? This is a word? I must write it down in my journal. Ha! I tricked you."

"It's a good word but not a good thing to do. I'm trying to train myself out of being clingy with men. The sooner I lose a quality like that, the better. Look! I'm reading this amazing old book; I think it's a classic in this type of thing. Maybe I shouldn't show you." She went to a pile of books on her floor and pulled out one called *The Rules: Time-Tested*

Secrets for Capturing the Heart of Mr. Right. "This book shows women how to remain aloof and mysterious and have men chasing after them; never taking them for granted."

"Ah," he said, picking it up. "This is how you will capture me: Mr. Right. I will read it, and will thwart you at every move. Give it here."

"No! I shouldn't have shown you my secret weapon."

"This is all manipulation. You know, Cali, there is nothing wrong with becoming attached: with expressing yourself to a man, showing love and getting into a relationship. Even if it might hurt or not work out."

"I think there *is* something wrong with it actually; at this stage of life, at least. We're here to learn, to improve ourselves, to set ourselves up for the future, not just hook up permanently with the first person, well nearly the first person, we like or sleep with."

"*Like,* only?"

"Love, a little?"

"Ah ha! So you do not want the man you love 'just a little' sticking to you like a chewing gum on the bottom of your shoe."

"Exactly. Or worse. Like when you *swallow* chewing gum and it stays in your colon, clogging you up inside, forever. Some people say that gum is not digested for seven years, if ever."

"Do you want me to go then? We can reclassify our evening as a one-night event. Never to be repeated again."

"No. Now don't be so quick to reclassify. Could we go for a walk before you go? Maybe go to the flea market? I've enjoyed this *a little*. I've hardly seen this neighborhood yet. The park?"

"I will join you to the park but then it's going to be a very simple goodbye. We won't promise that we're ever going to see each other again. Just leave things 'open'?"

"Well I, I don't want to say goodbye, exactly. I won't go into all the details, okay? But I find that I need to become more cultured, go to more museums and somehow become more sophisticated. And maybe we could do some of that together? But I really need to get fluent in several languages. And one of them being French, could you, could we sometimes…?"

"Have a French lesson?"

"Yes. On a regular basis. Until I'm super fluent. I can't afford tutoring but…"

"Ah! You don't want to get too close. But it is fine to use me for my native tongue. I see. My physical tongue was not enough. Now you need more. Frenching. I mean, French."

"God, yes, to everything."

"Cali, part of learning the French heritage involves a period of prolonged lovemaking; it's what we romantics call *amour*. Usually this takes place after the lesson. And when I visit, you must have good snacks and wine present. Usually, I like a Sancerre. And a Beaujolais Nouveau in that time of year. As a language professor I don't function well without wine."

"I can probably arrange something like that."

"And also, there is the matter of the length of your lessons. You see, I will never agree to something quick with you, sneaking out in the middle of the night to do this thing you call the 'walk of shame.' A short lesson is not enough for someone of your intelligence. We must take our time if you are to absorb the language. Of *amour*, I mean French."

"I would be willing to study all night with you, if that's what you insist upon."

"Let's talk more about it at the park. Get dressed, Snickelfritz."

"Snickelfritz?"

"I'm perfecting my Dutch idioms as well. So tell me, does this Italian-speaking Italian, does *he* insist on having – bah! I don't know – truffle pasta and red wine when he comes over to teach you Italian?"

"I refuse to answer that. We were having a perfectly great day until you started asking questions about other guys."

"Well, tell me this. Am I *ever* to be your ONLY boyfriend?"

"Could we start with something more casual, perhaps?"

"Ah, merde! Fine, casual it is. But it won't be casual for long, not once we take our masks down and start *getting real* with each other. You have a very pretty mask, but under it –"

"UGH, getting real, you are kidding me."

"No, I am completely serious. I want to know and love every inch of you."

After a lovely walk together in Prospect Park, as a chilly breeze rustled the tree branches, and they watched all the crazy dogs running free in the dog run, Cali and Jean-Chris warmed themselves with some hot apple cider purchased from a cart. Talking and laughing non-stop, she told him about how, as a child, she'd once dropped a cheap ice cream cone on the sidewalk. Her penny-pinching mother made her scoop up the part of the ice cream that wasn't touching the ground, then continue eating it off the top of the cone. "A little dirt don't hurt!" her mother had tried to convince her. She noticed Jean-Chris, the germ phobe, visibly cringe.

"You lived?!"

Cali explained how the indignity of such a moment had only convinced her that one day she needed to pursue a life of unbridled luxury, with unlimited scoops of artisanal gelato, probably a Valrhona chocolate consumed on the Spanish Steps in Rome, or a rich Madagascar vanilla *glace* served in a delicate dish while facing the Place des Vosges in Paris.

"Now I do understand why she was so often rinsing out your mouth with her soap bar. It wasn't just because you were compulsively trying to shock her with the F-word," he laughed, "She literally made you eat dirt! No wonder you have such a filthy mouth now."

"Ha! Very funny. I have to confess. I *really* enjoyed it when I finally got *here* and I could use the F-word all the time, as much as I want, without getting my mouth washed out with her soap," Cali mused.

"You know, you can use the F-word in bed with me. I do really like it," Jean-Chris teased. "Go, like, 'Fuuuuuck me!'" he gasped. "By the way, did you like it when I licked your, ummm, *trou du cul*?"

"What? God!" Cali sighed. "We just had our first time. Can't we just bask in that without 'ANALyzing'?"

"Ha! *That*, this morning, this was just an amuse bouche," he promised. "I have more and better for you. It is only the beginning."

"Promises," she sighed, trying not to smile too big in the street.

As they walked toward the subway station, where Jean-Chris would descend and she wouldn't see him again until their next "French Lesson," Cali suddenly remembered her weekend from here on out wasn't really about leisure. Besides copious amounts of homework for school, she had lots to do before her next Monday afternoon meeting with Hank Greenace. He'd given her several more pre-loaded gift cards to upgrade her look further before their next intimate 'lost hour.' Hank felt that her pores looked too large, and she needed to book into a good facialist.

She said, "I'll come in with you to town! I need to visit a spa before my next date…"

Jean-Chris stopped in his tracks. For a tiny moment he looked as if he was about to cry, but it quickly passed into anger. "Your date?" he nearly snarled.

"My work thing…"

"So sleeping with the CEO is now a work thing. So now you are a businesswoman?"

Cali instantly regretted her massive faux pas, her lack of finesse, her utter lack of romance and caring with regard to Jean-Chris. Had she been more masterful in caring for him, she would have just remained mysterious, taking an entirely different train into Manhattan. She shouldn't have exposed her best friend (and now lover) to her shenanigans. He didn't need her quasi-prostitution thrown in his face, and that's exactly what she'd done, and with a big 'Splat.'

"I don't feel well, I must go. Please take your own train in," he insisted.

"Oh my God! I'm sooo sorry. I shouldn't have said that!"

He made as if to go down into the station, but turned and tilted his face, his eyes dancing. "I should really leave you now. For good. You're a monster."

"I am!" she squeezed her eyes, as tears began to come. "I'm just trying to take care of myself, to become someone. Please don't drop me because I want to be comfortable. I want to finish school but really succeed with it, to have *things.*"

He sighed and shook his head. "I do understand where this is all coming from. It's the only reason I'm still standing here. I'm just a poor young student guy – *at the moment*. And I know that. And you're a girl who has been all alone, trying to make it here. But you'll see: someday I will be able to take care of you."

She plunged her hands into her pockets. "But you *do* take care of me. You're the fun in my life. Everything else is drudgery."

He approached her, grabbing her into a hug, and pulling her ski hat down over her eyes, holding it there. After a while she pulled away a little and put the hat back where it was.

"I don't deserve you," she sniffed.

He took a long look at her. "You really don't. Do you think I will still recognize you after you return from this magical spa?"

"Come over for my French lesson next weekend, and find out."

He sighed and nodded. "Saturday evening?"

"Yes."

"I'll go first."

"Go first," she agreed, watching him go down the stairs of the train station. Her eyes followed him, as she held back the urge to cry at how her life might change and her feelings might evolve after more weeks and months of being Hank's secret (somewhat kept) mistress. She bit her lip. It would be so much nicer and easier if she and Jean-Chris could just head toward boyfriend and girlfriend, without her getting lost in an increasingly confusing maze of questions about what she really wanted out of her life.

He turned around suddenly, as she felt he would.

He blew her a kiss, and she caught it.

Chapter Fourteen

The following Monday, after a weekend of feeling rather giddily in love with Jean-Chris, Cali came back down to earth to 'perform' for her usual visit with Hank. Once out of his embrace, and back home in Brooklyn, she had all afternoon to get herself ready for her weekly Italian evening sex/tutoring session with Tony, which now felt a bit tawdry compared to the intimacy she'd just experienced with Jean-Chris.

Often enough since she'd moved out to Brooklyn, on Monday evenings Tony left her well-sated, doused in sweat and limp as a ragdoll, repeating some new Italian phrase over and over in her mind. It was as if Hank provided all the non-penetrative foreplay during the afternoon, and Tony, with his sometimes brusque yet exciting style, sort of finished her off that night. But like a kid wanting a new toy, Cali wished she could exchange him for a newer, different plaything (or two). Though she knew women could often call the shots (i.e. walk into any given bar and ask some cute dudes to sleep with her, and be reasonably certain one may say yes) she still felt a bit awkward about how to get more new and different sexual experience. Besides, Jean-Chris was promising to become a regular, wonderful lover – and she desired more *of him*. Why be greedy?

The pattern was emerging where her days and nights were crammed with commuting, temping in offices, night classes, loads of weekend homework, a sliver of time to bathe and take care of herself – before falling into bed, exhausted. Fitting more boy-toys into her life felt a bit decadent (although still doable).

Today, she was still riled up about the fact that Tony was probably married, but she decided she would let it go. She should have assumed, asked, or investigated, but she'd chosen not to, and remained in denial about him. *My bad*.

However, she re-thought the so-called 'terms' of their relationship. In a hot bubble bath, she thought more closely of the fine print that discreetly underwrote their supposedly mutually-beneficial relationship. It seemed to be all in Tony's favor.

Does that Italian do anything to make your life any easier? Jean-Chris had probed, during their walk in Prospect Park.

She jumped out of the tub, and dried off, thinking that Tony should probably take some responsibility to help her through this difficult period following the wipe-out of most of her savings to pay for Clive's legal help, and until she could stabilize financially again (and, admittedly, manage her money better). She'd never dare ask Hank for additional help, as that might involve confessing that she'd tried her hand (badly) at high end hotel hooking. At least with Tony, he had some street smarts to him, and she could confess honestly as to what had gone down. He knew she'd worked as a stripper, and so might have been tempted by something more (and gotten in trouble her first time out).

Once she was situated in her kitchen, Cali stirred that pot of her thoughts while also stirring a crock of slow-cooking vodka sauce – yet again for Tony's oft-requested Penne alla Vodka. (It was the only thing she'd gotten good at cooking so far).

She sipped from the source bottle of Vodka as her mind roved over everything that was wrong with their deal. As she sprinkled a few pepper flakes and that expensive prosciutto he liked into the sauce, she realized fully that she felt slightly bored of fucking him. No, make that major bored. Did he feel the same way too? She was also sick of rarely going out in public with him, because he would cite the excuse that there were "eyes and ears in Brooklyn" (*hadn't that been a signal enough to tell you he's married!?*) Cali started calculating the *real* cost of dallying with Tony.

"*He's a waste of space*," Jean-Chris had tossed her way in the park, and the words reverbed in her head just as the doorbell rang.

"Hey baby," Tony said in English, before switching to Italian, which by now –with her concerted studies outside their lessons (and running Italian MP3s all night on headphones so she was completely immersed in the language for hours) – she got about 85% of what he was saying.

In Italian she asked him where some flowers were for her. "*I fiori, dove sono?*"

"No flowers, *I'm* your flower," he said back in Italian. "You got wine?" he asked, going to the refrigerator; happy to find as usual she'd purchased a good Montepulciano (at her expense) for their date. Right next to it was the much more special Sancerre she'd specially chosen for Jean-Chris' next visit, which she was looking forward to with a childlike anticipation. She ran her fingers down the bottle for Jean-Chris, struck with a deep, loving emotion in thinking of him.

"I'm gonna hit the head," Tony said in English, already unzipping his pants, and heading into the bathroom. "Get my glass going! Meet you in the bed."

But today she didn't meet him there. She stayed in the living room, seething. Coming out of the bathroom, he approached her on the couch. Tight and toned, he tore his shirt off. While his muscles and physique were appealing, she now balked at the almost automated way they'd fallen into a routine of fucking, eating, and speaking Italian while they were doing it, a bit hurriedly, with him usually leaving in under an hour – getting back to the Bronx and Tony's Wedge in time to not be missed.

Besides, Jean-Chris had proved out to be a fabulous, loving lover, *numero uno*; thus rendering Tony a far second…or third. (Clive had been a fabulous fuck, as fucks go, she thought, but there probably wasn't going to ever be a rematch with the celebrity attorney).

"What's wrong?" Tony sighed, "You got that look on your face, like someone just ran over your poodle. We gonna bone or what?"

"I don't want to sound fussy, OK?" she said, trying to sound reasonable.

"Ah, here we go. This sounds familiar. Yap, yap."

"No, come on; I'm not even going to bring up *your wife*."

"I was wondering when you were gonna ask…"

"No, but have you ever considered bringing me a nice gift from time to time or maybe helping me, financially, with something that's important to me?" she asked. "Couldn't you just offer sometimes? I do need help sometimes."

"Whoa, Cali! That's not what I thought we had going. I really like you, you know that? I think we have a good time together."

"Well if you really liked me, would you be concerned that maybe, possibly, I've just lost my savings? Or maybe something bad happened and I'm at rock bottom. And maybe you'd want to help me out for a little while till I graduate from school?"

"Whoa. Sorry, hon. I'm not sure I'm up for sponsoring your schooling. Wanna go back to dancing or somethin'? You were a great dancer, from what I saw. Just not at my club. You know how I felt about that."

She sighed. "Dancing is out of the question. If I'm going to ever go back to the sex business, I think I'll do something a little more lucrative and less grungy than *that*. There *are* other options, you know."

"Whoa! That's not what I want to hear," he tried to hide a quick peek down at his watch.

"Why are you checking the time?!" she whined.

"No, hon. I'm not checkin' the time. I'm checkin' the

condition of this watch. Look, it's not a Cartier, but it's a good watch. I'm gonna give it to you. Take it down to the pawn shop on Atlantic; see what he'll give ya for it," he said, sliding it off his wrist, and placing it on the cocktail table at the same time he reached for his clothes on the chair. "So, we're not gonna, you know, get it on?" he asked sadly, with a deep frown.

"Now *you* look like someone just put your German Shepherd to sleep." She stifled a giggle. This was all so ridiculous.

"Oh, I see how this is. Rage against poor Tony. I get it from all sides. The wife. And now you."

Ah, playing the guilt card. She watched in amusement as he pouted. She asked, "Is it OK if one time you come over, I opt out of fucking? Am I allowed to have an off day?"

"Yeah, you can have the day off but you're missing out. What was the whole point of me coming over, then? Your Italian's pretty damn good. Could be better. I'm trying to be nice here, and help you. So you want the watch? Cost me a pretty penny at the shop where I got it," he claimed, handing it over.

Cali gave him a tight smile. After window-shopping on Madison Avenue on a regular basis, and having been exposed to Hank Greenace's rotating collection of high-caliber watches, she could see from a few feet away that Tony's 'replica' watch was a cheaply-plated piece of faux horological crapola. "Thank you. That's so nice of you. I'm sure it will help."

"It's hard to part with, but you're worth it," he nodded, handing it over.

"It's a beautiful piece…" *of shit*. Why hurt the guy's pride or his taste in aluminum? *Oh my fucking God, I am worth SO MUCH MORE than this!*

"Let's get in touch," Tony said. "Hey, if we're not gonna ball today, can you make me a to-go box of the penne? Throw in one of your forks and a napkin to protect my shirt in the car? I'll bring it back next time. I'm runnin' late and there's a bunch of construction on the BQE."

"Sure," she said, returning to the kitchen. She'd *completely* forgotten to bitch more about him being married. Good! No more fucking a married guy for nothing. No need to nag him further with the fact she never intended to sleep with him again if he wasn't going to support her dreams and goals. GG's girls probably didn't put up with that shit; their rates were stated up front. Though she had no 'rates' to speak of, she wasn't going to stand for him getting off cheaply.

Fuck it! Men I'm not in love with aren't gonna sleep with me for free!

She tore open a kitchen drawer, looking into the organizer that sheltered a rather special set of vintage enameled flatware in an exquisite Majorelle blue. The floral ferrules gleamed and charmed her as much as they did the first time she laid eyes on them. She and Jean-Chris had hunted the set down together that first morning together at the flea market, gleefully jumping up and down after the seller gave her a more than fair price for the gorgeous set.

I'll never give up OUR set. Not for a well-off guy who has never spoiled me properly, and whom I'm probably never going to see again!

"Hurry up!" Tony called from the next room.

"Coming!" Cali called back. *Fuck you.*

She quickly grabbed a paper-wrapped set of wooden chopsticks, and then pulled off a few paper towels. She put them together in a sack with a plastic-covered dish of the Penne alla Vodka. She half hoped he'd get splinters in his tongue. *Try slurping sauce-laden spaghetti with chopsticks while driving on the BQE – Ha!* She gleefully imagined the mess it would make on his white shirt.

He was already waiting by the door. "Bout time," he sighed.

"Here you go," she said, handing the package over.

"You're the best. Love your pasta," he said, before slinking out the door… never to be seen again.

Chapter Fifteen

As the semesters went on, and Cali began to excel at interior design school, her Monday and Friday afternoon visits with Hank were equally educational. They always commenced with a long period of hugging, but also seemed to consist of some new honing: some new lesson that whipped Cali into 'fighting shape' to be his mistress (and perhaps eventually become a courtesan for several men, if that was the direction she was indeed headed; she dared not tell him about that).

In the litany of things that he taught her, she came to integrate certain behaviors into her being (and her notebook), as if they'd always been there and came naturally:

Show up with something to discuss. Read today's news or even a trashy tabloid, but have something to spark or spice up a conversation.

Be a good listener. Listen rapturously. Never interrupt.
Keep your word. Never be late.
Be impeccably groomed. No slouching.
Flatter, always.
Lingerie should always match.

Bring gifts for special occasions.
Know the names of the children by heart.
Clean up after yourself. Disappear when room service steps in.
Act like every time is the first time.
Never call the office.
Don't show up sick.
Pretend to be happy, even if you're not.

In the realm of *her* outside life, the one 'out there,' he'd emphasized that in school or in her future career:

Never take no for an answer. Go for what you want.
Less is more, in most matters. Don't overwhelm.
Never complain, never explain. No excuses.
No booze during network & schmooze.
Sleep your way to the top if you must. But you're smart so you need not.
Be an originator. And beware of the copycat.
Look, act and hesitate prettily, but think, decide and take action decisively.
Take control of the room the minute you walk in.
Success is an inside job. Start with thoughts of success the minute you wake up.

And *Live in 'day-tight compartments'* (to steal from Dale Carnegie: Hank's favorite inspiring person).

For Cali, living in day-tight compartments came to mean planning her days out with precision, including the days she took off from temping, thanks to Hank's largesse. She fiercely protected the time needed for preparation of a vast amount of design school work. She slogged through three days a week of temp assignments, and the indignity of being treated as a ghost in every office where she went. And she religiously attended her evening classes four nights a week.

She made her greatest priority be those two visits per week with Hank, which required a mental discipline she was beginning to master, in terms of crafting the 'perfect' experience she gave him. He rewarded her with his (unpredictable) financial sponsorship of her goals, which was enough to help her move forward but not enough to truly splash around with. She and her life had become a finely oiled machine, with every minute – and dollar – accounted for.

As her semesters progressed, and her first year in the design program at The Design Arts Institute turned into her second, Cali got even deeper into the routine of design school and temping work, and Jean-Chris.

At first it was heady stuff for her: the Monday and Friday afternoon interludes with Hugging Hank, which, for all his hopes and promises of sex, only ever resulted in heavy petting (and sometimes a happy hand job ending for him)… and then the full-on powerhouse of her developing (weekend) love affair with Jean-Chris. Saturday nights or long Sundays were usually spent with him, sometimes doing homework together. He'd groomed himself not to ask too many questions about her other days of the week, any other lovers, and especially about Hugging Hank.

But, one cold night in the middle of the winter, something changed as they warmed up together in a hot bubble bath after they'd returned from a long, freezing cold walk out in Prospect Park. That night in the park, they'd talked about deeper things than usual, like how her father's girlfriend Lacy had so deeply impacted her approach to life, and how as a result, she could never feel as close to her own mother. He recalled, too, how he'd felt so unguided and lost without a father, but felt glad he'd been so well-fathered by his uncle. Deep down, despite academic successes, he still suffered from a type of imposter syndrome with regard to his abilities.

Now in the bath, he wrapped his arms around her under the water, and asked: "Can it just be us from now on, I mean, besides Hank?" He spoke softly. "I realize he needs to stay in your picture for practical reasons…"

"You mean be exclusive? As in not sleep with other people…?" she smiled, thinking to herself that since her romp with Clive Vogelnest and her break up with Tony, there'd been nobody else, and she hadn't felt compelled to seek anyone else out (or be sought out). Contrary to her imaginings about how she'd move out to Brooklyn and go wild 'practicing' – shagging tons of different guys – she'd grown a little attached to Jean-Chris. Those notions of fucking lots of different men had discreetly left her mind.

He was slowly building up her sexual experience: with each and every long blow job she indulged him in, and with each snowflake-like (no two ever alike) sexual encounter she endeavored to have with him. It amazed her that the more she slept with just him, the more confident she felt in her ability to (possibly, if ever required) give pleasure to *many* men. Counter-intuitive, yes, but she saw that it was working.

"Yes. Just us." he insisted. "I'm happy with just you. I think I could be for a very long time. Like, forever!"

Forever? Forever seemed like a very long time.

"Just *me?*" she asked. The idea of having sex with just one person (possibly for the rest of one's life) was daunting, but *he* seemed to be handling it just fine. What planet was *he* from? She, on the other hand, was thinking of exclusivity as more of a temporary state of affairs while they grew up and changed their minds, and possibly moved on later (but she dared not hurt him with her true thoughts).

"This is serious, Cali. I'm fine sharing you with Hank. I know you said he doesn't hmmm, go inside you, and I know that probably in your mind it's just a type of job that gives you some comfort – but I want to know that *we're* exclusive, apart from him."

"OK," she agreed, seemingly easily, as yet another way to flatter him. Meanwhile, she was greedily thinking of how this conversation might quickly lead into the idea of deliciously going bareback (condomless) with him once they'd sorted out all the details of medical testing, etc. Feeling his cock inside her without that sheath of latex might just be addictive enough to actually consider *forever* with him, she thought, as she felt his fingers start to fondle her moistening flower.

She reached back and stroked him under the water, finding him already hard. Apparently going exclusive really turned him on, perhaps a little more than it did for her. She grabbed tighter around him and looked forward to the next ride (bareback).

As the semesters passed, Jean-Chris was growing tremendously in his education and his burgeoning career as an antiquarian. It was reflected in how little time he could devote to his flirtation with, going out with and making love with Cali. However, he called her whenever he could give her *all* his attention, even for a short while, and their bond was truly made in those telephonic conversations. They shared their most intimate thoughts and the developments in their studies; the love vibrations grew between them, which she felt in every fiber of her being. This only enhanced the moments when they saw each other face-to-face, and devoured each other in their more free-feeling state of exclusivity, which now included a more delectable skin-on-skin (and heart-to-heart) contact.

When they were apart, she missed the impromptu walks and dinners out that she and he had enjoyed more when they lived in the Hotel, before she moved out to Brooklyn. She longed to inject more leisure into her life, and secretly hoped for that time to be with him. On the other hand, she nourished her dreams and fantasies of having a life of glamorous adventures: a no-two-days-being-the-same lifestyle.

As her design courses became more technically complicated, Cali also wondered if the adventurous, glamorous, travel-filled life she dreamed of could be achieved by becoming an interior designer. Certainly other women who'd become wealthy at this profession had proven over and over that it could be, and her passion for the creation of beautiful environments was evident in her course work. Her portfolio of potential room designs had become quite magnificent.

Saffron seemed outrageously jealous. Despite everything – namely her bad behavior on their first night having drinks with Jean-Chris – they'd learned to respectfully tolerate one another, and even chit-chat on the many nights of classes, field trips to design projects and furniture manufacturers. They'd even gone out a few times for post-class drinks in the neighborhood from time to time with classmates (but never again with J.C). At those times, Cali always kept things cool and professional.

They would never be friends, but sassy Saffron was someone to observe and learn from. She had a certain charm and confidence about her, conversing easily with everyone. Cali watched (and from time to time tried to emulate) with interest.

One night in class, Saffron had exclaimed "I love that! You have something, some *je ne sais quoi*," she'd said, pointing to a particularly impressive computer-aided design and materials board that Cali had done for one of the 'pretend' clients they were to design for each week.

Mr. Takaya, in the week previous, had outlined this particular client in the design brief as being "a luxury hotel for cats" – which mandated that "at no time should there be animal motifs, themes, or any references whatsoever to felines in this boarding facility. Cats live there, yes. But humans will not be allowed to crap it up, or should I say, cat it up: with leopard spots, cat paw murals, or the like. Get it, folks?!"

"Can I take a picture? It's magnificent," Saffron had asked, pulling out her camera to snap a pic of Cali's cat lair before Cali could even protest. Feeling flattered, and while mingling among the other students, looking at their boards, Cali hadn't noticed Saffron *also* taking a photo of Cali's work plan, which sat on her desk – and included the source materials reference list, as well as a proprietary list of the pet-specialist contractors, fabric makers and special cat fencing manufacturer to be used for the project's outdoor garden, featuring a glass-covered temptation pool for the cats to interact harmlessly with fish.

As Cali slammed into the later, even more intense semesters of her college career, it seemed like all the spontaneity seemed to have gone out of her life. Temping in various offices and corporate settings was a nice, steady way of keeping herself in rent and food – but her deep discomfort each day as she sat stiffly behind a desk only brought into sharp relief the fact that she wasn't meant to ever become an executive, even a high-up, powerful one. All the corporate protocols and the office politics, the 'performance review' system, and tamping down of one's personality in order to fit in – it felt like ligatures around her creative mind. She was meant for something else.

So when Mr. Takaya announced the list of interior design firms offering the senior students interviews for paid internships after graduation, Cali balked a bit at the idea of more office settings (even if creative ones). But she pounced on the idea of getting paid to be trained, with an eye to soon enough striking out to form her own design consultancy someday. An internship in an especially prestigious or notable interior design firm was an instant entrée into the world of interior design, and the kinds of projects that would give her credibility.

If she could get along with everyone and not fuck it up.

But then her heart sunk when Mr. Takaya outlined the typical pay for such full-time traineeships, and it was much less than what she made temping (and taking care of Hank twice a week). If she took on an internship, she'd need *five* more days of temping, and *two* more Hanks in her life to afford doing an internship *and* not become homeless.

"*I've* already got an internship," Saffron sung, as she sidled over to Cali's desk during the break, to inform her of her latest good fortune.

Cali rolled her eyes. "Tell me more, Saffy. You're obviously dying to brag. Who are you interning with?"

"A paid internship, I might add. With Clara Z. Hilliard. Just found out last week," Saffron gloated.

Cali smiled and nodded but felt shot through with jealousy. Clara Z. Hilliard was her uber-favorite, most-admired interior designer ever, with a flair for gracefully integrating the work of artisans from around the world. She had a reputation for creating pale, feminine environments that both coddled and seduced – without becoming candy boxes. Clara had become even wealthier and more well known as a designer, by starting a lucrative side business designing custom fabrics and furnishings for the secondary market under her own brand name.

"That's really super, Saffy. Really. Congratulations!" Cali managed a big smile, before turning away to frown, while sipping from a hot drink over by the window. Fleetingly, and with an odd fascination at how her mind worked in the face of her jealousy of Saffron, she thought of dear GG and Kin – and how a stint in GG's was also like an internship, leading potentially into that independent life of a private call girl, with all its cash and 'no-two-days-are-ever-alike' possibilities, giving her the ability to start a business, invest in real estate, or whatever struck her fancy.

Being a call girl would give me all the cash I'd ever need to start my own design practice, and I could skip over the part about slaving away for other people's success.

Mr. Takaya wasn't done with his announcements when the break ended. "Listen up! I have another announcement to make. Something new the school is doing just this year to draw attention to the interior design program."

Saffron and Cali looked at one another and raised their eyebrows.

"There's a paid project available to the talented senior student who wins the Exhibition Competition Prize. There will be an exhibition of the competing projects during graduation and a panel of outside consultants – real world designers – will judge. The prize will go to the student who creates the most compelling proposal based on the design brief given for the competition. You can look at this in more detail in the handout."

Mr. Takaya walked around handing out the Design Brief as the students greedily tore through the pages, reading.

"OK, listen up, everyone. It's for a women's shelter. The design fee to the graduate is amazingly generous. But it's a pretty limited design budget overall. It must include space for fine art, either on the walls, or let's say, as a modality for healing the women's lives, like maybe an art therapy room installed within the shelter. You get it. This is for an *actual* women's shelter, I believe the, let's see here… the Hank and Esther *Greenace* Women's Center. You'll be hired to redesign the space, implementing the proposal you've done. This is tremendous. The Institute has never offered such a great gig before for the graduates!"

The rest of Mr. Takaya's announcement was lost on Cali. Mr. and Mrs. Hank *Greenace*?! *Oh my god! That's ironic.* She nearly choked on the tea she was drinking, already thinking of design ideas for her winning women's center. Wait until she told Hank! Oh, duh, he probably already knew. Was *he* behind this prize? Was it maybe rigged in her favor?

He had probably had a good laugh coming up with a sneaky way to challenge her. She'd really zing him about it the next time they met. Or maybe his wife Esther was behind it – or neither of them at all, just the charity. Hank might have been a generous donor to numerous charities, but he'd been careful not to 'spoil' Cali too much, knowing it was dangerous to take away her impetus to become a success at something outside of mistressing. This was her chance to show her stuff, to accomplish something that she wouldn't have to hide from others.

As Cali imagined herself in the near future, stepping up to the podium to win the Exhibition Competition goodies, Saffron interrupted her thoughts, "What's *your* idea for it? I can see it in your face. You have something already." Saffron was already circling like a vulture, seeming to think that Cali was stupid enough to share her plans with her.

"I have no idea," Cali lied, smiling tightly. "It's quite an intimidating brief."

"You're taking the piss. You're going for it, aren't you? I can tell," Saffron said, looking Cali up and down with a tinge of condescension in her voice.

"Why not?" Cali smiled, noting the strain on Saffron's face.

"Why not? Because you'll have to beat *me* to get to it. And I'm a better designer than you." With that, Saffron dumped a few items in her big canvas bag, and was off.

Chapter Sixteen

That Friday during Cali and Hank's 'lost hour' of hugging/giving him a hand job in bed at the Wendell-Astor Hotel, she nuzzled his neck, and tried to extract more information.

"Ummmm…"

"Don't ummm; say what you mean and mean what you say."

"Did you set up that design challenge competition with my school by any chance?" she asked, watching him carefully for any tells.

The edge of his lip twitched a little. "I don't know what you're talking about."

"Ah ha! You should never play poker, Mr. Greenace. I know you're the genius behind it."

"You'd better win it. But if the Director of the women's center doesn't like your proposal, you're screwed. I don't have any influence."

"Hmmm, you don't have a say in who wins?"

"No, damn it, Cali. Fair is fair. I just launched the idea

and funded the thing and they went running with it. If I wanted to just give *you* a high dollar contract to redo that space, I would have. But this is something you have to earn or WIN. On your own."

"You're no fun."

"Who says?" he smiled, guiding her hand to his lap as he gave her some gentle kisses on her cheeks. "Let me between your legs today…?" he asked, getting into position, but finding her unwilling to open her thighs to accommodate his desire to simulate sex. Usually all he required was a vigorous hand job, which took seemingly forever to bring him to a climax, but sometimes he enjoyed a rub between her fleshy thighs, finished off with some hand action.

He was still trying to pry her legs apart with his while she hesitated. "I don't know. If I have to work so hard for my success, you do too. Just *try* and get my legs open!"

"Oh come on, I'm just a sweet old guy who wants to see you succeed," he sighed, as she slowly let loose, and he was he able to snuggle his cock between her thighs. "That a girl," he smiled, rubbing vigorously, trying to use pleasure to allay his frustration with his weak erection. This went on for a while, and he struggled a bit for breath and energy, as usual, but ultimately he took his pleasure while she helped him along. As he seemed to hit his apex he said, "I feel strange…"

"Hank, are you OK?"

He sighed, "No. Ohhh," he seemed to be confused, as if the room was spinning around him. "I'm…"

"Seriously, are you OK?" she asked, watching as he clutched at his chest, and collapsed beside her on his side.

With a thud, his hand hit Cali's boob – and stayed there, unmoving. "Hank! Hank!" She shook him onto his back, hoping to rouse him. "Wake up! Hank, say something. Please?"

Nothing doing.

He was clearly dead; she checked with reluctance to find his pulse gone, his heartbeat nonexistent. For once in all the time she'd known him, he seemed perfectly at ease, not all wound up. He seemed to have finally gone on that nice long vacation he so deserved, but always put off taking.

"Oh…God…" She cried.

She squeezed her eyes shut, as tears streamed down, and took a deep dive for a while into the shock and sadness she felt over suddenly losing her wise, handsome friend. She thought over this sudden end of his life, and how he hadn't had a chance to say goodbye to anyone. Despite his temper, he truly was a 'people person,' always speaking of his family, his closest friends, his valued employees, and even his pets – and especially Esther, his beloved wife. This was sad stuff, indeed.

After recovering her composure, she sat for a while on the bed, observing him. She thought of calling his second assistant, Katherine, for some discreet advice on how to handle this discreetly – but Katherine might give it all away. She was a panicky type. Besides, how do you quietly move a dead man to a hotel lobby, a hallway, or even a sidewalk so it looks more like it didn't first happen in a hotel room (possibly with a mistress)?

There was Twyla, his first assistant – maybe Cali could

call her for help. But in Twyla's fastidious efforts to always do the right thing (and her penchant for gossip), she might actually fuck up his discreet passing *sans scandale,* and spill the beans to the wrong person. Cali thought hard. The last thing Hank would *ever* want was to appear on the cover of the New York Post with the headline, 'Big Pharma Hank Dies During a Yank.'

No, that wouldn't do. She needed to ghost right out of the scene. This needed to be neat and clean and enable those in the know to send the right message: *Hank Greenace died ALONE. He was a hard-working, exhausted man who treated himself to an afternoon nap twice a week in a nice hotel. Whether he was alone or not when he passed away from natural causes is of no real concern to the public or the family.*

Cali stood up, went and blew her nose in the bathroom, wiping away her smeared makeup, then throwing the soiled tissues into her purse. After dressing, she spent a great deal of time and effort fastidiously cleaning up any evidence of her presence or his desires for intimacy. *Always clean up after yourself*, he'd once instructed.

It might be discovered that she'd been there, of course. The DNA technology was certainly there to prove her presence, but a woman like his wife Esther wouldn't be all that interested in knowing *exactly* whom he'd spent his last breaths with. Knowing Hank, Esther probably already knew all kinds of details about Cali.

"She looks the other way and I don't throw it in her face," he'd once told her regarding the various flirtations he'd enjoyed during the later years of his long marriage. "She wasn't interested in sex anymore. Not even *touching*, which is a damn shame. 'Cause I'm a toucher. So here I am."

"Oh," Cali had frowned. It both sounded extremely familiar (like her parents) but also extremely unfamiliar to her deeper romantic nature. "For myself, I'd like a life long love. Not now, of course, but maybe later," she'd mused when confronted with Hank's practical approach to the vagaries of romance, wondering where Jean-Chris fitted into that.

"Nice work if you can get it," Hank had confirmed. "In theory, I believe different loves pass through our lives at different times, so it' not always just 'The One.' In practice though, I've stuck with one. And that's a form of love. *Love is a verb*, Cali. Remember that. *It's not what you feel, it's what you DO.*"

It took her quite some time to wrap her head around this idea, but she was slowly coming around to it. Often enough, she was asking herself, "I have feelings for Jean-Chris, but what would I be willing *to do*, or give up for him, if asked?"

Now that Hank was dead, all his shared opinions and teachings would take on a compendium-like presence in her subconscious, accessible at any time, well-absorbed.

One thing at a time. She pulled herself together, and stood up. She looked over at him as she took a washcloth and scoured over every surface of the room with it, hoping to remove her fingerprints or other traces.

She wasn't all that worried, but as the minutes ticked on, she felt the pressure on to leave the scene clean, and as soon as possible. She hoped any autopsy of his heart would tell the full story of his non-homicidal demise. However, a check of his heart would never be able to reveal the fondness he'd truly felt (and often expressed) for Cali, and the zesty inspiration he often said her presence brought to his life. On the days when she didn't see him she'd felt so peripheral to him, but on 'their' days she'd felt so front and center. Perhaps by knowing her place, she'd learned to manage her emotions better, as GG had once told her she desperately needed to.

He'd conditioned her with one of the main tenets of mistressing (or for courtesans with those VIP clients who needed to be handled with care): *know your proper place in your man's life, and don't be needy when he can't attend to you; focus on your own interests in the meantime, because at the end of the day, all you have is yourself.*

Once the de-fingerprinting was done, she tucked Hank more neatly into the bed, and carefully removed traces of her lipstick from her water glass, as well as anything else that might reveal their 'story.' She re-arranged the lunch table to look like just one person had eaten there, returning her water glass to the bathroom, and sliding her used set of silverware into her purse.

She felt grateful for all he'd taught her, and how he'd made her life so much easier and efficient over the last couple of years. Now was her chance to repay him, with her discretion. She clicked on the TV, and left a cleaned-off remote control beside his hand.

First things first. There's always an order to things.
She picked up the hotel phone and called 911.

"Hello. Hi, 911? Yes. I think a man here has suffered a massive heart attack. Could you please send your people over? He's in Room 405 at The Wendell-Astor Hotel. No hurry. He's resting peacefully. I just have one request. Please ask the paramedics to be discreet as possible with him, about contacting his family, if you know what I mean? Only Esther Greenace, his wife, should be contacted. Please note that. Thank you."

Cali found Esther's number in her phone and wrote it down with the words, 'My wife' on the hotel stationery. (She'd once taken the info down from the desk Rolodex on her first day temping, when she first felt Hank's interest rising – and wasn't exactly sure what to make of it, and whether leverage was needed). She tucked the paper into the sheet by his neck, where it would be easily seen.

She did one last quick mental and physical swipe of the room for any details that might be wanting – like earrings removed and put on the bedside table. She tucked Hank's favorite cuff links safely into his jacket pocket. And placed the towel she'd used to de-fingerprint into her purse. Taking out her sunglasses, she put them on, giving Hank one final look.

"*You're destined for great things, I can tell you that,*" he'd once said, encouraging her in her studies and life.

"Thank you Hank!" she whispered. "Love you, always. Bon voyage!"

Discretion is the greatest honor you can ever give another person.

With a Kleenex in hand to cover her tracks, she took a

big breath and let herself out of the room. Keeping her head down, she sought out the fire exit stairs instead of the elevator.

Chapter Seventeen

Cali stood on the street near the Hotel Wendell-Astor, after she had discreetly exited the scene of Hank's sudden departure. She watched the hotel's back service entrance from a safe distance. Over the arriving siren of the paramedic truck, in a rare act of desperation, she called Jean-Chris and found him at the auction house repair shop.

"Darling, I can't talk right now," he whispered. "I'm right in the middle of watching an expert restorer apply a gilded patina to a carved wooden frame encasing a priceless Soutine."

"Ah, OK," she sighed.

"Can I call you back? It's so loud there. Is everything OK?"

"It's a fucking fiasco!"

"Are you hurt?"

"No, I'm just shocked. I'm… well, Hank has died."

"Oh! Poor you. May I call you back later? He is using a historical custom-made recipe for the varnish."

"Sure," she said. Gosh, she'd expected a little bit more

comforting and concern than that. Yeah, *Poor me! Literally.* With that in mind, she called Surefire Temps.

"Misty Seemeister. What is it?" Misty droned over the line.

"Hi Misty, it's Cali Kistler."

"Oh, you." There was a long silence, as Misty metaphorically stared her down over the phone. Cali still felt raw from Hank's sudden departure, and Misty's hard edge made it even worse. Still, it was crucial that she get lined up with more work, if Hank would no longer be a support.

"Why are you calling me?" Misty was apparently still pissed off with Cali about the last 'incident.' It was based on a complaint received in a previous week about an altercation between Cali and her manager at one of her last temp jobs: a woman named Demi in the billing department of the Casberger Clinic for Ear, Nose, and Throat, part of a much larger hospital system.

The dispute began when Cali had complained that people there were smoking in the office. Normally this was a big no-no, especially in a hospital setting, but the office culture dictated that it was all OK as they were on the business side and far from any patients. It was extremely disturbing to Cali to work there, as the smell had seeped into her hair, clothing and belongings.

"I smell like a fucking ashtray, Demi! And I can barely breathe. It's not healthy here. This is a HOSPITAL for ear, nose, and throats, for fuck's sakes!" Demi, her short-term boss, at that moment, was blissfully sucking away on a cig a few desks away. "Now I have to go to school smelling like the Marlboro Man!" Cali screeched.

Demi, without looking up from her computer screen, had simply stubbed out her cig, then picked up the powerful electric stapler (Cali would learn later it was exactly the kind Jean-Chris used to adhere canvas onto wood frames). She'd pointed it Cali's way, finger on the trigger. "Would you like a couple of *these* in your forehead?" she asked calmly before giving Cali a taste of the stapler's velocity by pointing it away toward a partition. She shot it off, without flinching, as they both watched the staples embed into the partition with impunity. It hurt just watching.

A fiery anger at being bullied by smoky Demi tore through her. "Go staple your mouth shut, cunt! Better yet, while you're at it, go staple your cunt shut!" Cali grabbed her coat to leave for the day. Or, make that forever.

"OH, I'm a cunt now. I wonder what Surefire Temps will have to say about this."

Cali screamed so everyone down the hall could hear. "Call some cunt at Surefire Temps and find out! Cunt it up *together* if you want. I don't give a good goddamn. This is an unhealthy environment, and I'll be mentioning it to the board of the hospital. A bunch of Methodists run this place, and I'll bet *they* think tobacco users should go to hell."

"*You* got to hell."

"You go first. You invented it!" – and with that Cali slammed the hell out of there.

"Well, Kistler? What do you want?" Misty now growled over the line. Cali was also skating on thin ice for various *other* infractions, besides the most recent one with Demi. (Like not wearing pantyhose to the temp jobs, eating sushi and slurping soup at her desk, and once bringing leftover cold Sancerre wine in a thermos to work, which made her smell of alcohol; then there were the incidents of occasionally mouthing off to her superiors, à la "If you don't want me to sit quietly and read, and there's nothing else left to do, shall I just twiddle my thumbs here, or would you like me to go clean the toilets?").

In general, all her faux pas had amounted to a huge yellow sticky in Cali's internal temp employee profile at Surefire, which had the words, "INSUBORDINATE – FIRE?" scrawled across it. The only reason she hadn't been fired yet, Cali had once been reassured by Misty, was, "You work good when you work, you show up on time, and you dress nice. You type like a bat outta hell, and you're good on the software. You're sharp. But it's your shitty, insubordinate attitude that's, I'm telling you, gonna get you shit-listed." Apparently Cali's insubordination was dragging her nearer and nearer the sewer pit of a citywide, temp agency-wide blacklisting. "So don't make me shit-list you," Misty had threatened, after the incident with Demi. Now it was time to be sweet.

"Call anybody a cunt lately?" Misty asked.

"No, I have not. I've been on my best behavior," Cali promised. "Listen. Would you mind giving me more hours? Can you put me on for Mondays and Fridays now?"

"Sure thing, Sure Temp," Misty said.

"How 'bout a little hourly raise? You know I can be good."

"Ha!"

"Ha?"

"Ha," was almost the last thing Cali heard before Misty hung up, mumbling, "I'll see what I can do about Mondays and Fridays."

That night as she walked down the hallway at the Design Arts Institute, Cali still felt shaken from Hank's sudden exit, but there was no way she would miss class over it. Hank wouldn't have had it otherwise, as he'd once advised her (when one of his employees had died): "Cali, grieving is a waste of time. The person's dead and they aren't hangin' around. We should just be glad for 'em that they don't have to deal with all the pain of living, of being human anymore. And if they die in their sixties or seventies, sure it's a little early, but hey, life did them a favor and they got to escape the hell that can be old age, with people wiping up after them! We should just *be happy* for the deceased. Grieving is a purely self-generated behavior – you miss the person and you're pissed off they're no longer in your life – but it's of no consequence to *them* and the sooner you realize that, and rejoice in them moving on, the better."

God, can't I be sad for him just a little? Cali thought, thinking of Hank's clearly stated, if cynical opinion on the matter. She could still hear the echo of his pontificating voice in her mind as the students flooded into the classroom for Advanced Design Fundamentals.

Mr. Takaya was suddenly beside Cali, taking her aside outside the door of the classroom, to discuss something important. "We need to talk."

"What is it?"

"Cali, you know I can't name names and give all the details. But someone in your class recently got a very prestigious paid internship with a top interior designer. I mean, it's really quite above this particular student. And that designer called me for a reference. Usual thing. And, I have to say I was shocked when we started talking through the portfolio that was presented…" Mr. Takaya ran his hands over his face, nearly beside himself. "I'm so conflicted because everyone deserves to be successful. But I find stealing intolerable; yet I don't want to block the success of one of our students because she *did* receive the internship, based on the work she presented, even though I strongly suspect it wasn't *hers*."

"Oh?"

"It's good for our students to go on to bigger and better things. It would kill my reputation in the business if I admitted that we have cheaters in the school – in *my* class. But this hurts me, all of us."

"What!? Just tell me what happened. You know, I haven't applied for anything yet, an internship."

"YOU of all people *should*," he sighed, ruffling his hair nervously.

"So what happened exactly?"

"So the designer started raving about the projects in this student's portfolio, and she explained that this person had presented a cat boarding facility with a temptation pool with fish that just blew her mind. Then she was all gushy about the extremely femmy, glam boudoirs she'd seen in the portfolio, all illustrated so beautifully, the custom floral wallpaper designs…"

"OH God," Cali rolled her eyes. "I *knew* she was stealing from me!"

"You see what I'm getting at, don't you?"

"I do, and I really, gosh, I want to thank you for telling me. On the one hand, I'm extremely sad because I think it was a so-called friend who did that to me. And on the other hand, I'm incredibly flattered that someone like that designer would even consider *my* work as good enough to get that kind of internship."

"*You are* good! Hasn't it gotten through yet? I want you to take more initiative. Had you gotten yourself the internship interview with the same designer, she would have seen *your* work, not the work of a copycat. It's criminal. The only difference was that the person who stole your work was forthright enough to go out and try for the job." Mr. Takaya tapped Cali on the arm. "I'm sorry," he said sadly. "Think about being very protective of your work from here on out. The Exhibition Competition is just around the corner, and you know what that means. It could be the start of something great for you."

"I do and I will," Cali confirmed.

"Maybe find another studio, outside school, where you can stretch out and work, away from prying eyes, if you know what I mean," he smiled with regret.

"Thank you. You are tremendously kind to tell me about this."

Chapter Eighteen

When Cali met Jean-Chris that Saturday night, in Chinatown for dinner, he pulled her into a happy hug outside the subway station. He kissed her gently on the lips, and for a moment it made her forget all her troubles.

"Mes condoléances on the loss of your, how do you say, honey daddy."

"Sugar daddy."

"Yes."

"Don't you want all the details of how he passed away? Like, how I had to skedaddle out of the hotel room, and all that?"

"No. Why should I? This is a man who was giving you money to give him pleasure. I don't really care about this. About *him*."

Cali bristled a little with anger. It was bad enough she'd just lost someone she considered a good friend, a mentor. Hank had been the nearest thing to a personal coach she'd ever known, apart from Mrs. Havistock at the old town library, whom she still called every now and again for moral support and to continue their long-standing friendship. "God. I guess you can't relate to what I'm going through. How would *you* feel if your mentor at the auction house suddenly fell off his ladder and died?"

"I would rejoice! I'd step over him, take over where he left off, and start *slathering* the Soutine frames with gold. My boss is so stingy with the gold *vernis*! I do not agree at all with his approach to gilding, it is not historically accurate, the *connard*."

"I guess you don't understand the kind of effect this will have on my – God, I sound so petty – but my *lifestyle*, my ability to get through this last semester!"

Couldn't Jean-Chris even *try* to be more comforting and sympathetic about Hank's transition? She intuited that he would never admit to being jealous of Hank. Instead, he probably lumped him into a collective group of old farts with a lack of morals who he imagined were taking advantage of her at every moment.

"Where will you find your sugar *now*?" he asked.

"Why are you asking me this? Do you really care?"

"I don't care about him. I care about you."

She stopped and looked away, not even sure if she wanted to continue on with the evening. She tried to contain her annoyance, and seize the moment. After all, a person (even Jean-Chris) could die at any moment, as she'd just seen earlier, and it was probably preferable to make the best of the moments one has. "I'm not sure how I'm going to swing everything, and it's terrifying me. I think I depended on his *largesse* more than I realized. Now I have to go back to temp work full-time. It's the last semester. There's the Exhibition Competition to prepare for, and I still need to get good grades, to develop my portfolio more. You know how it is."

She imagined that Jean-Chris might feel some regret, having said numerous times how much he wanted to be a man she could rely on, in all ways. Maybe soon. But not soon enough.

"I do know exactly how this is. I am up to my ass in alligators before my graduation. And also I am trying to manage something else. I have just had some sad news…"

"What!?"

"Not yet. At the restaurant."

They walked west toward a very sexy new restaurant with moody lantern lighting, red silk walls, and intimate seating made of chinoiserie-inspired black lacquered wood. It was a little fancier and expensive than Jean-Chris usually went in for.

Once seated together in a cozy booth and sipping smoky cocktails redolent with Lapsang Souchong, and picking over some delicate seafood dumplings, Jean Chris shook his head sadly, lifted his glass and made a toast. "Here is to my favorite uncle, Monsieur Pascal Ozanne, the ultimate gentleman. The ultimate collector. I hope you pull through this one, Uncle Pascal. It's been a life well-lived, so far, maybe there can be more, much more."

"Oh!" Cali said, clinking glasses and taking a small sip. Weird to be toasting someone in some kind of trouble. "What happened?"

"He's at the hospital with heart troubles, for the first time in his life. My mother is there, looking after him. He was very much a bachelor all his life." He laughed suddenly. "I'm not sure he will have time for my mom between all his girlfriends he'll have visiting him. She is already very annoyed by them."

"Is it really serious? Sometimes these things are fixed easily, micro-surgery and all that."

"They've told him it's a 'massive' condition, too massive to fix, and to start saying his goodbyes."

"Oh," Cali's eyes shot down and back up again and met Jean Chris'. "You love him a lot, I know. I'm sorry."

"I do, he is like a father to me," he sniffed, shutting his eyes tightly, as a few tears came down. "I just wish I could be there with him. I would go, today, but he told me to stay here and be a man, basically. We've always had an understanding about these things, that I was to come over here and grab life by the balls, as he said, and he's the one who's been helping me stay here, sending some funding across." J.C chuckled a little and put his hands over his eyes. "He's the kind of guy who'd want us to have a great dinner tonight…"

Cali rushed over to his side of the booth, and took him in her arms, where they stayed hugging until the main courses arrived. He snuggled in, and then sat up straight, resigned.

"It is what it is," he sighed. "Well, you know all about this, now that your Daddy Hank has hit the road, as they say."

"Whatever, J.C," Cali rolled her eyes, letting her rice dish cool on her fork. "He was a good, good friend to me."

J.C seemed not to be listening at all, and continued on, "Uncle Pascal always said: 'Food and sex are the best medicine.' So bon appetit!" He dived into a sizzling platter of food that had arrived and finally stopped spitting grease.

When the bill came, they'd been given the option of sampling either naughty or nice fortune cookies as a marketing ploy to buy more at the front counter. Both chose a few of the naughty ones. As usual, they added the words 'in bed' to the end of each fortune for a giggle.

"You will soon be the motherfucking boss. You are rising to the top (in bed)," Cali's cookie read. Opening the second one, they got a fun shock with, "'When the stocks go up, the cocks go up. Ride the bull market to the top (in bed).'"

"Ha!" Jean-Chris laughed. "I'll read mine. 'Love is in the air, but cum is in your hair (in bed).' These are funny! Listen to this one: 'You are lost in a desert of horniness. Find your way to a wet place immediately (in bed).'" They laughed as they both bit into their cookies. It felt good to see him smile and to laugh too, despite everything.

"Gosh, they're totally delicious, like heavy on the vanilla, but those are really vulgar. I mean, beyond vulgar! How can they sell something like that?" Cali wondered.

On the way out of the Chinese restaurant, as a gift for her, he purchased some of the fortune cookies custom-made by the restaurant: one bag of 'Nice.' He carried the shopping sack, and put his arm around Cali. "I must find a warm, wet place…" he whispered in her ear. "Do you know one?"

They decided to take a slow walk up Broadway, and over to the Hotel Gram-Irving for the night.

On the walk back to the hotel, as usual they discussed all manner of things, but mainly how Cali planned to win the Exhibition Competition for the women's shelter. She'd start with some modest structural redesigns, like moldings and arches and whitewashing the existing drab areas with glossy white finishes. But her strategy – the one the charity client would love – involved donating all of the larger floral mosaics (about 5x5 feet each) she'd done in high school. Impressive enough to have gotten her into Preston School of Design, they were stunning, feminine pieces – something the women would respond to – and they deserved a good home.

The mosaics would be used as wall décor in the public areas, and as a backsplash for a soothing fountain and beverage station that would welcome the women at the reception area. She'd propose coordinating furnishings and fabrics to tie together with the mosaics. They were too large and heavy to ship from home in California without proper funding, which would come with winning the prize and the paid contract. So to represent her mosaics to size in her display at the final exhibition, she would use her old enlarged photos of them, mounted on poster board.

"To win this, you also need a model of this transformation in miniature, but to scale!" Jean-Chris insisted. "And I will help you do it. Just send me the room plans when you finish them."

"No, you have too much work."

"I insist. Where exactly are they now, the mosaics?" he asked, almost afraid to hear the answer.

"Stacked in a barn at home."

"Ah. Have horses or cats been pissing on them? Urine is very acidic to ceramic and glass works. One must always take care to keep the equine and feline urine away from fine finishes."

"No," she laughed. "I Saran-Wrapped them all before I took off on the bus."

Once in Jean-Chris' tiny room, he lent Cali his red silky pajamas while he wore his usual root beer-colored flannels. He took care in making her a decaf hot green tea using his electric kettle, and sweetened it just the way she liked it. He served it in a delicate vintage Limoges cup and saucer that appealed to her, with its delicate roses and vines.

"I saw this at the flea market on the Upper West Side and thought of you. I've been waiting for you to visit and see it," he said, as she sipped down the hot liquid.

"You think of everything, all the time," she mused.

His bed was a full-sized square of softness surrounded by several tables stacked with the architectural models from his earlier student days, before he'd decided to go fully into antiques. And now his tables were laden with thick illustrated books from the library, and notebooks filled with his handwritten observations. After finishing their teas, he turned off the lights, letting the reflected glow of the city at night filter through his window.

As they took off their pajamas, and found each other in

an embrace, their bodies fit together intuitively – almost too intuitively for Cali, who felt herself mentally resisting the routine of even this amazing relationship. But she'd never had an orgasm she didn't like with him, and would never complain about a handsome, dear guy like Jean-Chris wanting to make love to her. Over the last couple of years, during their 'French tutoring sessions' out at her place in Brooklyn, when they had sex, often enough she'd closed her eyes, and used her powerful imagination to slip into edgy fantasies of him as another person, without ever actually telling him: her indulgent kidnapper, a shy young student she'd seduced during gym class, a masked man engaging in ritualistic sex during a cult ceremony, some anonymous but attractive client at GG's.

Tonight, in her mind he was just plain old Jean-Chris, who needed comforting in the face of the imminent loss of one of his favorite people in the world. "Come here," she urged. He gently, slowly let his hands glide along the curves of her body as their legs entwined. Taking her into a deep kiss, his hands massaged her back and rubbed into the nape of her neck, finding her tense. As he rubbed away at her back and neck, she relaxed further into his embrace.

Her hands ventured to his cock, where she found him hard as ever. Wrapping her fingers around him, she squeezed a little, and gently rubbed him up and down – until he was nearly mad with wanting to be inside her. Less tense than before and filling up with wantonness, she became completely receptive; at that moment, he rolled on top of her, and gently massaged the outside of her wet, slick flower with his cock. She could feel her melting, wanting him completely, opening for more.

He pushed inside her, and found a slow but steady rhythm that kept her in pleasure for what felt like hours. When he felt her body stiffen, he knew that she was about to come, and he stopped – changing his rhythm slightly, before starting again and bringing her to a new height. When at last it seemed she couldn't take any more of his relentless teasing, he let his rhythm stay steady for a long uninterrupted period. This time she rode another wave of pleasure all the way to the shores of satisfaction, as he let himself be swept along as well.

"Come with me!" she begged, and he felt himself explode inside her in a delicious burst of warm heaven in his cock, while her vaginal muscles contracted around him in a gratifying way that confirmed their mutual pleasure. They collapsed and returned to entwining, speechless and spent.

Eventually he got up and brought down the shade of his window to make his room completely dark for sleeping. As they cuddled back together, he held her hand, and brought it to his lips. "I wonder what we will both be like in five, or ten years."

"Pretty changed, I imagine," Cali supposed.

"I wonder if we will even be together."

"Who can say?"

"You will be more changed than me. I know this," he said, with a tinge of sadness.

"You're not a changer?"

"I am a changer, but in a normal way. You are someone who could change wildly. Too much for me, maybe."

"Maybe. Who knows where I'll be or what I'll be up to."

"You mean, you don't know if you'll be a courtesan by then or not," his voice was flat. She didn't answer right away so he answered for her. "So I'm right. You know? Your *problem* is that you don't believe in yourself. You don't *see* yourself, how capable you are. This is what I HATED about that man, Hank."

"Hank? He just died, and you're bringing him up now?"

"Yes. Because he is a perfect example. Men like Hank should leave young women like you alone. Men like that make you believe that you can't become something without their help. They make life too easy, financially, and then you find loving someone like *me* too hard. Someone struggling to make his life."

"Too easy? You think it was easy being perfect for him all the time in exchange for his help?"

"I am not making sense. And I am not struggling. I am just starting. There is a difference."

"You do make sense, actually. I know what you mean, Okay? I know what you want to say about starting vs. struggling."

"Thank you."

"I'm sorry that you find it so wrong, that I had an older man in my life, like Hank, who encouraged me and helped me out and treated me as a friend. I learned so much from him."

"Here we go."

"No, not here we go. But if it weren't for Hank coming along and helping me get through school and paying for things, I might very well be back in California working for *my dad*, living in one of his shitty flophouses and holding people up with a .44 Magnum for their rent money!"

"Come on. I do not believe this. You don't see the person you're becoming. You don't see the rewards on the horizon if you just keep persevering on *a straight path*."

"Straight. Right…" She began to doze off, feeling rather annoyed by the conversation, but too tired to get up and get a cab out to Brooklyn in order to clear the air.

The next morning Cali woke up, feeling less annoyed with J.C than when she'd fallen asleep (he wanted only the best for her, after all). Even so, she yearned to return to her own apartment before too much of the day was lost. As Jean-Chris snoozed away, she quietly dressed, knowing he was probably eager to get on with his own day of homework. It was a lot of what he had called "the final thrust" of the last semester, which for him involved numerous verbal exams, research papers plus his on-the-job training.

"Don't go," he moaned from his nest in the bed.

"You know you want me to leave. Don't pretend otherwise," she teased, sitting down by him and tickling his toes. "Can I make you a hot tea?" she asked.

"If it means you will stay longer, YES," he smirked, then, "NO! I have so many things to do. You are bad for me, keeping me from my studies."

"I thought so."

"Promise to send me your drawings and measurements. In a few weeks I'm going to bring you a magnificent model for the exhibition. It's not cheating to have some help, right?"

"No, as long as I'm the mastermind behind it all."

"Will you have time to do everything now that what-was-his-name? – Hank – is no longer with us?"

"No. In fact, I had to add more days to my temping. I need to work five days a week now. All I can say is, it would be really sad if I flunked my classes or lost the competition, all because I had to go work as a temp at some fuddy-duddy corporation to pay my bills." It made her feel panicky just talking about it.

"Cali. Do not worry. Time and money expands to fit your needs, as long as you are diligent."

"I wish I could believe you." All this talk of what was before her, especially more temping, was making her feel frustrated and annoyed. Best to get home, chill, focus – and eat this (huge, imposing, stinking) elephant one bite at a time.

He pointed over to the bag of fortune cookies. "Take the cookies, as a snack, to fortify you, and to give you some guidance," he smiled.

"You had to buy the nice ones, didn't you," she laughed, putting the sack into her bag.

"I don't want to give you any worse ideas than you already have. You could *write* the naughty ones for them. So what is the point?" He looked down, fiddling with the sheets. "I really hate when we have to say goodbye, you know? Do you think there'll ever be a time when we don't have to say goodbye so much?"

She dared not continue with this conversation. They'd be there for hours longer, hashing it out, and they both had so much work to do. "I'll slip out. You won't even notice I'm gone."

Chapter Nineteen

That Monday, Misty Seemeister could barely hide her devious mirth when she woke Cali at 6am with the good news: she had an all-week assignment to fill for an administrative assistant at the Bible Bouncers Christian Preschool on the Upper East Side.

"Get your ass up there on time, or I'll nail you to the cross," Misty's raspy voice growled over the line. For a moment Cali wasn't sure if this was just an extension of the nightmare she'd been having that morning, or an actual wake up call from her 'madam' at Surefire Temps. Children weren't exactly her thing, but as long as babysitting wasn't involved, she was glad to have the extra income.

"What do I wear to this one? A clown suit?"

"Be nice to the kids, do what you're told, and no fucking swearing in there."

Right on time, using a special code, Cali entered an elaborate gate that led into the rather posh Bible Bouncers Preschool. The courtyard, overseen by a benevolent statue of Jesus, was outrageously outfitted with a massive castle-shaped playhouse, mini swing sets and a bouncy urban playground turf made of bright green, high-tech rubber, which protected the children against nasty falls.

Beats the pants off a rope swing hanging off a tree and placed over a manure pile, Cali thought to herself, half-fondly remembering her own childhood play area when she'd gleefully swing out over the manure and let go, falling into the soft, pungent compost heap. She had been apparently quite resistant to staph infections as a child.

Several 'yummy mummies' with designer bags and shiny shoes were just leaving through a side entrance after dropping off their... Issue? Offspring? Breeding results? *Oh, just call them children. Be nice.*

Often enough Cali contemplated the fact that, even at the so-called height of her fertility as a healthy twenty-year old, she could not bear the thought of ever having children. In the wacked world of her own mind, babies represented developing alien beings carried inside humans for a time, only to be pulled out or surgically extracted VERY uncomfortably – thus requiring a lot of other fixes, like healing of stretched abdominal muscles and/or a complete re-arrangement of one's life, schedule and possibly goals (if your main goal wasn't to have children in the first place).

Yuck. No thank you, she was thinking to herself, just as a group of friendly children playing in the courtyard suddenly surrounded her, curious and cunning like tiny gypsies on the take in a piazza in Rome. *They must be attracted to my red power suit. Or think I'm the visiting clown.*

"Move away, little ones," she tried to sound friendly, hoping they'd scamper away so she could make her way inside to the Administration Area. Then it occurred to her that – like the barn cats back on Tightwad Hill who used to surround her begging for the treats she held in a bag – they might like one, too. "Would anyone like a cookie!?" she said, trying to add some syrup to her voice. If she was going to spend a whole week here temping, she'd do well to make friends with the ultimate clients: the kids.

She reached inside her school bag and pulled out Jean-Chris' gift of the 'Nice' fortune cookies, which she'd intended to snack on as needed. Ah, brilliant. This would help them learn English, too. Kids these days in these kinds of schools were usually early readers.

"Me, me!" one little boy with an odd bowl-shaped haircut called out. Cali tossed it to him as if he were a dog.

"Meeee!" another little girl in a prim Bonpoint dress whined. "Me want cookie!"

Learn proper grammar, and I might just give you one.

"Don't eat the paper inside, just the cookie part!" she reminded them. Other little takers gathered around for theirs, opening up the cookies, biting in and enjoying the rich vanilla treats while discarding the papers on the playground or putting them into their little pockets. "No! Don't litter. You pick those up and keep them. Those are your fortunes!" Cali instructed.

"Thank you!" some said graciously as she made her way toward the Admin Office, feeling all charitable and good about herself, having so well-hidden her immense discomfort with the little brats.

Once in there, she was shown around by a nice-enough woman: a volunteer mother at the school named Kaley. "The staff is in a meeting right now but they'll be out soon," the woman said as she led Cali to a desk and chair in the corner where she'd need to sit idly for the week, probably leaving an indentation in the foam, not unlike Christ's bones in the Shroud of Turin. "Here is command central, where you'll answer phones and pass on any issues that may arise," Kaley said.

Just at moment, the bowl haircut boy pushed open the 'little door' inside the actual door, like a proverbial 'doggy door.' Everything in the school was apparently designed with children (or dwarves) in mind.

Must they be privy to everything? Cali thought.

"Mama! What does this mean?" he asked, coming toward Kaley, unfurling his fortune.

He sounded almost adult; this four-year-old must have been one of the smart, well-read preschoolers Cali knew existed now, but not in her day. In her small town, kids had actually gotten to be kids with more leisure time than they knew what to do with, and not aggressively over-scheduled and positioned by their parents for early entry to Yale. Jumping into manure piles and blowing up wood block forts with firecrackers (with other children inside, screaming) was perfectly acceptable for hobbies and play times.

"Well, read it to me, honey," Kaley encouraged him.

"It says: you are one lucky lad. Built like a jockey but hung like a horse."

"What did you say!! No, don't repeat it, Hanson! Hand that over!" she said, grabbing the piece of paper from his hand, and confirming what was written inside. "This is outrageous!" She wrung her hands to her chest, as if she'd just seen a Poltergeist. "Oh my God! I mean, My Gosh! Where did you get this!?" she asked him, kneeling down. "Tell mommy."

"The other kids got one too," he said. "Everyone has a different one."

"Who gave this to you!?"

Right about the time Cali heard Hanson read the 'hung like a jockey' phrase, she'd slowly reversed toward the door of the Admin area, ready to bolt, hopefully undetected, but then he pointed over at her. "*She* did, Mama."

Cali backed out the door, keeping her hands in front of her for protection and to seem more harmless. "I'm sorry – Kaley – it's all been a big mistake! I swear. You've got to believe me. Please believe me! I would *never* do something like that. I gave out the wrong cookies! I had no idea they were the dirty ones; I thought they were the NICE ones!"

"Really?" Kaley seemed conflicted, evidently not sure whether to believe this sly-seeming woman who looked a little too slick for this preschool environment.

Cali watched, wide-eyed, as Kaley glanced toward a nearby telephone, while also giving her the evil eye. "No, please don't, please don't call the…"

"I don't know if I should believe you." Kaley was still squinting at her.

"Really! They weren't supposed to be the naughty ones,

I swear! The restaurant where they made the cookies, they must have made a big mistake with their labeling. You can call the Ming Foo Dog restaurant in NoLita. I'm sure they'll tell you there's been a problem with their labels. I was only trying to be nice! Really. – Gotta go!"

It was like parting the red sea to run through all those wiggly little kids playing in the courtyard, and get the hell out the gate onto the street. As Cali hustled it out of sight, she was mentally already down on her knees, praying to God that Hayley wouldn't call the police. As she got a few blocks away from the scene, someone was calling *her*. She pulled her phone from her purse and answered. It was Misty Seemeister.

"Kistler. You are one sick puppy. You know that? Children, Cali? Children!" she spat out. "Shooting off the email now. THERE. You're fired – and blacklisted! You *insubordinate* little freak! Don't *ever* think of temping in this town again!"

Chapter Twenty

As Cali made her way far, far from the Bouncy Biblers Preschoolers School – she was in such a dither she couldn't remember the exact name – a swirly, sick sourness overtook her in her stomach. She realized that not only were Hank's gifts never coming in again, NOW her somewhat reliable cash cow of office temping was a no-go.

I'm never going back to Tightwad Hill! Never!

She sought some kind of immediate comfort. Something to eat, something to drink, somewhere to go, someone special (and hopefully understanding) to talk to…

She met Jean-Chris for lunch in an atrium a few blocks from his part-time job in the repair section of the auction house. She got there first and watched him as he seemed to swagger in, looking as if he might own the place.

"Why do you look so sure of yourself today?" she asked.

"Maybe I will tell you later. But first *what* is going on!?"

She launched in, detailing the story. "OH MY GOD! They thought I was a perv, that I was abusing the children, that I gave them the dirty fortune cookies on purpose!"

"Just relax, it's over. You're here with me now."

"It's all your fault."

"MY fault? Come on! I didn't buy the dirty ones – it was all a mistake."

"Whatever." Cali really felt sick now, mostly about losing control and drawing him into her dramas. But she was not so upset as to turn down the smoked mozzarella, basil and tomato sandwich he offered (accompanied by kettle-cooked potato chips).

He slid the meal over to her, poised on a tray in the balmy office atrium populated by palms and Ficus trees. "Eat this. You will feel better. You know what my uncle always says, about food and sex being the best medicine…" He shook his head, and watched as Cali launched in, savoring the meal, scarfing it down as if she hadn't eaten for days.

"How is your uncle doing?" she said between mouthfuls.

"He's sitting up and receiving all his visitors."

"Oh. That's good, right?"

"No. He's sitting up to say his goodbyes."

"Oh, sorry."

"So what do you do now?" he asked, deadpan.

"I've lost my job! *All* of my jobs. And I've been blacklisted at *all* the temp agencies. They put out an 'APB.' It's some kind of all points bulletin on us bad ones, never to work again. I mean, they think I did something really bad – and in fact I really did it – even though I didn't really. Oh, I'm going for broke, literally!"

"I shouldn't have given you the fortune cookies. I

thought I gave you the nice ones. It's all about the context in which you do naughty things," he mused, trying to lighten things up but it went over like a lead balloon.

"Context, right. It's really not your fault; I'm sorry I said that. At least they didn't call the cops. Or, not yet anyway. I told them at the school that it was all a mix up, that the cookies had been mixed up."

He sighed, seeming a bit tired of the topic already. "I'm sure it will all be OK. Let us look for the silver lining in all this. What is it, do you think?"

"For one thing, I didn't know *how* I was going to stay at that Bouncy Bible place another day anyway. I so don't like being around…"

"The Bible?"

"No! The Bible isn't bad; it's very literary, filled with – gosh, the teachings of Jesus are life lessons for us all. No, fuck, it was *the children*!" She tried hard to smirk, and then found herself giggling at the irony of all this.

Oh, the look on his face told her this was news to him. They'd never remotely even discussed children, apart from the fact she was on The Pill, and didn't worry about pregnancy.

A cringing look came over his face, but he could hardly suppress a joyful smile. It wouldn't be everyday he came across a woman who felt the same way he did. "I don't know how to say this without sounding like an asshole. But I think I would prefer a life without… *them*."

"That's nice," she said, thinking it was probably a little too non-committal for his liking. "Isn't it wonderful that we both don't want the same thing? Anyway, so what is your news, the reason you look so swaggering today?"

"Maybe now is not the time, considering that you just got, how do you say? Canned. Maybe it should wait?"

"No. Tell me."

"Well, just when you've LOST your job – I've gotten one. I've been invited to go back home to Paris after I graduate. I've been offered a very junior position at Christie's Auction House, in the historical furnishings and antiquities department."

"Oh! Congratulations, Ah J.C, this is soooo wonderful for you! That's what you came here to do: line yourself up for a place like Christie's!"

"It's excellent news. It's a place to get very grounded, very knowledgeable. It will not really pay me enough at first, but it has a certain prestige, and then we see from there."

They clinked juice bottles. "This is so wonderful!" she nearly cried. She suddenly felt like a person standing in an elevator when it drops a few floors down without warning. He was the most wonderful, sparkling thing in her currently dreary life of (now non-existent) temp work and a pressure-filled school career. And now he would be leaving. "I will really miss you."

He put his bottle down and took her hand in his. "Why miss me? Come with me to Paris," he said. "After your graduation. We can go together."

"Oh my God… I don't know…"

Paris. Yes, it was like a dream in her mind: Europe. She'd never been outside the US, and all its romantic charms beckoned.

"What do you think?" He seemed to want his answer now-ish.

"So you mean *live* together in Paris?"

"Yes. In a tiny garret, it's what I can afford on my salary. But it will be romantic, no? Maybe something bigger if we live further out, but what is Paris if you aren't in the center of things? I want to walk to work every day, like I walk to school here."

"Uh, I need to think about it."

"You must take so much time to think about living with me in Paris? Why not say yes NOW?"

"It's not just you. What would I *do* there?"

"Get a starting job in interior design! Do the same like you would here in New York."

"But how long could I stay over there without a visa? I think I'm limited to three months unless…"

"I am a French citizen. Perhaps…" and here a sweet, hopeful smile crossed his face. "I don't want to scare you about something more serious. But there *are* ways for us to have you stay in Paris long term."

She dared not utter the word *marriage*. It loomed in her mind like a large, square detention center for two self-deluded people. It had ugly connotations she couldn't overcome so easily after what she'd seen her mother go through at home as a wife, and all kinds of little observances along life's path.

"Ah, I'm not sure." She felt dazed. And confused.

Her mind flashed off to images of them alternately climbing up the stairs of the Sacré-Coeur, hand-in-hand…

followed by savagely arguing over something back at home (probably money or her needing so much "alone time"). That 'charming' tiny attic apartment could easily become nothing more than a romanticized human pigeon roost for two warring birds.

"You aren't coming to Paris with me." He frowned and looked away. It was like the lights in that beautiful frothy French building of him shut down. He went dark.

"No! It's not like that. I just, I need to absorb this. You know, we've never even told each other we love each other. You've never said, 'I love you, Cali.' You know that?"

"Our time in New York. It's been like an amuse bouche. I believe that if we started life in Paris together, everything new again, no more honey daddies, no more me living in the hotel, and you across in Brooklyn, no more Tonys from the strip club you may run into at any moment – we could truly fall in love and just *be*. Together. All the time."

"But if we didn't already fall in love here, and, whatever, *be* together most of the time – what makes you think it will be so much easier in Paris?"

"Well, how can people *not* fall in love and live together in Paris? It's *Paris*, a city made for people to share their lives. It's just in our culture. You are so blind. You don't know how much…"

"What?"

"How much I…" he seemed to struggle a little to find the right words. He sipped slowly at his drink, and eyed her over the edge of the glass.

She felt like he must be thinking she was such a *bad* girl, with lots of character flaws, really too many to name. How could she know if his heart raged for her and his body always yearned for her? She looked over at the dearest friend she'd ever known, the guy whose wry observances always made her laugh: whose hands, cock and mouth always made her come, but more than that, were attached to a man who made her feel cared for, even if she was always in a quandary about if she really felt deeply enough about him to forego her fascinations with more mysterious ways of life.

Her mind raced. Was her love for him enough to overcome the wild wanderlust and material desires and strange fascinations she felt gathering like a tornado inside her, kicking up and ready to potentially destroy everything?

Would a move to Paris to 'start over' and cohabitate (she even hated the word) be enough to slice through the heady thicket of deeply ingrained rebellion, familial dysfunction, sexual desires? She dreaded stopping at just a few lovers – and Hank had been just a Hugger. Was there an explanation, called Destiny, that could explain her lifelong fascinations with courtesans and now her split ambitions?

"I *do* love you," he said. "And I'm *in love* with you. And I love being with you. All the time if we could."

"Well, I love you too," she confessed simply, making no promises beyond that.

"But is it *enough*?" he ventured, fidgeting with his paper napkin. Pushing his chair away, he stood.

She looked up as he took his remaining sandwich half and a cookie off the tray. Then she looked away, unable to protest what deep down she knew was the truth. "I'm just not sure. And that's the truth of it," she said, trying to infuse it with a little promise. "Could we revisit this over the weekend when you come over? I need to figure out what to do next for money, anyway. Now that I'm *sans* job."

"Fine," he said, his voice a little icy. "I need to get back. The boss is showing me how to remove speckles of latex paint off of 18th Century copper lusterware, and I don't want to miss a minute of the excitement."

Chapter Twenty One

Cali traipsed away from the fern-filled atrium, planning to get on a train going downtown so she could spend the day at the school library, until classes started in the evening. Her mind was filled with images of her and Jean-Chris in Paris; how it might feel to start anew there, and get into the routine he was proposing.

But hadn't she just gotten the hang of being a New Yorker in this fabulous, buzzing isle of Manhattan?

As she moved along, she realized the naughty fortune cookie incident of the morning might not be over yet. She was still praying to God that Kaley wouldn't involve the police – or attorneys – in her major faux pas. Even if those worries proved unfounded, her temp jobs were gone, and she wondered how she'd find a new place to sell her office skills on short shrift.

A fleeting, rather erotic thought entered her mind: in a worst-case scenario, maybe she'd need Clive Vogelnest's help again in defending herself, which could bring about a chance to get nailed so well by him again. In her mind, almost like watching a porn clip, she saw them going at it. She marveled slightly at the audacity of her desire for Clive, considering she'd been so exclusive with Jean-Chris, and here they'd just been talking about committing even more in Paris. *Maybe I should investigate how easily my thoughts turn to sex with other men (or even strangers, if I'm being honest with myself).*

Feeling in a huge quandary about everything in her life, her thoughts naturally turned comfortably to the elegant townhouse tucked away on a leafy side street: GG's.

She wasn't far from it. It seemed to exist in a dream, or a movie she'd once seen, in which she, the main character, had slipped inside its glossy walls and felt immensely at home, secreted away with like-minded women, and an interesting, motherly person, GG.

She made her way to GG's street, and discreetly watched from a distance. It felt somehow consoling to look at its solid stone form. It was way too early for the house to be open, and it seemed very at rest: there were no long black cars out front dropping off male visitors. She half-wondered if GG was even still in business; perhaps she'd retired.

As she watched the front door for a while, hoping GG may come out, and also trying to imagine herself there again, it felt incredibly serendipitous when Kin, GG's assistant, came out of the townhouse. Kin skipped down the stairs wearing jeans and a black raincoat, carrying a large canvas shopping sack. Though several years older than Cali, Kin hadn't changed a bit, and was still jaunty with her shiny black hair and cutting-edge black clothing and large, black-framed glasses. Cali looked down at her own look: the red suit, the sensible shoes, a quality leather bag and tamed-down hair that was all one color (blonde). Would Kin even recognize her if she approached? A nervous wave passed through her being. *Go.*

Talking to Kin doesn't mean committing to GG's, she thought to herself, and Hank's words reverbed in her head: *Go for what you want. Don't take no for an answer. Own the street, own the room. Network, schmooze.*

"Kin?" Cali said, surprised by her own boldness; Kin was seemingly bent on getting somewhere quick, probably running an errand.

"OH, HI!" Kin said, "I remember you. California, right?"

"Yes, how are you?" Cali tried to seem genuinely surprised at the happenstance. "How have you been? It's so nice to see you. I really enjoyed meeting you that time. It feels like forever ago. You know, you made me feel so comfortable."

"Aw, thank you. I'm just going to get some snacks for the girls' room. Have time? Walk with me?" The two walked together toward the grocery store. "You look really good," Kin smiled over. "How is the City treating you?"

Don't complain, don't explain.

"It's great. I'm back in design school. I quit stripping. I'm making friends. It's good." *Be a good listener. Flatter.* "How have you been? Can I ask, are you in school too, or do you have other projects? I know GG's probably keeps you really occupied, but… just curious. You seem a bit, I don't know *intellectual*. I know it's more than just the glasses!"

"Oh, you're sweet to ask. Gosh, nobody ever asks me

about me, except GG of course. I'm a writer. I studied creative writing up at Sarah Lawrence, and then I tried to do an internship and get into screenwriting out in Hollywood. But *that* worked out badly!"

"Really? Why?"

"I hated L.A. I don't drive and I'm not much of a pitcher. I'd manage to finally get 'in the room' and I could barely talk. So I scampered back here to the City."

"Wow. There's no reason to live there much anymore, with all the technology."

"Maybe, and I'm more of a novelist anyway. And at GG's I'm swimming in great material, not a dull moment *there*. But now it's hard to find the time to write it all down."

"You have to protect your time, I think. That's just how you do it. I'm learning that. Just block it off, carve it out, and don't let anyone or anything distract you. *Nothing* is probably more important than you writing your first novel or screenplay."

"You're so right. This is exactly what I needed to hear. How weird that I was laying in bed this morning, so frustrated with my progress, or *lack thereof*, on my writing, and here you come along and remind me. Neat! You're like my messenger angel."

"Ah, here we are," Cali said, as the grocery store doors slid open automatically. *Less is more. Don't overwhelm.* She suddenly blurted out, "I'm actually thinking about moving to Paris. Have you ever been?"

Kin stepped back from the opening door and let it close up again. "Wow, no. I'd love to go, though. GG keeps pestering me to take a vacation and go experience *la belle vie*. So why are you just *thinking* about it? Why not *do* it?"

"Because I just need to graduate soon and… moving over, it involves a guy."

"Oh, them. They muck everything up. But they also make everything so much nicer in life. In doses. I do like it when they carry my luggage."

Cali giggled. "Can I ask you a question? What would you do if you were me? You're so much smarter than me. I can just tell." (*Flatter, always*). "Would you go to Paris, if it were a great guy involved?"

"Hmmm," Kin leaned on one leg, poising her hand on her chin, seeming to settle into the question. "So I don't know *all* the parameters here. But what I can tell you is that if you're even questioning it, then…? Hmmmm. Look. The best thing is always just to be clear with men. Or people, any kind of people! Just be honest and clear, totally transparent every step of the way, and like this, you don't hurt other people, you don't waste their time. You don't lead them on. And you don't hurt yourself. I have this really strong belief, actually something GG taught me: wasting other people's time is, like, one of the biggest sins you could ever commit. Because they can never get their time back. Money comes and goes, sure, but time is something people can never have back."

"Whoo! See? You're *my* messenger angel, Miss Kin."

"Happy to help."

The circumstances of just 'running into' each other might seem very suspicious to Kin, and so Cali held off on pushing for them to do something further as friends, like a drink or a meal out sometime. She'd let it happen naturally, or at Kin's request.

"I should really let you go and do your shopping. This has been sooo nice," Cali smiled, opening her arms to hug Kin, who hugged in. "I hope to see you again. I think…? Would you remember me to GG, say hello from me?"

"Of course! I know she really liked you. She brings you up in conversation sometimes, just wondering how you are. She'll think this is really neat, me running into you. I'll tell her you're back in school, if that's OK. She's strict, but it's why she's the best at what she does."

"It's OK. I didn't think so at the time, but her giving me two years is turning out to be a good thing. It's working out perfectly."

"Good, then! Come back and see us when the time is right, okay? If you don't go off to Paris with Mr. Right, or Mr. Wrong. I love a good destination romance." Here, Kin gave Cali a quick wink. Pushing up the glasses on her nose, she smiled mischievously, "Bye, hon!"

Cali nodded, as Kin waved and turned into the store.

Chapter Twenty Two

That Saturday night after Cali got fired, Jean-Chris came over to join her in Brooklyn. He sat in her living room sipping a glass of wine as she fussed with her hair in the mirror of her bedroom, exasperated. Despite his recent proposal that she move to Paris with him, she was still feeling lost and cash poor. And in comparison to him – now firmly 'having his ducks all lined up in a row' (professionally with his new job at Christie's, and all the future prospects it would bring) – she felt like a comparable hot mess.

"I wish I could go get my hair highlighted today, like I used to!" she whined, bemoaning the roots she'd have to live with a little longer in order to stretch out her budget a little longer. "I HATE budgets! I HATE not having money to burn! FUCK!"

She felt for a moment like throwing something. So she picked up a hair spray can, and aimed at the wall, but quickly put it down. *Self-control, remember?*

"You know, darling," his voice wafted over calmly from the living room, its patronizing tone already annoying her a tinge. "There are people in the world living in slums, squatting to use the toilet in the bushes, living in squalor and hunger, and here you are whining about a few stray hairs that aren't perfectly blonde.."

"Shut up!"

"You're gorgeous – don't worry about it," he tried to soften the moment, but it was too late.

She came out of the bedroom and plopped down on the couch next to him, seething silently about who-knows-what. She was trapped a little by his presence (and now his expectation for an answer on Paris). She felt as if she had a million other things she should be doing – in order to save her financial life – besides be his companion tonight.

Adding to her misery, like a sniper, he came out of nowhere with his take on things: "You know what *this* is, don't you? You crying and fussing now that you've 'lost it all'?"

Shit. He's getting on his high horse. Again.

"This…" he paused.

"This what?!"

"You *finally* getting fired; fucking things up so many times at your work so they had no choice *but* to fire you; and (by the way) you making no effort to get an internship at a design firm by now, like everyone *else* does at design school."

"What the fuck do you think it all is then, J.C.?"

"It's very simple. *This* is all self-sabotage."

Aaargh, the all-knowing, all-seeing tone of his voice had her imagining hanging him by his feet from the third-floor window. "The internships don't pay what I need to…" she countered.

"…To what? Live like a minor princess?" Here he looked around her apartment: the lovely furnishings and pricey antiques she maybe shouldn't have bought; the fact that it was four times the size of his room at the Hotel Gram-Irving. "You *want* to be forced into the life of an expensive call girl. You've got it all set up beautifully. Like a little house of cards. Like my little popsicle model house you almost tore down, remember? Just take out a few supporting sticks in your life and plop! It's all over. Permission granted to start life as a courtesan. I'm sure you've already got your contacts lined up, right? The madam, the little black book…"

She couldn't protest with him. It would sound tinny and she knew it.

"Am I right?" he pushed further. "I know you too well. You know exactly how you'll start and what you'll do. You've got your path all mapped out."

"It's not like that, really…"

"And it *doesn't* include me, does it? You don't *really* want to join me in Paris and be a real couple, sharing everything in our lives, living together. Am I right?"

"*A real couple living together?*" She acted like it was the first time she'd ever heard the words or concept in her entire life.

He rolled his eyes up into his head. "You are so transparent." He kneeled by her as she sat on the couch, so they were eye to eye. "I adore you, you know that? But I can't waste my time treading water here. It's so hard to make plans or envisage my future if I don't know if you will be a part of it or not. I've given this my best. I can't give you more than that."

"You have!" she nodded. "You're right." She thought of how stalled out she'd been feeling on moving forward with him, and how her indecision was probably wasting his precious time. She thought about what Kin had said. It wouldn't be fair to keep stringing him along further.

"Let's know that we adore each other, and I'm happy to see you anytime…" he sounded like he was concluding this venture, possibly leading up to something very decisive.

She shivered a bit at the thought but let it roll. "Anytime?"

"I think we should *both start seeing other people*." There, he dropped the bomb.

"Other people?" she smiled ironically. She didn't know men as well as she may some day, but in the world of urban dating 'seeing other people' was code word for 'let's break up.' It was only really a question of whether they'd stay friends or not, or perhaps after 'seeing other people' (and all of them sucking) they'd return to becoming a couple again, stronger than ever. "What is this *see other people* business?" she asked, somewhat mystified by this new development when he'd just proposed she join him in Paris.

"Let's see if we meet other people we might actually have a future with."

"Have you met someone? Why are you being like this all of a sudden?"

"No. What does it matter, if I met someone? If you're not jumping at the chance to join me in Paris, then what is the point of us continuing on like this?"

"Are you sure it's OK if we see other people. Me included. I mean, it's OK if I do, too?" As soon as the word came out of her mouth, she regretted it. She sounded like an eager kid asking if it was OK to take a cookie from the cookie jar.

"It's fine! It's only fair. I can't bear to know the details: what you get up to in your spare time. I'll never expect a total commitment from you, or from myself, until the day you decide."

"Right. Decide about what, exactly? Just to be clear."

"About living in Paris with me! About loving me, and *only* me, completely, wherever this may lead. Marriage maybe. I know you want to have experiences – whatever – with other guys, before you really settle down. And your backstop has always been this *insane* idea of one day becoming a courtesan. Which, I think will destroy you if you do it. But I'm getting to the point with you where I can't bear the thought of it. *Any* of it."

"Gosh."

"Move to Paris with me. Or don't. There's no in between here. You must decide."

His stern tone was way too serious for her liking. A part of her felt like a naughty child, being given an ultimatum by a much-wiser parent, some all-knowing patriarch who knew what was best for her. It made her want to run out of the apartment screaming, but she held steady. He was simply in love with her. Perhaps she was in love with him too; she certainly felt a chronic adoration for him often in her thoughts and feelings. But where was the *verb* in this, if, as Hank had once taught her, "love is a verb"? If love were actually a verb, wouldn't she be *doing* more to *show* him, to *do* for him, as in *packing* her bags and *moving* to Paris? It was only fair for him to want to know where he stood.

With time, perhaps she could wrap her head around the kind of relationship he proposed: a move into that tiny garret, that total commitment. Otherwise, they were free to see other people. Weird, yes, but nothing in their relationship till now had ever been quite normal.

"Could I have some time?"

"Of course," he sighed, sounding a little annoyed. "For the moment, I'm here. Waiting. But I can't guarantee it will be like that forever. Other women *are* circling, you know, I'm not completely undesirable."

Like buzzards, or sharks? *Oh, he got that spike into my heart. Well, I have it coming.* "When do you need to know?" she asked.

"I'm moving away a few days after your graduation, with or without you. I'll come and see you win that competition, and we can go out for a fancy lunch after."

"Of course! But I don't want *this* to be goodbye," she whispered, as he leaned down and kissed her on the cheek. Gathering his rucksack, he indicated he was about to leave. "Stay the night, won't you?" She felt she sounded like she was begging. *Steady on, girl, don't forget to play a little hard to get.*

"Not tonight. I have things to do," he said, playing a lot more hardball than she was used to.

"Oh, me too," she tried to sound casual, but then lost her cool completely. "Where are you going? I thought you were staying?!"

"No, not tonight," he said firmly.

"But I prepped dinner already."

"I'm sorry. I know it's rude, but I have another plan."

"Is this goodbye?"

"I don't intend to *ever* say goodbye to you. If you make the right decision."

Chapter Twenty Three

After the front door clicked behind Jean-Chris, leaving her in dark silence, Cali sunk into a rather deep funk; it was a bad feeling she predicted she couldn't overcome with her normal means of cheering herself up, like going out for a great slice of pizza in the neighborhood, or whooping it up at the bar with the local crazies during the Saturday night karaoke club, or even a bubble bath followed by warm, 'homemade' cookies made from a tube of dough hidden in the fridge.

No, this was very different. She just sat in her overstuffed chair, staring into space, taking in the absence of Jean-Chris from her home on their usual Saturday night – the absence of his handsomeness, his sexiness, his charm and his laugh. She felt the pending loss of his previously-pledged loyalty, now that he'd given himself 'options.'

This feeling sucked: it brought up an unfamiliar concoction of jealousy, lack of possession, and lack of control (all lower emotions she knew, but she indulged in them nonetheless). It wasn't a crying jag-worthy sort of feeling; she didn't have any tears or physical heartache welling up about the thing; no sobbing was necessary. It felt more like a dull realization that: 'his life is moving on with or without me,' and 'I'll soon need to face the music.' The music? Huh. Like a bad conductor of a lousily arranged symphonic orchestra, she turned her thoughts away from all the motley crew of musicians warming up their instruments in her head, ready to play their various songs and *not* at all harmoniously.

Fuck it. After heating up the dinner she'd prepared for the two of them – eating his portion, too – she left the dirty dishes in the sink (which was something J.C would never have allowed on his watch). *Fuck his requirement that we never leave the sink dirty.* She slunk off to the bathroom, and popped a rare, nearly outdated pain pill left over from dental work, which ensured a good night's sleep. *Fuck him for discouraging me from using the drugs I had at my disposal before they expire.* She climbed into bed in her clothes. *Fuck his preference for me to sleep in the nude.* Pulling up the covers – *Fuck it, now I can take up the whole bed!* – she spent the rest of the night half-brooding, half-sleeping... and half-fantasizing of what might be next.

The next morning, feeling better about things, she baked her chocolate chip 'tube cookies' for breakfast, and ate them alone in her living room: enjoying the pleasure of freely getting crumbs and melted chocolate all over her robe, which was destined for the washing machine anyway.

As she nibbled away, her mind raced over everything, but especially the stark fact that after all these months (two years nearly) of she and Jean-Chris dating, she was suddenly (seemingly) free to see other people, and that at the same time, she was also woefully out of work.

First things first. Money!

She wrote down the details of all her accounts and debts, including the remaining cash she kept at home. She contemplated the state of her dwindling resources now that Hank was gone, and the fact that any immediate temping work wasn't readily accessible. Hotel hooking, obviously, was out of the question. That one night at the Penultimate Hotel had been such a shit show. No more disasters like that one without the benefit of more experience and training as an escort.

It brought back all those feelings of lost-ness and desperation she'd had when she'd first set foot in Manhattan, just off that Greyhound bus. Unlike then, when it was somewhat exhilarating to fly by the seat of her pants (and show her panties to the strip club guys), she now felt sheer terror at being well on her way to stone cold broke. She kept a small cushion of emergency cash stashed away in a savings account, and in the apartment, but it was only for emergencies.

Wasn't *this* one?

No. Not yet. It can't be! But is it?

YES!

A return to strip-teasing, she reasoned, could always work as an injection of liquidity in her life but it felt so grungy, such a step backward: no longer *her*. And she'd *promised* herself not to. Stripping had had its place in her life, and now it was *over and done with*. She'd used the wiles she'd learned while stripping to become the mistress of a powerful man: one who made sure the basics of her life were well-covered so she could study and hopefully become an interior designer. Opportunities like that didn't come along every day. So how do you go out and find another gem like Hank, and leapfrog onto the next career move? By hoping to meet a gem like him at GG's?

Perhaps she was now ready for a return to GG's. But *now* – during the last crucial weeks of design school? No, talk about self-sabotage! A move like that would be completely disruptive, assuming GG would even have her – which was probably not yet, and certainly not without having completed her studies officially.

I'd damn well better win the Exhibition Competition now – and enjoy all the options it might bring to save me from the life of so-called debauchery that I'm oddly so magnetized to!

To Cali's mind, surrendering to GG's to become a professional companion was not something one should approach or do lightly. She disdained any kind of namby-pamby, dilly-dallying, pussy-footing around about becoming a modern-day courtesan. Women who dabbled in and out of prostitution seemed amateurish, and that seemed like sacrilege to her. *Either go big or go home*, as they say.

Giving herself up to GG's – IF she were to go ahead with it as she'd had in mind over the last two years – must be embraced with some pride and panache to the thing. An entry into The Life, as her old colleague Sugar had once described it, echoed the idea of becoming a nun: renouncing all that had once been, and taking up a new, cloistered life with all the components of faithfulness, secrecy, and service.

Sugar... Brown Sugar. Sugar Brown. Cali thought of Sugar's latest venture: Sugar's Divine Mind spiritual center. Sugar had definitely walked the walk and talked the talk of a 'different' kind of spirituality, one that Cali was endlessly intrigued by. Why was it that it always seemed to take those extreme 'come to Jesus' moments to bring a girl to her knees?

Cali recalled how she'd seen once seen Sugar *on her knees*, in that greasy auto garage, at that ill-fated bachelor party, and how Sugar had ultimately lifted herself out of addiction, slavery to substances, and the accompanying shame; lifted herself into a seemingly joy-filled life as a minister to women in jail, and as a source of teaching and inspiration to those who sought to tap into the power of the Universe hidden within their subconscious minds.

Cali had once read through Sugar's website, intrigued by its insights, but she had never attended a service. Maybe tomorrow was a good time to go visit Sugar and her Divine Mind Center, and to dig into what it was all about…?

On Sunday morning, Cali pushed into the heavy brocade curtains of the Divine Mind Center, hidden away in the basement apartment of a brownstone on a crooked street in Greenwich Village. She was welcomed like an old friend: no judgments, no forced donations, no rules or regulations or expectations apart from seeking inner peace and interacting with the other 'students of joy' in a mindful way.

The space was gladly lent to Sugar by its owner, who lived

upstairs and was happy to lend the space for the advancement of spiritual practices. The basement in the huge brownstone resembled an old English library – with wood wainscoting and frayed Tibetan rugs and large pillow seating on the floor. Sugar had warmed it up with a faux gas fireplace and a free lending library of spiritual books donated by its members.

During the service, she spoke on the oddly apropos topic of "The secret to finding and keeping romance in your life." She quoted from an old Spanish proverb: *Take hold lightly, let go lightly, this is the secret to felicity in love.*

As Sugar spoke, Cali wondered if she should go off to Paris, and take hold of Jean-Chris *tightly*, not lightly. He was the only one so far she was as happy to sleep with as to talk to. Later, however, during the meditation service, while being brutally honest with herself (as her wily still-undisciplined mind wandered over various cocks and tongues she'd enjoyed) she had to admit that she'd also relished her purely lustful times with Tony, Clive Vogelnest and, to some extent, Clark Gent. Hugging Hank was a phenomenon unto himself, of course.

A huge part of her wondered, too, who would be next: the next lover she could explore, the next much-older sugar daddy whose life she could light up (without sinking into some day-to-day drudge). These thoughts prompted her to doubt if this tigress, man-eating part of her – which so dominated her character – could *ever* settle down nicely in a small garret in Paris, even if it was with the "perfect man" (as her mother had termed Jean-Chris after Cali had first described him).

During the meditation, Sugar prompted her students of joy to ask their innermost beings: *"What do you want?"*

What do you WANT? WHAT DO YOU REALLY REALLY WANT!? Cali asked herself. What she *really* wanted to do in life – her fascinations with courtesans and call girls, and women who enjoyed a great lifestyle by being feminine and sexual and pleasing a variety of men – puzzled and troubled her. She'd never shared how invasive her obsession was with a psychiatrist or counselor, and she held it deep inside: unable to pull it up and look at it in the light. But she felt it there, like a crouching tiger, ready to spring.

Shouldn't I deeply want to design rooms and homes and spaces… or move to Paris with Jean-Chris, be a wife and work as a designer there? That's what I'm now trained to do, what I seem to be good at. Shouldn't I want to merge paths with such an amazing young man?

Once out of the meditation, Sugar continued on with her teaching. "Stop 'shoulding' on yourself, people," she said. It was as if she could read Cali's mind. "It's OK to want *who* or *what* you think you shouldn't want. Let your *yeses* be real *yeses* and your *noes* be real *noes*. The minute you say yes to a no, or no to a yes, you've set yourself – and others! – up for pain. Don't commit to something, or even somebody because you think you *should* say yes to it, or them. Stop the shoulding, and *feel* into what you *really* want. Just DO what you really, really want to."

Cali looked around at the many relieved faces of the other spiritual seekers. She'd learned that much of Sugar's group consisted of top-performing Type-A professionals who'd found their way to the teachings of Science of Mind when the outer trappings of success hadn't brought them the joy they wanted.

After the service, Sugar made an announcement before everyone crowded over to the kitchen area for her famous hot cocoa made with real melted chocolate and a sprinkling of cinnamon. "I've got a special treat for us today, for during the social hour," Sugar said, looking out at the group of students. She smiled and pointed at a paisley sheet draped over some tall furniture, creating a tent-like effect, and now glowing from within with pink light from a salt lamp. "I've invited Miss Kali, from the East 20's. She's a seeer, she'll be able to see into all the possibilities for your lives. Just a small love offering today will make her day, as she shares her insights."

Some people – those who didn't believe in psychic powers, and/or love offerings – moaned slightly, and headed toward the kitchen. But Cali remembered *her* Kali from the East 20's: her pink den of intuition and how helpful she'd been on Cali's first day in Manhattan, nearly homeless, broke and ripped-off. *Miss Kali*.

"I'll go!" Cali said, approaching the tent.

Inside, sitting on some stacked pillows, was a new and different Kali. This one was younger – tall and wiry thin – and wearing a hot pink turban with an attractive iridescent jewel embellishment. The old Kali had resembled a wise, fat female Buddha sprinkled with sparkles.

"Kali?" Cali asked nervously. "You look so different since last time I saw you. Did you join Weight Watchers… or start injecting Human Growth Hormone?"

"We are changing all the time, no?" Kali confirmed, speaking in her thick Indian accent. "We are all of us capable of incredible transformations, yes?"

"Ah, yes, I suppose so," Cali said, taking her seat on a pillow. "What do you see for me?"

"Long version or short?"

"I'm low on cash, so the short," Cali said, sliding a small bill along the floor, which Kali tucked under her skirt.

"I see two islands. Turbulent waters under. I see many unfinished bridges. When I see this it means that you want to go from here to over there, okay?" Kali took Cali's hand into hers, and closed her eyes, concentrating. "I see you build one bridge, but then you stop. You build a new one, then you stop. Bridge after bridge. And so many bridges but nobody going across."

"Hmmmm, what does all this mean I wonder?" Cali asked, taking note of some bejeweled brooches for sale on a shelf behind Kali, with price tags displayed on a velvet panel. One of them could be gorgeous on an evening dress one day, swishing around some ball in Venice or on a cape for a Renaissance Faire in Edinburgh. "If I buy a brooch from you, will you tell me a little more about what you're seeing?"

"Yes dear," Kali nodded as Cali slid over some more cash.

"So what does all this bridge stuff symbolize?" Cali asked.

"It's meaning for you to build one bridge only; just keep building so you have one bridge all the way, all the way, all the way to the other side. Now is the time to focus. Yes, *focus*!"

"OH."

"And they want me to tell you something more."

"Must I pay for that, too?"

"It's a freebie. I know you are a good customer. Come back to see me at my parlor in Little India sometime?"

"Oh yes. I've been before and it was very helpful."

"They say to become *comfortable with the uncomfortable* – in your uncomfortable, you must become comfortable. Remove comfort, and you can build the bridge. Like the master bridge worker: he sleeps on the half-built bridge until it is finished. He doesn't go home to be comfortable. He stays on his bridge until his bridge is built and he can cross to the other side."

"Wow, OK. I must be doing something right. Because I'm *really* uncomfortable right now."

"Not uncomfortable enough," Kali shot her a look. "Get *more* uncomfortable."

"More? How? Oh…" Cali suddenly felt woozy. She suspected exactly what she needed to do, and it wasn't going to be pretty.

"Which brooch you want for the evening dress for the ball in Venice or your cape for the faire?" Miss Kali asked brightly, her eyes twinkling as she pushed the display of jewels closer to Cali, whose own eyes widened in shock. "Eh, what is new – I know things!" Miss Kali shrugged.

Chapter Twenty Four

The next morning Cali swung into action. She would allow nothing and no one to get in the way of graduating with high grades, and securing the Grand Prize in the Exhibition Competition, not to mention that first lucrative design contract. From there she'd have options, and if she *did* go to Paris, she'd be going with some oomph behind her, career-wise. She only had a few more weeks left until graduation, and planned to make every second count, money or no money, Jean-Chris or no Jean-Chris.

First, the apartment had to go. She was wasn't in a position to pay the immediate rent due, and it was better to get out while the going was good, rather than crash her hard-earned credit score with an eviction. She couldn't afford to pay rent anywhere anyway, until she'd secured some form of paid work again. Who knew when that would be? Work had to be put on hold until school was done, her college degree in hand, a new paid internship opportunity found, or *whatever* it would take to level up.

Whatever it would take. Her teenage crush, Dr. Reddy's

words reverbed in her head. He'd once said something to her like, "What's great about you is you're willing to do *whatever* it takes to get what you want." Her mind ventured to the inner sanctum of GG's: the lush bedrooms, the interesting adventures one could have, the cash that could fuel her raging wanderlust for travel and waking up in new and different places (with new and different men?). She imagined pumping at that fountain for the funds that could put her on the express route to starting her *own* design business someday. Fuck all those so-called gatekeepers, those internship interviews with snotty design people mulling over her portfolio (as great as it was), and questioning her skills and abilities or – now very checkered – past. Would a stint at GG's help her get her to her own firm faster as more of a lone wolf?

Whatever was next: it required focus, building one bridge only, sleeping on it until it was absolutely done, so she could cross to the other side. Leveling up would require simplifying and streamlining her life in such a way that it rendered her free from the distractions of looking for work until she won the Exhibition Competition (with her first design contract in hand). Or, she tried to keep the thought at bay: until she returned to GG's and began her career as a…

No, don't think about that. Not now, anyway. Be a designer! Or act as if.

She pulled out her one 'reserve' credit card, new and never used; it was shiny and with plenty of credit to get her through the next few months (although she planned to use it judiciously). Nearly shaking, she called the Hoard and

Store In-Town storage facility (*what a name, she thought*) and used the card to reserve a 24/7 access, 200-square foot storage unit in lower Manhattan for her things… And her, of course, but they didn't need to know that she'd be staying, too.

Then she called Monty, her landlord's representative, and left him a message to let him know she needed to leave her apartment lease early and, understandably, he could keep her security deposit. "Please, I just ask that you don't come after me legally since I got out early?"

She was somewhat amazed when he called back and said he was "cool with that" and that they wouldn't penalize her further. No need to drag "good old Tony" in on things as her guarantor.

Whew.

Now Cali was on the phone with Barry, of Barry's Art Loft, who had given her the first job she ever had in New York City, as a nude model for his revolving studio times. "Barry?" she cooed, when he picked up. "Not sure you'll remember me, it was a few years ago but I modeled for one of your groups, and that big fight broke out with the guy who hated your refreshments."

"Ah! Yes. Cali Kistler. Lovely little Cali. The model who doesn't spread."

"Well, I spread now. And how. You have a photographic memory."

"I'm a photographer, that's why. What can I do for you?"

She prefaced it all by saying, "It's really OK if you say no; I'm just pleased that I feel comfortable enough with you to ask for help." She shared details of her financial plight with him, and said, "It's OK, I have a plan. I'm not asking to borrow money, but I'm hoping you might be able to assist…" She outlined how she wanted to focus and give it her all during her last semester, by saving money and moving into her storage for a short while, "Just a short while!" Then, she explained how that nasty Saffron had presented her work as her own to gain an internship (and how there was the possibility Saffron might steal her Exhibition Competition ideas again, if they both used the shared studio space at school).

"Say no more!" Barry assured her. "I get you completely. You'll use my place as a crash pad. Free." He was in it to win it with her. "I'm all for the underdog! Or the top dog being hounded by the underdogs, whichever the case may be."

Cali marveled at how people were so willing to help, when you needed it and took the risk of asking for it. Hank had once told her the story of how, as a young man, he'd been loathe to seek out a mentor to help him professionally, but struggling immensely with his progress, one day, he said *fuck it* and took a chance on contacting a highly-placed executive he'd never dreamed would ever respond to him. The man was happy – delighted, in fact – to take him on; and Hank's career took off after that.

"Kid," Hank had said, nuzzling Cali's neck as he told the story, "Your willingness and capacity to ask others for help is usually directly proportional to your ability to one day give help to others."

As someone who hated asking others for help, this idea

took some getting used to, but once she got it, she had lost her fear about asking… and now found herself on the phone with Barry. He was a rather random person to ask, but he sounded delighted to help her out.

"Here's what we're gonna do," he said, excited. "We're gonna give you one of the sectioned-off workspaces, and – since you'll probably need a shower – you can use the bathroom here as much as you like. Now, I know you may be sleeping part of the day in your, uh, let's call it your *studio apartment* – but just sign up to nude art model for me from time to time if you're around and available. I'll pay you like I normally would. Just for a few weeks to a few months max. That OK?"

"Perfect!" She was thrilled it could work out. The extra funds would sure help.

"Love it," he said. "You know, I don't live in the loft; you can stay as long as you like, and come and go any hour of the day. It'd be great if you could manage that goddamn bottomless coffee carafe and the snack table for the painters. Fartists! They're a bunch of dirty monkeys, leaving their sugar wrappers everywhere."

"Of course. Wonderful! You're saving my life here," she sighed gratefully.

"It's nothin'! And don't worry about me coming on to you in there. I'm one of those quiet gay men marinating in my catholic guilt."

"So are you an underdog or a top dog?" Cali teased.

"Ha! I like both. I remember your sense of humor now! Hey kid, would you be interested in modeling for me personally, though? I'm doing more boudoir stuff, but with attractive couples. I'm working on a kinda multi-cultural, diversity series of large panels called 'Entwining.' You being so pale would be so great with Melvin; he's so dark. You remember Melvin, the model?"

"Hmmm…" Cali pretended not to remember him, but how could she forget? He was an Adonis dipped in dark chocolate. During his modeling session all that time ago, he'd climbed up and sprawled on the tufted chair like a proud panther. "I think so." She stifled an excited cough. "So, uh, Melvin and I would be modeling together for some, hmmm, sexy photos?" She tried not to sound too excited. "There won't be any video, right?" she ventured gently, not wanting to have anything to do with that world. She'd always felt that celluloid was forever, and steered clear of the notion of doing porn.

"It's not porn, honey. Art photography. It'll make people feel amorous to see people of different races entwining, but it's not porn per se. It's artful expression of the erotic subtext of unity, of coming together. No video. I wouldn't know what to do with a video camera if I had a gun to my head!"

"Sounds fine, Barry. I'll call you when I'm on the way over."

Finally, Cali called Jean-Chris.

"I just need to let you know that I'm going to go 'incommunicado' for a while," she explained. "Just… I'm going to disappear into my work and focus for a while." She told him she'd be spending most of the next few weeks working out of Barry's Art Studio, near school. She gave him Barry's address in case he needed it.

She skipped the part about abandoning her apartment in Brooklyn, and her plan to sleep in her storage unit during the morning into early afternoons when it was safer to do so. He'd especially balk if he knew she was doing all this following a psychic's vague instructions on focusing, and building a bridge (sleeping on it, in fact).

J.C was one of those gallant young men in shiny armor, and he'd never allow her to do such a thing if he knew. He'd insist she stay with him in his tiny room at the Hotel Gram-Irving. And that was out of the question. Relying solely on Jean-Chris over the next few weeks until graduation was far more than she could bear to ask for. He was already working from his own limited resources, and she wasn't completely sure if he'd broken up with her, or they were still going to be friends, considering he'd proposed that they seek out others who might want something more serious.

"You sound so sad," she said, picking up on the strain in his voice when he spoke.

"I think I just had my last conversation with my Uncle," he sighed.

"Aw, I'm sorry. Do you want company?"

Instead of answering, he just said, "In due course. I'll bring over the architectural model for your exhibition soon, to Barry's studio, OK? It's going to be one of my best. Your field measuring and drawings are impeccable. The model will win this for you."

"Thank you! But are you SURE you don't want

company? I could come out later on."

"No," he said curtly, then softened his tone. "I need some time to myself."

After a local charity store came to remove her furniture from the apartment, Cali cried a little at her now-empty nest. It kind of broke her heart to let her pretty antique pieces go, but she felt certain the Universe would restore it all soon enough. Sugar had once spoken of the phenomenon of divine restoration of all that was lost ("This or better," she was to chant). Cali had to just trust that it would be true for her, too.

There was something else, as well, that got her all misty-eyed: all her memories of Jean-Chris' visits during the last two years, their weekends of doing homework together there on the living room floor, and their overnights having great sex under the pretense of his teaching her French. So often – usually after she went to the trouble of cooking something for them – he would push for more i.e. hint how nice it would be if they could *always* be like this. She would then push back, feeling somehow claustrophobic every time he mentioned commitment, and would change/evade the subject.

She sighed and rose to finish taping up a few last boxes. As Kin had pointed out, "If you're even questioning it," maybe it wasn't the right thing to do.

Sitting in her living room, boxes packed up, and about to leave the Brooklyn apartment for good, she took one last look around. It was over in that bed that she'd gained quite a good proficiency in all things sexual, mainly with Jean-Chris, and a bit with Tony the Italian. With Clark Gent and Clive Vogelnest, she'd learned what it was to take on near total strangers, and give them pleasure (and take some for herself, too).

Despite her bond of friendship with Jean-Chris, had she just been practicing at sex, and not really participating with her heart enough over the last two years with him? Had she been practicing (or even pretending) at playing house with him on the weekends? Had she just been passing the time with him, meanwhile always secretly yearning for more action, a more adrenaline-fueled kind of life and sexual variety? Had unsuspecting Jean-Chris been the sexual and emotional equivalent of training wheels or a flotation device until she felt comfortable to ride on alone and/or deep-dive into the pool of adventures and even more new and different men?

She felt the looming need to decide and commit, to *something*.

In a rare move, later that day, she called her mother and caught her up on the pending situation with Jean-Chris and Paris. Cali's uncertainty was met with no understanding whatsoever. To make matters worse, she'd caught Pearl working in the marking room at Rags to Religion, and all the ladies were listening in.

"If you don't go to Paris, and commit yourself to that young man, you'll be thumbin' your nose at God – the God who brought you *a good man*! You go get your butt on that flight, get over there with him and marry him, or ELSE *I will!*"

"We will too!" the elderly ladies (none of whom had ever traveled yet) piped in from the background.

Her mother quickly clicked off, citing the fact that Vera had brought her amazing Watergate Salad, and they were going off for a snack break. Cali felt that Pearl, as much of a believer in a Higher Power as she was, had always operated from a sense of entrapment, of limited resources that – if left untapped – would dry out. The good men were scarce; the good jobs would disappear; the best vintage thrift store goods would be gotten by somebody else if she didn't act fast and now.

Cali, on the other hand, was very conscious (and getting more so as she studied Sugar's teachings of Science of Mind) of her freedom to choose everything in her life. It was probably impossible to make truly wrong decisions, as long as they were things that were definitely decided, and not just *in*decision left to stagnate until no other options existed except one. Different definite decisions, made well, could only bring about good outcomes.

I'm not ready, no, I'm not at all excited to entwine lives with one man, as great as this one is. I'm not ready to keep a home for him, to be his rock. I'm not ready to quickly become his wife, to mistakenly embrace what might become mundane.

WHAT DO YOU WANT THEN?

That question, again! When would she be ready to answer it?

I AM ready to be blissfully, luxuriously solo – and venture into something more exotic, something more unknown… even if I find out it's not all I think it is.

This idea felt so much more exciting, but also decided and definite; nearly vibrating with a magnetization to her solar plexus. If felt *good*. Risky, yes, but *good*.

She then pictured her handsome best friend J.C – in his blue wool jacket, the jaunty scarves he often had wrapped around his neck, his brown eyes so often laughing and making fun of her, yet tinged with a slight sadness, easily overcome by his ambition.

I'll need to be clear and transparent with him. It's a sin to waste his time. But it's also a sin to trouble him or break his heart just as he is in his final most intense weeks of college. The timing needs to be right.

Her doorbell suddenly buzzed loudly, indicating that the van service had arrived. This noisy intrusion into her thoughts didn't jar her at all. Something that had been whipping up inside her now felt settled, and she was ready to go build her bridge.

Once she and her things were trucked over to lower Manhattan, Cali moved into her storage unit at the temperature-controlled, secure Hoard and Store. She placed her boxes and her smallest of antiques in a very specific way that would allow her to access all her clothes and shoes, now kept in wardrobe boxes, as well as to enjoy her Queen size mattress nestled inside a fort bordered by her boxes.

She cried a little as she made her bed with her nicest sheets, feeling terribly alone now. But hunger and a drive to succeed eventually pulled her out of it. She gathered her purse and various necessities she'd need for Barry's Art Studio, and pulled down the gate.

Once outside, she found her way into the edges of the trendy meat-packing district. There, in an unassuming pizza joint, she nearly dove upon a crisp, cold salad accompanied by a perfectly-done chicken parmesan hero sandwich dripping in a rich marinara sauce. It would become her 'go-to' comfort food restaurant, open 24 hours a day, serving all the right – but *oh so wrong* – carbs for a lady trying to power through the intensely demanding end of design school (and possibly the end of a beautiful friendship).

Chapter Twenty Five

Once ensconced in her workspace at Barry's Art Studio, often working through the night (and returning to the storage unit to sleep the next day), it amazed Cali what she could accomplish with her new allotment of spare hours by no longer working as a temp. Now that where she 'lived' was located so close to her classes and Barry's studio, this new building of the bridge idea seemed more do-able.

An art modeling gig every few days or so at Barry's helped keep her in light meals, without having to hit her credit card. Her discreet daytime sleeping-at-the-storage hack was working out pretty well, too, with some earplugs and a blindfold (in case neighboring unit renters showed up with the ruckus of moving things in and out).

Sleeping on Barry's couch wasn't cool, as she didn't want to impose on him any more than necessary. And she secretly enjoyed the cave-like, protected feeling of covertly napping in the storage unit. She'd gone a bit upside down on her schedule: working on her final projects or modeling at Barry's in the mid-afternoons, going to school as usual in the evenings, and then returning to Barry's late night to work on her projects into the wee hours. Then, when the storage unit place was less deserted, she'd sleep from 6am until 1pm, change clothes and pretend to herself that being homeless and sleep-deprived wasn't slowly driving her nuts.

As the weeks continued on, Cali often found solace at Sugar's Divine Mind Center. She would listen carefully to her and the guest speakers' lectures on the transformative and healing powers of the subconscious mind, tapping into intuition, and communing with a Higher Power. In addition, the guided meditations and the singing and chanting of positive affirmations all contributed to Cali's new awareness: *she* could choose how to feel. *She* could choose how she communicated. While she might not be able to control things that happened, she was always in charge of her *reaction*.

Sugar taught: "Between every action, and re-action, is a space: for transformation. To change the way you might normally react, for the better." This one life-altering idea seeded in Cali's fertile mind. During the meditation portion, she attempted to become more proficient at escaping her often-indecisive 'monkey mind.' But despite her efforts, her thoughts often drifted to Jean-Chris. They were both so busy ramping up to their graduations now; she sensed him out there, somewhere. Perhaps he was waiting, purposely giving her enough space to miss him (and to hear her decision about Paris). Or was he feeling quite free now to see other people? Was he, indeed, doing just that: slowly forgetting about her?

Take hold lightly, let go lightly.

She'd wait until Jean-Chris surfaced again from his final push of schoolwork, dealing with his uncle's illness and preparing to move back to Paris. She'd wait until he made the first move to prompt her for her decision on Paris. Maybe *he'd* already changed *his* mind. She would know that soon enough. He'd promised her the architectural model for the Exhibition Competition, and she'd sent him an invitation to her graduation, and she'd received the invite to his. Sooner or later their paths would cross, and she would need to answer him face-to-face.

One thing was certain: Cali's plans for the Exhibition Competition were working out beautifully. Each graduating student competing was to be given the equivalent of a sizable trade show booth space to propose and exhibit their visual answer to the revamp of the Esther and Hank Greenace Women's Shelter. Within the space, the graduating student could display anything that would convince the judges that their proposal was the winning one, including models, photos, swatches, drawings, even video. What Cali had planned was spectacular, and Jean-Chris' model (she knew instinctively he would still come through with it) would cinch the deal.

As Saturday evening crept in, and Barry's Art Studio cleared out, Cali sat behind a large partition that separated her from the artists who came and went all day. At her own large work table, she worked on her presentation boards, budgets, and scope-of-work documents; and she carefully mounted sizeable photos of her original mosaics (the ones she would donate) onto boards that would post up nicely against the backdrops of each wall.

Jean Chris' architectural model, to be displayed on a table in the center of her booth, would show in three dimensions how she would transform the women's shelter from drab to rad. Cali even bought several yards of a crisp white denim to be a convincing background to cover the dark-black of the booth walls, and to highlight her colorful fabric choices. All this would visually convey the ambiance of the inspiring space she would redesign for the shelter.

"Cali! I'm home," Barry called across the loft from the loft's front door. "And I've got Melvin here. This hunk of Big Puma is making me look like a scrawny side dish of curly fries."

She heard Melvin's deep voice laughing. "Barry, you better be careful. I'm not putting up with you comparing me to a jungle cat."

"Sheesh, Melv. It was *a compliment.* Go get undressed. Come out when you're ready. As usual I'll be fiddle-diddling with shit on my camera for hours. I'm so ancient I'm still using film. You kids remember film? NO, of course not."

Melvin called out, "Hi Cali! Wherever you are."

"Hi Melvin! Nice to see you again," Cali said, coming around the corner in her dressing robe. She felt a bit transported by Melvin's firm touch when they shook hands; there was no doubt that he remembered her from two years before. Was the look on her face that obvious? As in: *Take me, I'm yours.*

"Good," Barry said, watching them, pretending to shiver. "I'm feeling the chemistry already." He set off to mess with his camera equipment and the lights that were set up in the corner. He'd be aiming at the entwining couple set against a grey background. "Have a drink, you two!" he called across the loft. "Wine's in the fridge. Loosen up; I'm gonna be here for a while. My apertures are all fouled up. You don't mind if I light up?"

"You lighting up our lives with your sparkling personality?" Melvin asked, winking over at Cali, who was secretly feeling a little weak in the knees as her eyes glossed over his rather triangular physique.

"NO. I'm lighting up a joint, if you don't fucking mind!" Barry growled. "Where the hell did my reflector go? I had a gold reflector somewhere, gives everyone that Baywatch look."

Looking over at Melvin, trying not to stare, Cali thought to herself that perhaps a new experience in the sexual realms was called for – now that she felt she'd so well grasped the basics (among other things) with Jean-Chris. And he'd recently informed her that they needed to see other people, hadn't he?

See other people, indeed, she thought. I'll see *this* one!

Cali followed Melvin to the small kitchen. They started laughing when all they found in the fridge were half a dozen half-open wine bottles, of unknown age, precariously rattling around on the shelves. Finally, they found a new bottle of red in a cabinet. "I asked him if he wanted me to clean all those out of the fridge," Cali giggled as Melvin uncorked it.

"But he said he's old enough to remember Prohibition, which still haunts him, and to just leave them 'the fuck' alone. He has a 'system.'"

"OH, a system," Melvin chuckled. "Gotta love Barry. So, what do you do when you're not modeling?"

"You first," Cali hedged, as Melvin poured out two plastic cups of wine, and they sat down together on a nearby couch strewn with various international textiles Barry had picked up during his hunt for the world's best cannabis resins. She lifted up a striped piece of scratchy red and black wool, and set it aside genteely. "See this blanket? I don't mean to sound gross, but Barry confided in me that he got dysentery back in the 60's while crossing the Sahara desert with some nomads who refused to stop for a Gatorade break. Then, when they finally made it close enough to the outskirts of Marrakech to kick him out of the caravan, they made him buy *this* blanket for some exorbitant fee. He said, their philosophy was: 'You poo'd on it, you pay for it!' He's still angry about it, let me tell you. But I think he's had it dry cleaned since. I really hope so"

"They had Gatorade back in the 1960's in Morocco?"

"Yes, it sounded suspicious to me too."

"Barry!" Melvin yelled over to Barry's corner. "Were you drinking Gatorade back in the 1960's?"

"Yeah, dammit! It was an experimental drink back then. The astronauts were all taking it; the government didn't want people to know about it. They were testing it out on nomadic sheep-herders. I saw some UFOs out there off Ben Guerir, too. Another thing the government didn't want us to know about! What's it to you, Melvin!?"

"Nothin' – just asking," Melvin said, as he and Cali cracked up, falling back into the couch.

By the time Barry was ready for his models, Melvin and Cali had worked through most of the wine, and had learned a great deal of silly stuff about each other, including the fact that Melvin's day job was actually a night job as an IT consultant for the Federal Reserve Bank, whose transactions flowed through the wire room at all hours.

"I like coming to Barry's, gets me out of my head, or more in," Melvin confessed. "When I'm stuck in a pose up there, it's like I can really think deeply into things. Can't do anything up there but ponder one thing at a time. And I love being naked. I'd be naked all the time if I could be."

"Me too," Cali agreed, looking forward to seeing Melvin naked again.

"You kids ready for your close ups?" Barry finally yelled over, interrupting their engrossing conversation.

Melvin stood and began unbuttoning his shirt. Cali reached up to help him.

"Let me help you with that," she smiled.

"Oh, thank you!" he said, holding her shoulders as she used the excuse of unbuttoning him in order to sweep her hands over his broad chest. She felt a bit tipsy from the wine, and a lot less pent up than usual. It was all for the sake of some great photos, wasn't it? "Let me help *you*, with *that*," he said, undoing the tie on Cali's robe, and sliding the silky piece off her shoulders, discreetly laying it on the couch.

"Let me help you with *this*," Cali said, laying her hand

on the zipper of Melvin's pants, and slowly zipping down. Melvin pulled off his pants, revealing a sleek pair of back undershorts clinging to his bulging package of…

God I want to fuck this guy.

"Oh, take your time undressing, guys! I have all night," Barry said sarcastically while walking away.

For a long moment Barry didn't exist, and Melvin's fingers strayed down the inside of her robe discreetly. He rubbed her clit softly as she rubbed her fingers along his hard cock. Suddenly, he picked her up, and wrapped her legs around his waist – pressing his hard cock against her through his underwear. In such a position, he carried her over to Barry's corner; the momentum of walking caused his hard dick to beat against her clit, driving her crazy for more. He deposited her on the grey backdrop, and slid down his underwear, while Barry turned up some sexy mystical lounge music.

"Oh, you've started without me," Barry mumbled, looking through his lens. "Just do your thing and I'll shoot. Just entwine, guys. I know you've got a big hard on, Marv. The camera's not gonna pick up on that. I'm not showing it, just the hint."

"Should I…" Melvin ventured. "Should I hide it somewhere?"

"Like, inside me?" Cali giggled, as she and Melvin got into a spooning pose that had Melvin's cock nestling in Cali's butt crack, and his big hands completely covering her breasts.

"No," Barry said. "No funny business. Let's be professionals."

"Right," Cali agreed.

Barry shot away for what felt like a long time, flashes firing, as Cali and Melvin nearly danced horizontally, slowly making their way into various entwined seated and prone positions. His skin contrasted beautifully against hers, while his raging erection poked into her flesh at every turn. It reminded her that as soon as Barry had his money shot, and was out the door, she and Melvin could take it all the way.

"OK, it's a wrap. You did good," Barry finally said, packing up. "I'll straighten everything up tomorrow. Just… turn out the lights when you leave," he smirked, loading up his favorite camera into a special bag, and slipping out the door.

Chapter Twenty Six

Meanwhile, as Barry headed home, Jean-Chris was cabbing it down to the Studio with the architectural model for Cali, which was carefully placed in a protective box. And he had a surprise bouquet of flowers and a bottle of chilled champagne… He came bearing big news; he hoped to tell Cali about it over supper in Soho, if it wasn't too late for her.

He rehearsed in his mind how he would tell her. "My uncle *did* die, it's sad. The thing is, he had no children. And I've just learned from the *notaire* that he's left me quite well off, with his vast apartment in the 9th Arrondissement; there are just a few charges every month, nothing I cannot handle. I also inherited his antiques business and all his merchandise. It's a wonderful thing! I cannot believe how perfect it works with the education I chose. I guess I had a good instinct when I changed my studies. So now I would have the job consulting at Christie's *and* the antiques business *and* the apartment. Please say yes! Come with me! It will all be perfect now…"

The cab slowed to the curb as Jean-Chris' daydream of

Cali's positive response to his good fortune faded into the background of the gritty city noises. The way he was puffed up as he slammed the cab door behind him indicated that he felt rather full and sure of himself. He looked up at the lighted fifth floor of the loft building. He was certain she must be up there working away, and desperate for a diversion. Champagne and life-altering news now being the perfect diversion!

True, she *was* up there, but blissfully not alone. After Barry had departed, she and Melvin had turned the music way up. "Cause it's gonna get loud in here," Melvin had promised, taking her hand and kissing it, looking over at her with his to-die-for brown eyes ringed by long, lush lashes.

They'd made their way to a shaggy rug in front of the couch nearest the front door. Finding her wetter than he could imagine, and legs spread for him, Melvin slid on a condom, climbing on her – trying not to suffocate her with his weight, and yet bearing down enough that his ample cock felt like a dream as he inched it inside her; then pumped her slow and steady as she grabbed his ass, and clung her legs around him.

Fucking another near stranger, love it, she thought as they slowly accelerated their pace until they were at it like wild animals on the floor. *How I love fucking strangers. I wonder what it's like to fuck hot strangers AND get paid for it. THAT must be the ultimate high…*

As the pleasure overwhelmed her, she found herself screaming out, so free in a place where nobody could hear.

Her first orgasm hit her like a shot of heroin, while another one, slower and more delicious was quickly behind it as he slowly but surely jammed into her with his huge, hard tool. Melvin kept up a rhythm, and she felt overtaken by him, as if he were that stealthy UFO in the Moroccan desert, overshadowing her and drawing her into the deep, dark mysteries of the Universe, multiple orgasms and a lust-fueled evening she'd never forget. She had lost track of time, and had lost all her sense of hearing…

Just as Jean-Chris pushed inside the unlocked loft door, she was deep into her screaming and moaning, which intermingled with the loud music, and Melvin the Puma's own calls of the wild. This was mating at its best.

For a moment, Jean-Chris stood there stunned, watching Cali and this other man getting it on in a passionate way she and he had never experienced together, not really. Half of him was strangely attracted to this wild underside of Cali: a young woman capable of doing whatever the fuck she wanted with whomever she wanted to, no apologies. The other half of him felt heart-broken, repulsed, and deeply disappointed in her as his future lover, possibly even *wife*. Was this a woman he could ever introduce to his *mother*?

But he'd not been lied-to. She'd never promised her fidelity or their future. And, every step of the way, she'd been relatively honest with him about her reservations about committing. He'd come upon this scene uninvited, a private moment. Now he felt ashamed of himself for showing up there by surprise, and having such high hopes that maybe she'd commit to him when she heard about the goodies awaiting her in Paris. If she truly loved him, wouldn't she have agreed (right away!) to go live together – even in a tent with him in a refugee encampment by the canal, if that's what it took to stay together? Wasn't *he* enough?

Jean-Chris continued watching the oblivious couple for a few moments more. He caught the 'New York Knicks' tattoo seared into Melvin's bottom, which was now pumping on Cali. He had an almost murderous instinct to go over and throttle the guy to death. But Melvin was faultless in this. (Definitely; J.C sensed Cali had a knack for picking men up whenever she wanted).

Jean-Chris set the box down in the hallway of the loft. Next to it, he laid down the bouquet of flowers. Despite what he'd just seen, he reasoned that she didn't deserve anything less than some of the best architectural modeling work he'd ever done, inspired by how much he cared for her.

Pulling away, he slammed his hand into the wall in the hallway, bracing himself as he held himself back from the brink of committing a crime of passion. He pulled the loft door shut. It made a loud thud that seemed to reverberate through the building.

So much so that Melvin and Cali stopped fucking for an instant, listening. And then Cali heard the sound of the fire exit door slamming hard, and someone running down the stairs.

Jean-Chris descended the long sets of stairs, holding tight to the champagne bottle, and found his way out of the loft building. He decided it would be fruitless to go back to the Hotel Gram-Irving and attempt to sleep. It would first take a copious amount of drinking from his champagne bottle, alone in Washington Square Park, to forget what he'd just witnessed. Wiping hot tears from his face with the handkerchief he always carried, he hoped to find a lonely alley or corner somewhere, to break down and let it all go.

And now Cali was standing in front of him on the street, in a robe and bare feet. "Goddamn it, J.C! Why didn't you just call me first!?"

He launched in. "You weren't even wearing the bracelet I gave you while you were... screaming out. I can still hear it, your pleasure." He covered his ears, and turned away, letting himself go, sobbing. "I shouldn't have come. I assumed..."

"The *bracelet*? That's what's bothering you?"

"Yes! You aren't even sentimental. You don't have a heart. If I'd at least seen my bracelet on you while you were shagging that athlete (what is he? A football player?)... God, if you'd just been wearing the bracelet I gave you, it might be better."

"This is nuts. Why didn't you give me some notice you were coming over? It's just part of being the way we are. Right now, the... parameters."

"You were liking it too much. You've never acted like that *with me*."

"Oh God. Come sit. Please." She motioned for him to sit down on the ramp of a low metal portico adjacent to the loft building.

He slowly approached and plunked down next to her, hands over his face, collecting himself. "I'm going to forget what I just saw, OK? It's my fault, for pushing you away. I will only ask you one more time, because things have changed, for the better."

"What things? Are you sure you want to ask me *anything* after what you just saw? You never should have come over without calling first. That's Rule One of 'We should start seeing other people.' Or didn't you get that memo?"

"Please. Stop going on about that. I am fine with it. I can have open relationships with the best of them."

"I don't think so. You're not like that."

"Let's change the subject. My uncle has passed away, OK? Oh, thank you for asking…"

"I meant to. I was waiting for you to tell me if you had news."

"Right. And of course I am very sad about this. He was such a great guy."

Here, despite his better judgment, and feeling like some kind of *brocanteur* – selling an idea to her like some old relic – he told her about all the inheritance goodies that would alter his lifestyle. Like a list of assets, he detailed the big apartment, the business, all the perks.

But it all sounded like gobbly-gook to her, now filtering through a mind that had already decided not to go with him. The material stuff didn't matter to her as much as he might think.

"Wow, that's so wonderful for you!" Cali gripped his hand.

"Wonderful *for us*. What do you think?" he asked sweetly. "Come with me to Paris?"

She was a little shocked at the turnabout. Here was one more thing to tick off on his list of amazing qualities: he didn't seem to hold grudges or hold on to sexual jealousy for very long, and was focused on the bigger picture.

She sat pondering 'the offer' for a long moment, feeling inside herself for a heartfelt answer. She searched desperately for something to say yes to, like a woman reaching deep into a cluttered purse in search of a favorite lost lipstick, but finding the one in the wrong color instead. Living well in Paris with Jean-Chris was really the kind of offer or package that would make any woman swoon. But that was just it: it felt too much like an offer and a package; it bordered on the venal, despite the fact that Jean-Chris was such a love. He was *such* an amazing person – but perhaps *too* amazing for her.

This felt like him appealing to her material, practical needs for shelter, comfort, a predictable entry into a new lifestyle and career. His proposal didn't hook into her on some deep, visceral or spiritual level: that inner spring where passion and risk and adrenaline – where go-getting and self-sufficiency – lived and fueled her. It felt a little too easy. Something about the whole thing made her feel dull inside. She often hated her 'scrappy' side (the one who chose to do things the hard, sometimes dangerous way), and yet being so scrappy on this journey, so far, had brought a lot of wonderful moments and authentic learning.

It was all too complicated and potentially hurtful to

explain all this to someone so dear, so sweet (so perfect for perhaps *another* time in her life. Or, at least, perfect for *someone else*). "I can't," she stated simply. "I'm so so sorry, my Jean-Chris." She slid from the portico, stood up, and turned around, as he stood, too. "I'll only disappoint you. You must avoid me at all costs."

"Please, Cali. Come to Paris."

"I'm saying goodbye." She gave him a long, soft kiss on his cheek. His hand continued to cling to hers. "This is the part of our romantic comedy where our paths go in different directions."

"Are you sure?" he asked.

She was already nodding *Yes, I'm sure*. It was so hard, the thought of possibly never seeing him again. She let go as they looked at each other, and she counseled herself to hold it all in check until she was back in Barry's loft and alone: that instinct to cry, to impulsively change her mind, and maybe change it back again! Melvin was still up there, and she'd need to not burden him with her romantic dilemmas. He seemed like the type of sensitive guy who would understand all this completely, but she'd confide in him some other night perhaps.

"Bye, *mon amour*. Good luck!" she said softly, walking away. She turned and watched from a few steps away as Jean-Chris sat there trying not to weep. And once inside, she stood at the window a few moments longer, observing him slouching up the street, hunched over in immense emotional pain. She hurt for him, but knew it was far better than the hurt of moving in with him, and doing the same thing a few months – or years later – if they hadn't got the basics right.

Once back upstairs in the Studio, Cali felt shaky and utterly drained.

"You gonna be OK, Cali?" Melvin asked, now dressed and coming toward her at the front door. He was genuinely concerned about her. "You ran off. It wasn't something I did? You sure?" His big eyes enquired in a way that made her have faith there was still a lot of softness and sweetness in the world. "I'd never hurt a girl. If I touched you the wrong way, or was I too much…?"

"No, Melvin. You're so sweet. It wasn't anything like this. It was just an old friend. He saw us, you know, in action."

"OH. Ooh, I see." He looked over at the box and flowers. "I get it."

"I really enjoyed this," she reassured him, and smiled. "I'm sorry it ended up like that. Could I, could we have a replay sometime, you and me, Mr. Puma?"

"I got plenty of Puma for you. And a panther too," he laughed easily, and she felt sure that they could be friends, maybe lovers or more moving forward. But for now, she was still seeing the pain she'd just witnessed in Jean-Chris' eyes, and the profound disappointment that showed in his posture as he'd fled the scene.

After the door clicked behind Melvin, Cali carried the box from Jean-Chris that had been left in the front hallway.

Setting it on a table, she unsealed it, and peered down inside. There sat an exact replica of her proposed design for the Exhibition Competition, in miniature, with delicate thoughtful details: like lighting fixtures and plants displayed in mini-3D. It was amazing. Masterful, like him.

She removed the model from the outer box, and placed it on her large worktable, admiring it. Then she lifted the model up – looking for something, she wasn't sure what, *a sign* maybe.

And there on the bottom, in Jean-Chris' classical script, were his words: "Dear Cali, on the occasion of your final Exhibition and College Graduation, may I wish that you forever realize that *you* are the architect and designer of your life. Love is the base of solid construction, friendship makes the supporting walls, and the rest is just details. Love, J.C."

She put her face in her hands, and cried.

Chapter Twenty Seven

A few weeks later, it was the morning of Cali's college graduation – and she prepared for the ceremony in her 'studio apartment' (actually, the cramped confines of her storage unit). In her wardrobe box, she located her best lingerie: a very expensive black lace bra and panties set, one of Hank's gifts. It made her feel powerful, beautiful and... *lucky*? "Luck favors the prepared mind," was another favorite quote of Sugar's, and Cali had come to believe that pre-paving any occasion with good thoughts and visualizing best outcomes was definitely the best way to go.

A slight wave of panic went through her, thinking how the day might end, but she pushed it from her mind. It was all up to her. She slid into a versatile little black cocktail dress and matching low heels that could go glamorously from day into evening. Should some wonderful 'unknown' happen at the Exhibition Competition – like a job offer, a dinner invitation for networking afterwards, or actually winning the Grand Prize – she would be ready for anything.

She also tucked a pair of sheer black thigh-high lace-topped stockings and an exquisite black lace garter belt into her purse. *You never know.* She'd also be ready for *other* possible unknowns. She reminded herself that of all the days of her life thus far, this was the day to remain *gracious, unfettered and unflappable.*

A cocktail reception for the graduating students, their guests and the judges of the Exhibition Competition was scheduled right after graduation. There, Cali would verbally present her project inside her booth where the judges would be given ten minutes to meet her, examine her proposed ideas, materials and visual representations.

She'd spent the previous evening ensuring all the details of her booth were perfect – and impressive. Furthermore, it was important that her presentation bore in mind the needs of the 'client:' the women's shelter. Cali felt that the winning combination of donating her large, feminine mosaics to the charity for use in the shelter as wall art, combined with her masterful re-working of the space – and budget-effective design plan – would gain her this first contract as a paid interior designer.

She opened a plastic package with her name on it, and pulled out the loose-fitting graduation gown and the matching square graduation cap. She put everything on. Her walk up to the Institute combined with the humidity in the air would be enough to naturally smooth out the wrinkled gown just in time for the ceremony.

As she closed the gate of the storage unit, and made her way clicking down the concrete hallway, she felt confident in the booth she'd finished preparing until late into the night before. A tiny ripple of fear went through her that perhaps Saffron might have snuck into the exhibition hall, tampering with her presentation between then and now, but who would do such a thing at 3am in the morning? If so, Saffron would need to be tampered with, too.

In it to win it: that's me.

As she walked up Seventh Avenue, heading toward the Institute, her thoughts turned to Jean-Chris, whom she thought of with a twinge of heartfelt pain. Perhaps staying friends with him was not going to be possible, as she hadn't heard from him, not really, since they'd parted ways at Barry's loft. She'd left numerous phone messages thanking him profusely for giving her the amazing architectural model for the competition, and he'd merely texted back, "You're welcome," followed by a mysterious, "I'm so sorry but I've had to un-invite you from my graduation. Not enough places. X, J.C." He'd once mentioned that given space limitations, every graduate at his school was limited to two guests for graduation. Perhaps, she thought, his mother or some other family were coming across from Europe to show their support. Or (she felt a sense of hurt deep inside) he simply never wanted to see her again.

She thought of what his graduation must have been like for him. The one thing that probably made the day truly great was knowing that he'd accomplished what he'd come to NYC to do two years earlier: mix into the vibrant city scene, of course, but also to emerge with the credentials, professional connections, and kudos he could take back home to Paris with him. She intuited that it must be such a fine feeling to have secured the first, rather prestigious job of his dreams.

I wish you well, wherever you are, J.C.

The graduation ceremony was about to start. There was a buzz in the air as Cali and the other graduates sat grouped alphabetically in a special section of the auditorium. She watched a little jealously as Saffron so expertly worked the way down her row, waving to friends, hugging and congratulating people (that ever-present exclamation mark in a balloon above her head). She was so very good at being the social butterfly that one needs to be in order to succeed in the upper echelons of interior design.

While Cali yearned to be more like the socially-savvy Saffron, for the first time in her life she acknowledged that it might not ever be *her*. She might never have the bubbly charm of a Miss Congeniality. Instead, she would aim to be a self-styled, self-controlled, rather reserved and respectful young woman who took time to warm up to others (except in the case of already-hot guys). She was someone who listened well, expressed sincere, authentic interest – when appropriate – and someone who'd *done the work* to call herself an artist, a design professional, and – soon perhaps? – a discreet, sought-after sensualist.

Everyone started quieting down as the officiator of the ceremony and key members of the school's board took their seats on the stage. She looked around. Someone was frantically waving, trying to get her attention from many rows away. She gasped as she waved back. Jean-Chris was *there*.

Delighted that he'd come around, she waved back and took a second look. He was seated next to a young woman who was clearly *not* his mother surprising him with a visit from Paris. Cali zoomed in. The way they were sitting together was not two strangers who happened to be seated together. The striking young woman, upon seeing Jean-Chris waving at Cali again, made the awfully smug choice of sliding her long, skinny arm under his. *He's mine, bitch*, that said.

Cali turned back toward the stage, and squeezed her eyes shut, feeling a new kind of heartbroken. Mr. Takaya, her favorite professor and the Chairman of the Interior Design program, took to the podium for a rousing speech before handing out the diplomas.

After graduation, Cali quickly made her way to the foyer hall of the auditorium where her Exhibition booth was located. The cocktail reception for the graduates and their guests was already getting into full swing. Free wine and food was swirling, and the 'secret' judges would soon begin their rounds of visiting the competing booths. Nobody knew exactly who the judges were, only that the esteemed interior design professionals would be looking around and conversing with the presenting students, judging them on their interpersonal skills as well as their design proposals for the women's shelter.

As she stealthily approached her own booth, Cali saw

Saffron and an unknown, very glamorous-looking woman (in a hot pink, ruffled wrap dress and impossibly high heels) having a poke around at Cali's work. *Of course,* Cali thought: Saffron was already baiting one of the judges against her. Coming up behind them, Cali overheard Saffron say, "Such a talent. Too bad she's had such a troubled past. Poor thing, she's really overcome a lot to get here, having been a stripper and all of that. What do *you* think of this project?"

"Hello Saffy," Cali said casually, quickly throwing off her graduation gown to reveal her gorgeous, clinging black cocktail dress beneath. She caught Saffy's friend's eyes all over her. "Don't you need to go over to your project in case a judge or two shows up?"

"No, I don't have a booth. I had delivery glitches," Saffron pointed across the hall to an empty booth. "I'm around today to boost the team. I don't *need* to win. I mean, it would be nice, but I'm already interning with Ms. Hilliard here. Clara, meet Cali Kistler," Saffron gushed a little too sweetly.

"Ah, Clara Hilliard," Cali smiled, taking her hand warmly. "Your reputation precedes you. I've always admired the way you use De Gournay. And the collection of stain-resistant silk velvets you did for Kravet. Those greyed down, sea-inspired colors were transporting enough, but the *hand* on them – like spun silk but with the long life of a sturdy velvet! I'm a huge fan."

"Awww, thank you!" Clara's long eyelash-rimmed eyes flashed, and she licked slightly at her wet-looking lip gloss. Cali picked up a distinctly "lipstick lesbian" vibe, as Clara's eyes seemed to take in her curves and drink her up. In a nano-second Cali observed those eyes half-close with some secret thought of shared pleasure. Clara's gaze then settled on Cali's lips for a small moment, before she collected herself. "You know my work so well," Clara moved her head to the side to express modesty.

"And you know *mine* really well! You've seen it before," Cali gave her a knowing smile, and returned a short gaze that all but said *I might rub pussies with you some day*.

"Let's go, Clara, we really should be going," Saffron said, nearly pulling Clara's arm off.

"No, I'm a glutton for flattery. Go on, Cali. How do I know *your* work so well?"

"Cali, please don't do this," Saffron begged.

"No, no. I really think Clara deserves to know *the truth*," Cali said calmly. "I think we owe our industry all the honesty we can bring to it."

"Gosh, this sounds ominous," Clara chuckled uncomfortably, as Saffron tried to laugh along too. Clara rubbed her thighs together, shifting the weight on her heels, while Cali appreciated the mysteries contained within her Victorian-inspired dress with its deep V-neck.

For a moment, Cali imagined how beautiful Clara would look if (or when) she slowly unlatched the front bow, and let the dress drop, revealing what must be coupe-de-champagne-sized, upturned breasts. Cali loved men, but more and more she was wondering if she was a little, just a little, pansexual. Perhaps Clara felt the same way, too.

"Whatever she tells you, it's not true!" Saffron

interjected. "She's a stripper and a liar!"

"Shush," Clara said, holding up a hand dismissively, her undivided attention on Cali. "I posed for Playboy once a few years back, if you can believe it, and the money I earned enabled me to start the firm. So go on!"

Cali *could* believe it (and planned to search out *that* magazine spread pronto). She continued, "Clara, you'll be shocked to know that the work you saw in Saffron's portfolio during her interview – the work that compelled you to hire her? – well, that was *mine*. *All* mine."

Clara's eyes widened in shock. "Really?"

"Absolutely," Cali confirmed.

Clara looked around, making that quick, synaptic connection between the quality of work and artistry she saw in Cali's booth, and what she'd seen in Saffron's *faux* portfolio. *Same person.* "Out, now! Saffy." She pointed at Saffron, and Saffron slunk away like a shamed dog. "I'll be in touch, Cali," Clara assured. She took Cali's hand lightly to shake it, and Cali returned her grip, feeling a little bit of electricity as they touched. "I'm very sorry about this," she insisted, as their eyes locked for a small moment. Suddenly, a couple of women who 'might' be judges approached the booth as Clara stepped away. "Gorgeous!" she gushed to them as she was leaving, "You'll fall in love."

Whew. "Hello," Cali said to the potential judges. "Welcome to my proposal for the Hank and Esther Greenace Women's Center."

"Tell us more," the women said in unison and winked.

"Sure…" Cali launched into a very pointed, short-but-interesting presentation of how she would donate and integrate her entire collection of gorgeous floral mosaics. They would be shipped from 'storage' in California, and installed on the walls of the shelter, coordinating with a whole floral theme, including a living garden wall. As she spoke, it suddenly occurred to her, keeping in the mindset of a winner-to-be, to get a formal shipping estimate to use a white-glove moving company to truck the mosaics from California to New York City.

After the women looked around, one shook Cali's hand, and said, "Thank you for sharing this with us! It's a stunning, charitable idea. If I were a woman needing to live in a shelter for a little while, THIS is where I'd want to live."

"Thank you," Cali nodded.

Meanwhile, some more people, who behaved like design experts, possibly judges, came through, and Cali presented the same excellent, short spiel. But a niggling little voice in her head kept prompting to step aside and call her mother as soon as possible, to check on the actual status of her high school mosaics. She'd always just assumed her gorgeous works, the ones that her whole project depended upon, would still be there, sitting out in the old barn, but…

A good professional interior designer would double check on such a thing!

When the individuals (hopefully judges) left – seeming happy and impressed – Cali called her mother, but her father picked up.

"Dash Kistler here, what the hell do you want, whoever

you are?" he growled over a screeching rant of Judge Judy on TV.

"Dad, hello. It's me. How are you?" she asked gently. "How have you been?"

"My daughter? The one who's off high falutin' it in New York City?"

"Something like that," she rolled her eyes.

"What's all that noise? Sounds like you're takin' off," he said, "Let me turn the damn boob tube down. You at the airport, jet-setting around, flyin' by the seat of your panties? Doin' a little gold-diggin'? You a high-priced hooker yet?"

God, he'd always been that way: pushing her into it, fascinated by them himself.

"No, not exactly. I *am* trying to take off, in a sense, I guess. I'm at my college graduation and my Exhibition Competition – in a booth showcasing one of my design projects."

"Hey now, and you paid for it all yerself. See? I knew you could get yerself through college. Where you livin' now, at the California Kistler Embassy?"

"In a storage unit."

"Oh. Shit. Don't ask for *my* help. You obviously got yourself into this predicament. You got a good lock or two?"

"That's not why I'm calling. Please listen. I just need to know if all my floral mosaics are still out in the barn? The ones I did in high school that got me into Preston?"

"Nope, not here!"

"What?" Cali said flatly. She could feel herself winding up into a major tantrum. An entire young lifetime of resentment at her father could not be overcome with a few months of Science of Mind studies at Sugar's Divine Mind Center.

Breathe in the love, breathe out the hate.

"Nope, don't got 'em. Now don't freak the fuck out. I'm really sorry. But I sold the mosaics. I didn't think you wanted them anymore, and I figured you owed me for all the gold you stole…"

"You *sold* my mosaics!" Cali was already hyperventilating, struggling to breathe, hoping to God no judges would step into her booth just at the moment. "But my whole project is predicated on my donating those mosaics to a women's shelter!"

"Yeah, I got that. NOW, now you tell me! Shoulda thought of all those ladies with abusive husbands *before* you made off with my gold coins!"

"Where'd you sell them?! Can I get them back?"

"Uh, it was some collector guy from the Bay Area. He was damn excited about 'em. I thought we'd haggle, but he outbid himself! He paid MORE than I asked, he was so happy to have 'em."

Suddenly her mother came on the line. "Honey?"

"Mom! I'm dying over here! Are you SURE the mosaics are GONE!? Why didn't you tell me?"

"OH, honey, your dad swore me not to tell you. You know how it always is, walkin' on eggshells around him, lyin' to his face about the smallest crudola, lying to *your* face to keep the peace between you two."

"You are so co-dependent!"

"Back in *my* day that was a compliment, Miss Cali!"

"Just tell me. I don't have much time. Where are they?"

"Aw, the guy was sooo handsome, hon. I couldn't believe my eyes. The guy drove up from the city to see them, and he bought them on the spot. He was like someone out of a novel. He drove some kinda car that looked like a space ship; I don't even know the name of it. I'm SURE he's one of them tech millionaires…" and here Pearl put Dash back on the line.

"Cash Kistler here!"

"And you didn't send me any of the money for my work?"

"Why, no. Did I OWE you money? In fact, I got back MORE than you stole from me! I made a tidy profit off all them *fleurs*. Those things were worth *gold*. The guy acted like he'd hit the freaking mother fuckin' lode! Just oohing and aahing over the florals. And he sure didn't seem gay, neither! Your mom was creamin' her panties over him."

"Oh God."

"Said he was gonna install them in his house on Nob Hill. Kind of freaky if you ask me. He was asking all about *you*, the artiste, looking at your old pictures we keep on the shelf, but we kept our mouths shut. You know, let the mystery simmer. I'd never divulge details about my ward."

"I'm your daughter, dad."

"Couldn't take his eyes off you, askin' all kinds a questions."

Cali took a deep breath. Karma was a bitch. *Steal, get stolen from.* It was a page from the Divine Mind Science playbook. She took a seat on one of the periwinkle blue, leather-covered poufs she'd installed in the booth. "Dad, I want to thank you for your honesty. And for taking the time to talk to me. For showing me by your example just what an asshole is, so I can detect it quickly in other men and avoid them at all costs!"

She couldn't help herself but to laugh. The mosaics were long gone anyway. And she did kind of need to pay him back for what she'd stolen. Now they were even. What was the point of filling up with bitterness?

"Ha! Shit, kid!" he hooted on the other side. "You sure do put a spin on your words. Was that a compliment or what? I knew keepin' you cooped up in that library all those years with Mrs. Gloria Havistock was good for *something*. A smart mouth."

"Yes. Thanks for Gloria."

"Congratulations, Cal. You did it. All on your own. Now go get that prize or that guy or whatever the hell you want out of life. Bye kid."

"Wait! Put mom back on…"

"Yes, girl?" her mother purred. "I'm so proud of you today."

"Thank you. What was his name? The buyer?" Cali asked, holding her breath, hoping they'd kept the fellow's name at least.

"Hmmm," she heard her mother rustling through some papers. "I got it right here. Xerxes Bingham. He was real sweet. Sent up one of them special moving services to pick it all up. They were nice as could be, all in uniforms, I offered 'em my nachos and –"

"OK, OK! Tell me about it later!" She clicked off. *Tits up, chin up*. She'd have to act as if she actually still had the mosaics (and a civilized, gentlemanly, generous father). She'd have to check out this Xerxes Bingham too, and see if she could get hold of him. Maybe the situation wasn't completely hopeless.

Just at that moment, Cali heard a loud cough behind her. Jean-Chris and his very pretty, very clinging vine of a date were standing there. His new companion smiled wanly – or was it swanly? The lithe, flat-chested gazelle was taller than him, and a solid seven to ten years older. Up close, with her hair tied back in a chignon, she was even more of a creature from Swan Lake than she looked from halfway across the auditorium.

"J.C! Wow, thank you for coming today! It means a lot." She wasn't sure how formal to keep her behavior, now that this new woman was in the picture. Cali clasped her hands together loosely, bowed slightly and remained somewhat aloof when Jean-Chris didn't come in for a double kiss on each cheek or any of his usual Frenchy funny business. She approached and extended a hand toward his new friend. "Hi, I'm sorry if you overheard any of that. Family! You can't choose them," she laughed. "I'm Cali, nice to meet you! And you are…?" She made a big effort to sound gushy, taking a cue from the social expert Saffy.

"Cali, I'd like you to meet Lamrine," Jean-Chris said, as the woman shook Cali's hand back weakly. It was one of those warm and wet, fish-like handshakes – without a word or eye contact, something Cali found intolerable. Lamrine's perfume was Miss Dior, and she'd apparently plastered it on with a professional paint sprayer. Cali took her hand back quickly, as if she might get it bitten off.

Lamrine seemed a bit bored with the whole exhibition, not giving Cali the satisfaction of even looking at or admiring her work. "I will go look around a bit. Find me?" she asked Jean-Chris in fast French, which Cali struggled to decipher.

"Lammy. A kiss goodbye first?" Jean-Chris said, speaking in French too, as if it were their own private language, exclusive to just the two of them. He made their kiss extra loud and obvious as Lamrine leaned in, barely touching his lips. Cali winced.

Once Lamrine – and her aura of Miss Dior – was out of sight (and smell-range) Cali spurted, "You brought *a date* to my graduation, *and* she's rude? Good going!"

"She is more than a date. She is moving with me to Paris. Tomorrow."

"Well, you didn't lose any time in finding some unsuitable bitch to fit into your uncle's apartment." That possessive part of her brain, which she usually kept locked up tightly, was now blinking with the red panic mode light. STOP, DON'T GO THERE, STOP, DON'T MAKE A BIG DEAL… But she couldn't help herself. "Were you speed dating or something?"

"No. I met her a while back at her retirement party from the ballet; someone from school invited me."

"*When?*" Cali's eyes narrowed in on him. "We only really

broke things off the other weekend, at Barry's!"

"*Amour* happens fast, when it's right," he shrugged.

"WHEN!?" she raised her voice, suddenly realizing this was all lower ego talking at the point: pride, jealousy, pettiness. Still, she wanted the so-called facts of the thing.

"Some people don't need an Ice Age to decide what they want."

"Damn it. Tell me. When did you first meet 'Lammy'?"

"Around the time I said we should start seeing other people, okay? Just a coincidence, the party was that night. But we didn't – how do you say? – start dating or *get together*."

"You mean, fuck her."

"Well, this is a very rude way of putting it. But yes, I only began 'fucking' her since the last week, after I saw you at Barry's. I was really down, and she cheered me up that night."

"She? That *ice queen* cheered you up?"

"I broke through. We've been quite inseparable ever since."

"Ah."

"I don't even know why I came," he sighed. "To say goodbye, I guess. To make sure my model was installed correctly. OK, and yes, to see you one last time."

"That so?" Cali asked, walking to the edge of the booth to peek out for any approaching judges. There were supposed to be two more coming through at any time.

Forget him and his so-called date. I must focus now. In it to win it, remember –not win him. GG's ideas about learning self-control and regulating one's emotions reverbed in her mind. *If I can't practice it now, I'll never be ready.*

"Are you too mad?" he seemed almost hopeful she would be.

"Look," she said, officially embracing a generous attitude. "I only want you to be happy, *and* Lamrine too." *Whooh! That was extra generous, if bullshitty.* She turned and sighed, "If Lamrine makes you happy, then I'm happy. Even if she strikes me as a… You could really date someone with more meat on her bones, personality-wise, you know? Someone who's *nice*. Someone who makes a little effort with your friends."

"She doesn't *have* to be nice. To anyone. She was *a lead* in the American Ballet Theater, if you must know. But she's willing to make a go of things in Paris. For me."

"Good for her," Cali sighed. "Retiring from the ABT at thirty. Just in time to move to a vast *appartement familial* in the 9th with you. After just meeting you! Sounds convenient for *her*."

"For both of us. Please don't be like this." He looked around the booth, taking in every detail, impressed. Trying to change the mood, he said, "Your project is breathtaking. Like you."

"Your danseuse is the *real* star of this show," she said with a hint of sarcasm. One more jab, to satisfy her lower self, and then she promised to take a higher road again. "Does she do the splits on you?" she spat out. Oops. *OK, now I will be nice.*

"You are jealous, I know it."

"A little. I admit." She let it sink in, but things were

definitely over with him; she needed to move on.

"I knew it! I knew you would be." Suddenly, Jean-Chris' hands were around her face, and he was kissing her passionately. Just for a short moment, she was kissing him back, perhaps out of habit. Then she pushed him away.

"Stop it! We can't *do* this. The judges may come by at any second! Sheesh! Do you want to mess this up for me? AND your new girlfriend is right out there somewhere. Do you want to mess things up with *her*?"

"Let Lammy walk in on us, and I'll suffer the consequences."

"No. I don't operate like that. I'll not be a party to that."

"That's why I'll always love you," Jean-Chris sighed, seeming beside himself with wanting. "Even if I am with Lamrine now. Always, Cali – really – I will be waiting for you over there; I know you'll come to Paris some day."

"God! You're going to move in with someone you barely know because she seems like a good fit. And you're in here kissing *me*? What does *that* tell you about how you feel about Lamrine?"

"I am sure I will find much to love in her. I just don't want to be by myself anymore, do you understand? Lamrine is ready *to settle*."

"Knock knock! Sorry to *coitus interruptus*!" a man's voice beckoned, and she and Jean-Chris quickly separated.

"Talk later! After you win!" J.C whispered as a flamboyantly-dressed man came in, with his partner and/or colleague, looking around curiously.

"I like what I'm seeing! Tell me more," Mr. Flamboyant said, and Jean-Chris slipped out of the booth while Cali continued with her presentation, trying not to seem flustered: glossing over the part about donating the (now nonexistent) mosaics.

Chapter Twenty Eight

"Ladies and gentlemen!" the voice of Mr. Takaya called over the microphone from a small platform that had been placed in the center of the auditorium foyer. "I'm about to announce the winner of the Exhibition Competition…"

Everyone gathered around, as Cali was joined by Jean-Chris and Lamrine. Despite everything, she was thrilled to have him there for moral support, even if Lamrine lent no sparkle or sweetness to the occasion.

"…As you know, the prize involves a paid contract to implement the design project *for real*, at the Hank and Esther Greenace Women's Center. This is a magnificent start to any interior design career – and it will pay well, too: the going design rates for this type of project, plus any commissions from the manufacturers. And it will mean, let's not forget, career recognition and a living, breathing portfolio piece out in the 'real' world! I wasn't sure if she would be able to join us today. But Esther Greenace herself is with us, and she'd just like to say a word and announce the winner."

Esther, a petite, solid woman in her seventies with a platinum blonde bob, made her way to the microphone as Mr. Takaya lowered it for her. Laden with pearls, she was wearing a nubby pale grey Chanel suit, and chunky-heeled grey leather shoes, rounded off with a cute handbag. Cali felt as if she knew her, as Hank had so often spoken of his long-suffering wife, mother of his adored children: a woman who no longer desired him sexually, but made it clear he was free to keep playing discreetly if it made him feel alive. It was so surreal to see Hank's 'steel magnolia' in person, and Cali felt a pang.

Esther, a little shy, looked down at a notecard. "First, I'd like to say God bless my husband Hank, who passed away not long ago. He came up with this great idea to donate to the school, and motivate all of you."

The audience clapped loudly before dying down.

"Well, I'm here to say that the judges had *quite* a time deciding on the winner today. There were so many great projects, innovative ideas, and impressive presentations. But one student's work stood out above the rest. Not only for her style and substance, but for the extraordinarily generous spirit of her project. Her proposal met the shelter's needs on so many levels. Not just from the perspective of a great new look. Her proposal embodied the sharing spirit of our center, as we rehouse and rehabilitate women in need, with no cost to them.

This design proposal keeps us looking glamorous but well within the budget we seek – given that we would not need to purchase any new art for the renovation. The fact that this designer was willing to donate her gorgeous floral mosaics to grace our center, well, that sold us on her project! The idea of such an incredible donation working so well into the project convinced me – and our entire board – of *who* the winner should be. So I'd like to award this year's Exhibition Competition contract to… California Kistler!"

Jean-Chris grabbed her into a hug, glowing with pride. "You did it!"

Noting the sour look on Lamrine's face, Cali pulled back slightly. Looking up at him, she smiled sadly, and squeezed her eyes closed, speaking over the din of applause, "Thank you. And good luck in Paris!"

Jean-Chris kept clapping and yelling the loudest for her. She was a bit stunned; everyone clapped and hooted and vibrated with congratulations as she made her way to the stage. She should have been floating on air, but instead she felt as if her feet were dragging in wet cement. With a heavy heart and hunched back, she slunk up to the podium.

I'll need to tell the truth about the mosaics.

She leaned in toward the microphone, which was already at the perfect height for her. "Thank you everyone: Mrs. Greenace, the board members of the shelter, and the designer judges. I just want to thank you for this HUGE honor. Gosh, I'm so pleased to have been chosen. But…"

I don't actually have the mosaics.

Cali took a deep breath, and the microphone reacted with an unpleasant boom.

The whole room seemed to gasp at once in anticipation of what she might say. She looked around slowly, and her eyes fell on Jean-Chris. He looked up at her, smiling and nodding, and used his hands as if to say "Go on!" The look on his face, knowing hers so well, said: "Whatever it is that's wrong, don't give up or give into it just yet!" That was so reassuring. He was such a gem, and a great part of her success today.

"Uhhhh" Cali drew back a bit of magic into herself, and continued. "I'm so sorry. I didn't write an acceptance speech beforehand. And I don't have the words right now to express my gratitude. So for now I'll just say THANK YOU! And congratulations to all the students – no, make that the *graduates* of this fabulous program! Mr. Takaya, and all the other great professors at the Institute, thank you for believing in me – in us! Happy Graduation, everyone. See you out there in the design world. But first, let's celebrate!"

There was a resounding applause as Cali left the podium and made her way outside to get her breath. She stepped out onto a wide balcony that ran all along the outside of the auditorium, facing onto the courtyard of the school, which was fresh with spring plantings that were now blooming.

Just a few weeks ago, she recalled, the roses had been buds, and now they were in full flower. *Isn't that the way of life? Maybe I'm ready now, too, for what comes next.* She looked out, breathless; her entire body was blushing from putting herself 'out there' among so many people, all without stumbling over her words. A wonderful spring breeze rustled through her hair under her graduation cap, as she focused on the beauty of the garden. She stood looking out at the green space, debating if she should go back in there and tell everyone what a loser she really was, having lost the requisite mosaics.

"Congratulations," she heard a gentle female voice say from her right side. It was Esther Greenace, perfectly coiffed and perfumed: a mature doll of a lady, who was also looking out at the garden.

Cali turned, suddenly nervous in her presence. "Thank you Mrs. Greenace."

"Please don't be so formal. Call me Esther. And I know who you are," Esther said. "Everything about you, in fact. Hank thought the world of you. You lit up his life a few times a week. Which meant you lit up mine. He was never so easy to get along with as those days when he saw *you*."

Cali shook her head. "How can you be so wonderful and understanding? I was his… well, you know. How can you accept…?"

"That's love. Lifelong love. It's not always perfectly black and white. He had my blessing, in a way. He wouldn't have been with you if I hadn't encouraged him."

"Hmmm, I'm still learning about love. I don't know much. And I feel like I've just failed at my *first* love."

"At this age, your first love should be *yourself*. You still have plenty of time to learn about romantic love. It comes. You're very talented, Cali. It thrills me to see you win the prize. Hank meant that prize to be for *you*. He knew you'd strive for it. And win."

"He taught me a lot, your Hank."

"I must say, you really handled his death at the hotel with aplomb. I'm not sure I could have done a better job myself.

You were discreet. I'll always be grateful to you for that. And I was watching you today. The way you were so warm with the judges in your booth. It was fascinating to hear about you when everyone was deciding on the winner. They kept saying how gracious you were. Designing rooms is one thing. But being the picture of calm, grace, and class – that is another, entirely."

Calm, grace, and class; that's what it's going to take in this next adventure.

Cali felt ready now, better equipped really (now more than ever): ready for stepping into her true calling. Esther's words only confirmed it for her. "Wow, thank you. I haven't always been this way. I guess it comes when we figure out that losing our temper and making a mess of things usually never gets us what we want."

"Who's us?"

"Mistresses. Women with the soul of the old-fashioned courtesans."

"Ah," Esther nodded, taking in the information. "Is that what you're thinking of doing? In lieu of designing?"

"Not in lieu of, but as a way to fund my own design firm one day. I'm so 'insubordinate,' I'm not sure I could ever work for someone else. I'm still visioning it all out in my mind, how it might work."

"Well, if you make men as happy and motivated as you made my husband, I'd say you're on the right track. That's a skill, a talent unlike any other. But nobody understands that. Don't expect appreciation or accolades for *that* in the eyes of society. Just do your job well. Rewards come. But they're private. Keep everything private. *Especially* if you attempt to keep a foot in *both* worlds. Everyone reveres the great designers. But few people appreciate what it means to be a fabulous *professional* companion to men in this day and age. People put it down, and they don't understand."

"People can sure hate, can't they?"

"They can and they do. But if you do your work with love, whatever *kind* of work you choose, you'll be protected – and you'll prosper."

"Have you studied Science of Mind, or Law of Attraction? That lingo sounds so familiar."

Esther smiled and turned toward Cali. "I *do* know about the power of those teachings. I'm a believer. But we both belong to a secret society of women like us who, hmmm, know things about how men tick; sometimes we know more about them than they know about themselves. And we use it to our advantage!" Here, Esther laughed to herself; the soft tinkling quality of that laughter reminded Cali of the sound of fine crystal being tapped delicately with a spoon.

She intuited then that Esther was the kind of woman who would never admit completely to her very distant past as a 'good time girl,' but the lessons she'd learned as – perhaps – a professional companion had stuck permanently, and now informed her every move.

Esther motioned that she was about to go. "You won't need luck, so I won't say 'good luck.'"

"It was nice meeting you," Cali said, absorbing this wise woman: crystalizing the memory of her in her mind.

"I'm sure we'll meet again. I'll see you at the shelter

reveal," Esther said, gliding off, waving delicately.

"Wait!" Cali came in closer, making sure nobody could hear their conversation. "I need to tell you something, about the project. I don't think it would be right if I didn't tell you. But maybe we could keep this our little secret, and you won't tell the shelter's board members about it. Until I can fix it? I'm sure I can fix it."

"Ah, a delay already? Isn't this always the way with you interior designers?" she mused. "What is it, dear?"

"OK," Cali took a deep breath. "Actually, I don't *have* the big floral mosaics, anymore, to install at the shelter. I *just* learned about this. They do exist! And I think I can get them back, but it may just hold up the project a little."

"Oh! This changes things. Where are they?"

"Apparently, they're at some young tech entrepreneur's house in San Francisco. He purchased them from my parents and he's very fond of the collection and…"

"How much do you know about this *collector*?"

"Nothing. I just looked him up briefly online before the announcement. I saw that he's known for being very eccentric and reclusive. He's single, and he looks like one of those brainy guys who doesn't know how cute he is, not deep down, you know what I mean?"

A sly smile crossed over Esther's face. "Hank had been just that way, before I laid hands on him, and instilled him with the confidence he so needed," she shook her head, remembering. Then her gaze narrowed and settled on to Cali, giving her a head-to-toe glance.

"Esther. What is it? What are you thinking? I'll

understand if you need to fire me. I'll return the prize. We can go in there right now and announce it together, before everyone leaves."

"Ha! *Fire* you!? No way. This project just got *a lot more fun.*"

"How so?"

"Well, go and *get the mosaics back*! I'm sure you know just exactly *what to do*. Work your charms on that man, whoever he is. The board wants the renovation done – including the installation of those gorgeous mosaics – in six months, eight if you're lucky!"

"I'll get them back," Cali said, but her voice betrayed a little lack of confidence.

"You've got *everything* it takes to get the mosaics back from that man, *and* get the design job done. So don't dither."

"Thank you." *I'm ready. For all of it.*

"I'll want every delicious detail." With this, Esther smirked and turned on her heels, clicking back into the auditorium.

Cali quickly headed toward the front entrance of the school, past the blooming rose bushes, and exited out of the school's gate to the busy city street. She left the school auditorium behind. And most of all, she left Jean-Chris behind: the closest thing to true love and romance she'd ever known. She would relinquish him back to the library of life, like a rare, well-loved, collector's volume. Who knew when she might pick him back up again? Thanks to her spiritual studies with

Sugar, she now had faith in the Universe to bring J.C and her back together again someday, if that was part of the Divine Plan.

***

Cali clicks uptown along Madison Avenue, enjoying a long, brisk walk – feeling as if with each step she's leaving her old self, her old life behind.

She realizes that it's another day free from working in an office: the first of many. Maybe it's the beginning of *never* going to another office *Again*! Her heart is singing. She is nearly breathless with what it means. People might say, "What the hell are you thinking, Cali Kistler?"

Yes, my interests are strange – socially unacceptable to some – but it's me. It's what I feel led to do.

She turns into an elegant street of flower-boxed townhouses on the Upper East Side. She begins to walk faster as she gets closer, her heels clicking louder along the sidewalk. Cali all but skips up the street, remembering to remove her graduation cap from her hair.

I'm on my way to being an interior designer, yes. But right now I will surrender myself to learning a new way of being.

Let the lessons begin!

She stops. She stands looking up at GG's townhouse for a long moment.

It is a grand adventure I want. And as the author of my life, I am choosing this adventure.

A gate decorated with golden paint and small birds slams shut behind her.

She bounds up the stairs.

Maybe THIS is my true calling.

She rings the bell three times and says the password. *Her* password.

Kin buzzes her in. In the inner vestibule, GG is waiting; she gives Cali a big hug, and ushers her in.

Home for now.

The door closes.

And a new chapter begins…

END

If you truly enjoyed reading Call Me Cali: Book 2: *Becoming* by Lana Gold, won't you please send a star rating or short review (even one line would be amazing!) for this book to http://www.Amazon.com (anonymous reviews are possible and easy; just find your previous purchase in "orders" and fill in the review form with your desired alternate name). Thank you!

Please visit Lana Gold at http://www.LanaGoldBooks.com for freebies, updates, and to join the non-Spam newsletter to receive book updates, and to order ebooks or paperbacks.

What's Next for Cali?
Please read Call Me Cali: Book 3: *Performing* by Lana Gold

If all the world's a stage and men and women merely players, then Cali Kistler is about to lose herself—in a new starring role

Cali's first season as a performer at GG's exclusive bordello is fraught with drama and fantasy as she develops a taste for the finer things, honing her art of providing sensual, erotic and emotionally-nuanced experiences to lonely, needy men. But in her spare time, what hot guys will provide the romance and take care of *her*?

When fantasy and reality begin to blur... where do you draw the line?

Driven by her desire to recover her lost mosaics, and finish her debut interior design project, she seeks out the eccentric, powerful man who holds her artwork captive. Can she play all his role playing games and get them back...or will he convince *Cali* to become part of his permanent collection?

"There's no business like ho business"

Will juggling two different careers, and her many different personas at GG's, wreak havoc on Cali's carefully crafted career plans – not to mention her sense of identity?

And will the lucrative, ball-of-a-time with the girls at GG's come to a screeching halt, forcing the intrepid Cali onto a new independent path where she can be truly more herself?

What happens when the mask comes down and the show is over?

CPSIA information can be obtained
at www.ICGtesting.com
Printed in the USA
LVHW051602220621
690864LV00010B/912